Chaos & Calamity

Hannah Till

JacBen Books

Published in the United States by Hannah Till

Cover design by JacBen Books

Character Artwork by Mayhara Ferraz

Cover Design by Hannah Till

Editor: JacBen Books

Copyright © 2025 by Hannah Till & JacBen Books

ISBN 979-8-9857674-7-6

www.hannahtill.com

Content Warnings:

ADHD/Neurodivergent

Cancer/Death of Parent

Explicit Sex Scenes

Explicit Language

Domestic Violence

Dear Reader,

First and foremost, I want to thank you for wanting to read this book. Before you dive in, I want to specifically state that this book is intended for adults only. It is my job as the author to make sure you know what you are getting into when you pick up my books.

Please know this book contains explicit consensual sexual content (on page), adult language, mentions of cancer/death of parent (on page) and domestic violence (off page). These sensitive situations may be triggering or inappropriate for some audiences. As always, your mental health is most important.

If you or anyone you know is suffering from domestic violence, please reach out to the National Domestic Violence Hotline at 800-799-7233 or text START to 88788

Contents

Dedication

To every one who was told they were too loud, too talkative, too messy, too cringy, too ... too... too... much.
To everyone who received the "talks too much" on their elementary school report card. To everyone who has a closet full of half finished crafts. To everyone who loses their keys on a daily basis. To everyone who can't seem to figure out how to finish the laundry. To everyone who felt as though they needed to change who they were in order to fit someone else's ideal.
You never needed to change. You were never too much.
You were always just right.

"I just wanted you to know
That this is me trying..."
-Taylor Swift

Prologue

1 Week Prior

Emily

It's a falsity universally acknowledged by the absolute worst parts of society that a single woman born with a neurodivergent brain must need someone to save her.

Well ... Fuck that.

Single or not, I did NOT need saving. What I needed was a large cup of coffee ... or maybe a shot of tequila. Though the tequila wouldn't help my current mental state. That being one focused on how exactly to secretly commit murder on the east wing of the hospital while not losing my nursing license or being incarcerated in the process.

"Miss Truce ... " The charge nurse, whose name I could never remember, snapped her fingers in the air. "I'm quite shocked."

At that moment, I finally accepted, through no fault of my own, I was being fired.

Though the thought of losing this particular travel placement had crossed my mind exactly seventy-four times that morning, I'd recently been too focused on the chaos to let that possibility sink in. I'd spent the last few hours in a haze after finding Dean, my now ex-boyfriend, half naked and all of three inches deep into a fellow traveling nurse on my unit. We hadn't been together long, but I'd taken this remote Arkansas assignment because it was where he lived.

It turns out it wasn't my scrubs and barely held-together messy bun driving him wild and keeping him returning to the hospital for a spur-of-the-moment lunch. It was the new girl he'd been screwing in the clean linen closet after he kissed me goodbye.

There were the obligatory slew of apologies from the two, and a rushed rearranging of clothes, but it didn't matter. The deed had been done ... literally.

The vision of walking in on that scene almost made me forget about the hours-old vomit from the premie on the west wing that was somehow still seeping into my shoes and settling between my toes. *He-who-shall-never-again-be-named* was far from impressive ... what was impressive was how far a newborn could projectile vomit. However, not impressive enough to warrant my desire to be covered in it.

Add to that the now blood-stained scrubs from a recent delivery, broken stethoscope and missing favorite pen that had all been borrowed from a fellow newborn nurse that morning with the promise of a pristine return after my shift, and this was quite possibly rounding out to be the absolute worst day.

"But, I didn't—" My cutoff words landed on deaf ears before they were spoken. It was a perfectly practiced rebuttal that begged to be stated. One I had, in theory, rehearsed a thousand times in the shower in hopes of never having to implement. It wasn't until the actual attempt that I realized no words, furiously practiced or not, would help to get me out of this situation.

"This is health care." The charge nurse practically glared through me with each word. "We hold people's lives in our hands. I can forgive one small mishap. I can even excuse a few mishaps here and there, but this is a trend I don't want to continue."

I buried the words I wanted to scream.

In truth, I'd been treading water for the last month, and this was the wave that would take me under. What had started as a ripple in the dawn of the early morning turned into a catastrophic tsunami by the end of the day. I'd slept past my alarm for the fourth time, worn the wrong color scrubs for the designated unit I'd floated to, left my supplies on the RV table, and forgot to clean up the spilled coffee as I rushed out the door.

My brain hadn't clicked into place until the sweet new nurse on the unit, who was starting in a few days, tapped my hand and pointed to her arm.

It was a tiny routine skin prick, a procedure I'd performed a hundred times if not more. All new employees were given a tuberculosis test at hiring, and due to a medical emergency in human resources, I'd been designated as the nurse to give them that week.

I stared at the injection site in confusion, not realizing what had transpired until what was supposed to be a small dot under the skin ballooned into a large, puffy bump that seemed to expand with each passing second. I'd snatched the tiny vial from the table only to realize it contained the solution for the tetanus vaccine and not the tuberculosis test.

"Miss Truce!"

I startled, leaving the wretched memory behind, as my charge nurse's voice rose. From the frustration hidden behind my name, I could only guess this wasn't the first time she'd called out to me.

"I think it's time for you to leave."

The RV door shut behind me just as another alert sounded. I had seven missed calls, and if I waited just a few more minutes, that number would only continue to grow. I sighed, knowing there was no way I could ignore Becca much longer. If I didn't reply in some form before falling asleep, she was bound to make the twelve-hour drive in under six and be at my door by sunrise.

The phone rang for an eighth time, and I held my breath as I mustered up the courage to answer. The screen went black just as my finger hovered over the button.

I grunted as I flung my now dead phone onto the unmade bed and hastily kicked off my right shoe. A string of mumbled curses flew from my lips as I fought with the unbudging left one. Once it finally sprang free, I chucked the offending sneaker somewhere off into the distance, resulting in a loud horn erupting to life as it bounced off the steering wheel.

I didn't flinch at the sound. Sudden noises had become my norm, except all I wanted to do right then was bury myself underneath the covers where it was nice and quiet and never come out. But then that newly freed sock-clad left foot hit the floor where I'd spilled that morning's coffee. The same coffee I'd mentally promised myself to wipe up and then, as usual, forgot about.

I screamed as I slipped backward, only able to reach out and claw at the drapes covering the door as I went down.

Outside lamp light from the small RV park poured into my tiny refuge as my ass hit the coffee-soaked floor, and another round of curses tumbled outward.

"You okay?"

I jumped at the unexpected voice coming from the other side of the RV door.

When I twisted to look out the now drape-less window, I found a familiar weathered face belonging to the elderly man from one spot over staring me down. A moment later, his more than unpleasant wife poked her head from behind to invade my currently imploding world.

I swallowed as I forced myself upwards to open the door. It was a battle not to cringe at the cold wet coffee that caused my scrubs to cling to my thigh.

"I'm fine." I lied.

"Don't sound too fine to us." The older woman, hair in curlers and arms crossed around her thick middle, countered. "It's almost ten at night, girl." The woman, whose name I also couldn't remember, tisked in disapproval.

Maybe she was related to my charge nurse? They had similar surly-looking features, and both somehow resembled that green lady from the Pixar monster movie I'd watched as a kid. They even had a matching mole and a –

"We were trying to watch TV but couldn't hear a thing from all the cursin' and hollerin' in here." She added.

I sighed as I closed my eyes and let the glass slipper slip into place. That was how I saw my mask.

It was as if I were Cinderella, hiding the ugly truth of who I was behind a shimmering façade. Every single day was spent preparing for the ball, but there was no charming prince awaiting me, only the crushing weight of expectation. Expectations I could never meet. And God, I was so tired of it all. The constant performance. The careful words. The meticulous actions. They were all to project an image, a lie, instead of the messy, flawed reality of me.

A deep breath shuddered through me as my internal self-hate reached its peak. Then, something shifted.

Maybe it was the spilled coffee, the disgusting shoe, or the fresh wound of unemployment ... I couldn't pinpoint the exact moment. But a tiny fracture appeared in the glass slipper and as I placed my weight within, the crack widened and splintered, until the glass shattered and the mask was gone.

Every proper and not-so-proper Southern phrase had already raced through my head when I opened my eyes. I knew kindness would've probably been the best decision, but then the memory of that cranky older woman not so accidentally knocking down my hanging tomato vine the week prior came bursting in.

Did she know how expensive tomatoes were in this economy?

I huffed in frustration and reeled in all that kindness to settle on good old-fashioned sarcasm with just a hint of Southern flare.

"Oh! I'm so sorry." I batted my eyelashes in mock sweetness as I freed that southern girl. Then, I had to blink a few more times when I realized the false lash adhering to my right eye was starting to come unglued. "I do apologize." I'd spent the last eighteen months trying to water down that thick southern accent as I traveled the country from hospital to hospital, but nothing could get it to come roaring back to life like a well-placed cunt in need of a backhanded compliment.

I placed a hand over my heart for emphasis. "I promise it's lights out for me, and you can return to your show." The woman had just started to turn when I added. "And while we're discussing keeping the noise down, I would sooooooo appreciate it if you could make sure to take out the dentures before you suck his wrinkled dick tonight; I don't feel like hearing him yell about your teeth again." I gave the woman my fakest smile and slammed the door shut for an added punch.

But then I noted the curtains were on the ground, not creating a much-needed barrier between their appalled faces and mine, and did the only thing I could think of.

At the ripe old age of twenty-eight ... I stuck out my tongue.

The woman recoiled in shock at both my words and gesture as she stepped backward, mouth agape, and stammered something under her breath about today's youth. I could only smile as I reached down, grabbed a nearby towel, and shoved it into the still-somehow attached curtain rod hovering over the door to serve as a new barrier between me and the rest of the world.

A wave of exhaustion, or perhaps it was madness, crashed over me. Or maybe I'd just forgotten to eat lunch, and my blood sugar was dangerously low.

I turned to lean against the door, then slid into the still-spilled coffee and burst into roaring laughter with no care as to which neighbor was around to hear.

But then the laughter died out, and a quiet reality set in.

I was alone in the dark in an RV park filled with people who had perfected the senior discount in a town I barely ventured into.

There was nothing for me here. Not anymore, at least.

I needed to get out.

But getting out meant dealing with another problem altogether. I was supposed to be in this no-name city for another two weeks before my next twelve week travel nursing position opened up. I contemplated drinking and sleeping the next fourteen days away, but without the following two weeks' income, I needed to save what I could.

Maybe I could just sit and stare out the window while reading the most depraved alien smut I could find and procrastinate every possible decision until the absolute last minute?

But maybe that was my problem?

I'd spent so long relying on my ability to procrastinate and adapt to the chaos of the situation that maybe I'd forgotten the purpose of it all. Even though I refused to voice the thought, I knew the idea behind it. Maybe if everything were a last-minute, non-thought-out decision, it would be easier to accept my inevitable failure than to know I'd put work into something that would never work out.

That morning, I woke up with two weeks left in my placement. But that night, I was going to sleep with no idea what the next day would bring.

Chapter 1

Present Day

Emily

I lay motionless, buried in a cocoon of pink and purple pillows, staring at the ceiling of my RV where a string of cheap Christmas lights shimmered. They were a worn-out strand a neighbor had tossed out a few rotations back. One bulb malfunctioned, giving the lights a mind of their own, causing them to flicker and dance in disorganized rhythm.

Sometimes, I'd lie inside my RV, aptly named Ramona, and stare at that same motion for hours, trying to guess which light would flicker next. Was there a hidden sequence I hadn't noticed, or was it all a mindless whirl, and no matter how hard I tried, I'd never guess which of those twinkling lights would spark to life?

"Emily!"

I jolted from my trance at Becca's voice having no idea how long I'd left my best friend sitting silently on FaceTime. I'd become so absorbed in the movement above that the rest of the world faded away.

"Sorry," I muttered as I turned to face the brightly lit screen. "I don't understand. When in the hell did they start fucking, and how did I not notice?"

"Honestly, I never liked him anyway. Besides, are you going to marry someone named Dean? Really?" Becca scoffed.

I hummed in agreement, not wanting to revisit the full extent of what had happened.

"And it's been a week. I never want to speak of or hear his name again."

"Ditto." She agreed.

I swallowed as I pushed his face from my mind for the last time.

"It's not the end of the world," Becca added with a sad smile and so much love pouring from those deep brown eyes I swore I could almost feel it. "Maybe travel nursing isn't your thing? What if you switched to a more permanent position where you wouldn't have to change things up every twelve weeks? Learning an entirely new facility so often has got to be exhausting. Plus, you might find a group of friends you could actually bond with."

I shrugged.

I didn't want a permanent position, and I didn't need any more friends. I had Becca, and she understood me more than any random fellow nurse I met at work ever would.

But most of all, permanent meant I couldn't run. And if I'd figured out one thing over the last few years, running was just about the only thing I was good at.

"I'd be bored." Though it was nowhere near cold, I pulled the covers up higher on my shoulders as if I could hide from the lie.

"That's an odd pronunciation of *scared*." Becca countered and I rolled my eyes.

I'd always wanted a big sister, but then I'd found a best friend in Becca and realized those big sister moments didn't need DNA attached to them.

"Scared?" I scoffed.

"Yes. You're scared."

"I'm not scared. I'm —"

"What are your plans for the next week?" Becca cut in, saving me from coming up with another bald-faced lie. "You have what? One, maybe two weeks until you have to be in Florida."

8

I cringed as I curled further in on myself and hoped Becca couldn't see the movement under the protection of the blanket.

Seven days had passed since Mercy had unceremoniously dumped me, and my life had become a blur of DoorDash, Chipotle and cheap boxed wine from the corner store. The inside of Ramona screamed "broke college student," and not "responsible adult with her shit together."

Tonight was the last night before my rental agreement expired and Florida had been my next rotation. But then came the shoe incident, the spilled coffee, the wrath of the cranky old woman—a trifecta of disaster. Shortly after, a terse email informed me the traveling position I'd been anticipating was permanently filled. Then a second email, this one from my travel manager, requesting an "urgent meeting to discuss my future with the company" came in.

My future. With this company? I'd scoffed internally. That was code for, "a future that absolutely does not involve you." Instead of facing that grim reality or replying, I'd spent the night lost in a sea of Franzia, staring at the twinkling lights on Ramona's ceiling.

Becca didn't need the full, agonizing details. The early firing and the cheating ex-boyfriend were enough of a burden for her to carry. Before our daily call, I'd desperately tried to distract myself from the crushing weight of the past week and the terrifying unknown that stretched ahead. But my mind refused to cooperate. It was a relentless engine of worry. Sleep had offered no escape and my eyes remained glued to the ceiling until the first rays of dawn peeked into my tiny home, and Becca's voice, sharp and insistent, pulled me back to reality.

"Are you going to turn that quick pit stop into an extended visit? Maybe you can come up and visit me?" Becca asked in such a motherly voice that I pulled the covers over my head as I mumbled a reply. "I can't hear you," Becca called out.

I smiled as Becca knocked on her phone screen, feebly attempting to get my attention.

"I don't know. I'll figure something out." I answered as I peeked my head out. I did want to visit Becca. Maybe that could be my answer? I could make a quick stop at home and then drive up to her and Liz's for a few days while I figured my life out.

"Babe," Becca said with such fragility I might as well have been a barely held-together piece of fine china. "You can't run away forever."

My face went taut. Every muscle pulled so tight I was sure one breath would shatter me into a thousand pieces.

"Yes, I can," I whispered, unsure if the words made it to Becca's ears.

Chapter 2

Present Day

Emily

I closed my eyes in frustration to silently await the next blunder when, sure enough, an eighteen-wheeler drove by and splashed a mountain of sludge onto my favorite pants and threadbare Pemberley sweatshirt. I'd traded last week's newborn projectile vomit for today's mud.

At least it was a step up.

"You've got to be fucking kidding me!"

A scream tore from my throat. It was a raw, ragged sound, swallowed by the barren trees and frozen ground flanking the road. All consuming fury, hot and violent, clawed its way through my bones.

This close. I was this close! Less than ten miles from home, and of course, *of course*, Ramona had chosen this exact moment for her grand meltdown. It wasn't just the engine sputtering, spitting and coughing like a dying animal; it was the simultaneous eruption of two tires as I wrestled her off the highway.

Everything was happening at once. My jaw ached, a tight, throbbing warning and I knew, with a sickening certainty, that I was teetering on the edge, moments from shattering completely.

The distant rush of cars horns became a frantic, angry chorus as they filled my ears. The biting January air, mingled with the heat boiling beneath my skin. It was a suffocating combination that made me want to tear myself free.

I glanced down at my Converses, now soaked thanks to the perfectly placed puddle I'd landed in while exiting Mona and a shiver of disgust ran through me, not just from the cold, but from the sticky residue of the entire catastrophe.

Okay, maybe today wasn't such a step up after all. The longer those seconds ticked by, the more that newborn vomit sounded like a welcome paradise.

A strangled sob clawed its way from my throat as I flung my arms out, coated in thick, clinging grime, in a desperate, futile attempt to shake off the filth that had found a new home. These past few weeks … they'd easily claim a spot in my top ten worst life experiences, maybe even top five. It wasn't simply bad luck; sometimes it felt like life had a vendetta against me, like nothing ever quite landed the way it should.

Most would look at my life and call it decent. Except for the gaping hole where my mother used to be. That was unequivocally, undeniably horrible. But I refused to acknowledge it. I wouldn't speak of it, think of it, or dream of that frozen moment in time. It was a ghost I wouldn't let haunt me, a wound I refused to let fester … or heal. As far as I was concerned, it had never happened.

The thought of her death, unwelcome and intrusive, crashed into my mind, and I shoved it back down, burying it beneath the layers of sludge that now encased me from head to toe.

I looked down to find the brand new sparkly jeans I'd just splurged on with what little money was left after my student loan payments, an utter disaster. The intricate design that had drawn me in at the store was gone, obliterated. I was sure even the pockets now held a handful of revolting mud and dirt. It was a perfect, agonizing metaphor for my life. Or rather, what my life was becoming: a flawlessly crafted, shiny exterior constantly being smothered, rendered damn near unrecognizable by every conceivable mishap that hurtled its way.

Prior to this most recent bump in the road, I'd had high hopes my life was about to take a massive left turn into something positive. But this wasn't just a bump in the road; this past week had turned into a full-blown, screeching halt to any hope I'd clung to for a better future.

Each step I took around Ramona was a careful, tense dance, avoiding the lingering puddles and mud left by a recent storm, then paused as a flicker of self-doubt burrowed its way in.

Had I truly taken my adderall a few hours ago?

The question nagged at me, a small, insistent burr beneath the surface of my thoughts. But I guess it didn't matter now. Though I longed for the calmness that dopamine kick provided, I knew there was nothing that would help the frenzy I had catapulted into.

These emotionally explosive episodes, though now infrequent, still possessed the power to unravel me, leaving me feeling like a discarded doll, tossed haphazardly in every direction.

A sharp, guttural cry escaped my lips as I stumbled onto the passenger running board, my gaze snagging on my reflection in the side-view mirror. The sight that met me was a cruel mockery of my former self. My once-gleaming blonde hair was now a multi-hued mess – a greasy, chaotic blend of dirt and mud that screamed "dumpster fire" louder than any actual flames ever could.

This could not get any–

"Nope! Nope! Nope! Nope!" The words exploded from my throat as my hands shot into the air in mock surrender to whatever cruel deity delighted in toying with me. No. I was not about to make that mistake again and let the universe prove me wrong one more.

I scrambled for the greasy fast-food napkins scattered across the car seat and scrubbed at the sticky mess coating me. I was so hyper-focused on erasing every last trace of my blunder that the world seemed to fade. I didn't even register the car pulling up beside me until a horn blared. Before the sound could fully penetrate my haze, I recognized the familiar, infuriatingly calm voice of my older brother, Anderson.

"What in the hell happened to you?"

I froze—still bent over and midway through wiping that yuck off my right thigh.

There was definite shock and genuine worry in every word, and once I gathered what was left of my dignity, I slowly, agonizingly, straightened, postponing the inevitable: facing Mr. Perfection in all my current, disastrous glory.

I'd regretted texting him the moment I'd hit send. It was as if crossing back over into the townlimits of Masonwell skyrocketed me right back into that helpless teenager I'd fought so hard to escape.

My stomach churned, a familiar, sickening twist, and the frustration I'd been desperately trying to suppress began to bubble.

I was twenty-eight . . . twenty-eight fucking years old and despite every desperate attempt, I still didn't have my life together. Now I had to turn around and face my brother who would be the very embodiment of competent adulthood in his impeccably pressed suit and gleaming dress shoes. Or maybe he'd be wearing those idiotic surgical scrubs, a constant reminder that he'd effortlessly achieved everything he'd ever wanted.

But then a second thought emerged. My anger wasn't truly about his success. If anything, I was proud of everything he'd accomplished. What gnawed at me, what festered and poisoned my thoughts, was the sheer ease with which he'd done it. He'd simply ... arrived. While I flailed, struggled, and stumbled through life.

A faint smile tugged at my lips. Apparently, the thousands of dollars I'd poured into virtual therapy over the past year hadn't been entirely wasted. They'd actually taught me something about processing this warped, twisted relationship we shared.

I counted to ten, willing my heart rate to slow, then inhaled a massive, deliberate breath, a desperate attempt to find some semblance of calm. But again, nothing ever seemed to go as planned, and that deep breath only heightened the frustration as I realized exactly what I now smelt like.

"Oh, you know. No job. No Ramona." My voice was a hollow echo against the backdrop of my pathetic refuge. I kicked the deflated tire of the thoroughly broken-down RV, a physical manifestation of my shattered state. "And no—"

"Soap? Clean clothes? Deodorant?" Another wildly unexpected voice finished my sentence.

"Jesus. Fucking. Christ." The words were a low, desperate plea under my breath.

I fought to maintain some semblance of composure, to will the building storm of nerves to recede, to stop my skin from prickling with unwanted—excitement? It was a losing battle. My entire body seized up at that voice.

The voice that was *not* my brother's.

The voice that haunted my nightmares and colored my dreams.

The voice that had once set every fiber of my being ablaze, only to then plunge me into an icy abyss.

Maybe I should have endured more therapy sessions before returning to this place?

No. No. No. No. No. No. No. No. No.

This couldn't be real. This wasn't happening. The universe couldn't be this cruel. I hadn't even finished the thought a moment ago ...

But when my eyes finally found him—the one and only Ford Edward Thomas, standing next to Anderson and casually leaning against the side of Ramona like he owned the damn thing—I had to admit that it was most definitely happening.

It had been eighteen months. Eighteen months since we'd even occupied the same state, let alone breathed the same air. And yet, there he was, standing not ten feet away.

The world tilted on its axis.

My heart hammered against my ribs.

The ghost of his touch, his scent, his laugh, all flooded my senses in a tidal wave threatening to drown me within the memories I'd fought so hard to bury.

Mr. Three First Names was in the flesh.

Fucking hell.

A kaleidoscope of memories assaulted me. Some painted in hues of joy, others in shades of pain. But the one that crystallized the moment our eyes met was the memory of his face the night I'd laid my soul bare before him. Every hidden thought, every unspoken feeling, every fragile dream had spilled from my lips, a torrent of vulnerability I barely comprehended myself. In that moment of utter exposure, he'd looked at me with nothing but bewilderment, and with that one look, he'd shattered my world. He'd peeled away every defense, every layer of self-preservation, every ounce of hard-won confidence and trust I'd spent years building.

But what twisted the knife deeper was the insidious whisper I couldn't silence. He'd burned my world to ashes months ago, yet seeing him standing there looking as beautiful as ever, he still lit a fire in my heart.

And I hated him for it.

No.

Perhaps hate was a lie I desperately clung to. The truth was, I wanted to hate him, but I knew I never could. I hated the agonizing truth that the hatred I wanted to feel remained forever out of my grasp. Because hating him would have been so much easier than remaining in this empty space where he would always be just a hairsbreadth out of reach.

His arms were crossed, and though he was nearly ten feet away, the muscles of his biceps seemed to invade my space. I drew a shaky breath, failing miserably to tear my gaze from those infuriating arms and the even more infuriating chest they guarded. That was a grave mistake. My eyes traveled upward, and damn it all ... they locked on his face and I *really* looked at him. The sharp, sculpted line of his jaw, the perfectly styled hair, the dark, seductive shadow of his beard, the sun-kissed skin dusted with freckles – a masterpiece of cruel perfection.

The tattoo, the one I'd spent countless hours tracing with my eyes, the one I could probably still draw from memory, peeked from the open collar of his white shirt. And he looked just as devastatingly beautiful as he had all those years ago.

Couldn't the universe grant me a single, measly favor? A tiny, insignificant miracle? A beer gut, perhaps? Or maybe an awkwardly receding hairline? I would have welcomed anything—*anything*—except the infuriatingly perfect specimen of a man standing before me, a veritable Greek god sent to torment my already fractured heart.

"How ya doing, Chaos ... "

My chest tightened with the stab delivered on the breath of a single word. The one word that would break me. But maybe he hadn't noticed because that devastatingly handsome smile on his devastatingly handsome face never faltered as he added, "or should I say, EATs?" He asked with a smirk that, at one point in time, would have had my panties around my ankles in three seconds flat.

Thankfully, the newly open wound on my chest mixed with the well placed sludge somehow caused my clothes to remain solidified to my now shaking form.

He tilted his head as if testing the waters, daring me to respond.

"I *hate* that nickname." The words were a brittle shield, a desperate attempt to mask the vulnerability clawing at my throat. I didn't specify which nickname, praying he wouldn't dissect the vagueness as I crossed my arms, mirroring his stance. But that only caused the sludge, clinging to my skin like a second layer, to become a sticky mess, binding one arm to the next. A physical manifestation of the invisible chains he still held me captive with.

Ford's low laugh vibrated through the air as if it was a cruel symphony conducted solely for my torment.

It was a deep, throaty sound that somehow managed to simultaneously slice directly through the gaping wound he'd carved in my heart while also landing right between my thighs. My breath hitched as every fiber of my being screamed to clench my legs together at the sound.

"I've been thinking—" He stepped closer and the air between us became charged with a tension that stole the oxygen from my lungs and a chill raced down my spine. "I feel like most parents would test out the initials of their soon-to-be baby before signing the birth certificate. Why didn't yours?" Ford's head tilted, a mocking gesture that twisted the knife already lodged in my heart, while Anderson, his loyal shadow, simply rolled his eyes.

A suffocating wave of grief-fueled rage crashed over me, threatening to drag me under.

Who did he think he was?

Eighteen months. Eighteen agonizing months spent piecing my shattered world back together, brick by painful brick. And he thought he could just waltz back into my life as if he hadn't been the one to wield the hammer in the first place? The memory of the man I'd convinced myself he'd become—receding hairline with a beer gut—was a flimsy illusion, a shield crumbling against the raw reality of the man standing before me. The man who had the power to undo me with a single glance.

"Would you like to ask my mom?" My words were a venomous hiss. "I'm sure you remember where the grave site is located."

Ford's smile vanished, replaced by a look of stark horror as he recoiled. A tremor of remorse ran through his voice, and for a fleeting, treacherous instant, I entertained the impossible—that it had been an accident. "Em, I didn't mean–"

"Stop," Anderson's voice sliced through the air as his body became a sudden, unwelcome barrier between us. "What is this, some kind of twisted anniversary? It's been almost two years since you've even been in the same state, and you still hate each other this much?" He threw his hands up in exasperation, then made a clumsy, aborted attempt to pull me into a hug. His fingertips brushed my arm, recoiling as he registered the substance coating me.

"Seriously," Anderson's voice held a note of bewildered disgust as his hand gestured towards the mess. "What happened here?"

I instinctively tightened my arms around my middle, uncaring that the movement only smeared the foulness further. A scalding shower was the only thing separating me from complete despair.

"Eighteen-wheeler decided I was its personal target the moment I dared to step out of the driver's side door."

"Hmm." Anderson's gaze shifted to Ford. "Guess we should have taken my truck."

"What?" I stared as my heart pounded against my ribs. Five steps to the left revealed the chilling truth: my brother's battered, beloved truck—the one he swore he'd never part with—wasn't behind Ramona. Instead, gleaming under the unforgiving winter sun, sat a pristine, impossibly expensive sports car.

My eyes rolled skyward. Of course Ford had a fancy new car. It was the perfect, sickening punctuation mark on his fancy new life.

He'd craved a life unshackled from the poverty and despair that clung to our town like a shroud. He'd dreamed of a life where money was no object, a sanctuary built on solid foundations, not the crumbling promises held together by WD40, duct tape and whispered prayers. He'd yearned for a real pool, a shimmering oasis and not the precarious plastic monstrosity that trembled with every summer storm.

We weren't poor, not exactly. We existed in a middle space, somewhere between scraping by and almost comfortable. It never truly bothered me. Our tiny homes on the fringes of town felt like havens from a world that threatened to swallow us whole. But to him, they were shackles, reminders of a life he desperately wanted to outrun.

I guess he'd finally achieved his ambition, severing ties with a past drenched in sorrow and disillusionment. I just never planned for the past he wanted to leave behind to include me.

But one agonizing question haunted me: *Why did he stay?*

He'd attained his dreams, earned the coveted letters after his name, yet he remained tethered to Masonwell. He'd simply relocated to the affluent side of town, a superficial shift of zip codes.

I shook my head, resigned to the fact that I would never know the answer. I was an outsider now, even if I never fully understood why.

The throbbing ache in my jaw intensified as I clenched my teeth, fighting back the torrent of bitter words that threatened to spill forth.

There was no way I was accepting a ride in Ford's fancy new car, one that likely cost more than everything I possessed.

"I can just wait for the tow company. They said it would only take an hour or two to come get Mona. I'm sure they–"

"It's just a car," Ford cut me off and my eyes shifted to his. "We aren't leaving you out here on the side of the road just because you're a little ... " He swallowed and then smiled, "dirty."

With that final word, a shiver, not of cold, but of something far more insidious, snaked down my spine. I knew what he meant. I knew, too, that a part of him, buried beneath all those layers of ice, reveled in the exquisite torture of pushing me to my breaking point. It didn't help that I'd replayed the memory of those very words, uttered by those very lips, far too many times. Though, under very different circumstances. And maybe also had gone through and entire pack of batteries for my favorite battery powered toy in the process. But, no one needed to revisit that thought.

"Do you have any towels in there we can use to protect his leather seats?" Anderson's voice cut through the tension, but he didn't wait for an answer, already opening the door to Ramona and stepping inside. Then, for the first time in years, we were alone.

Ford took another step closer, and I had to fight the traitorous urge of my body to lean in. The roar of passing cars, mere feet away—cars that moments before had assaulted my senses—faded into the thrumming of my own heart. A million things could have been happening around me, but the only sound I could hear was the desperate pounding of my blood in my ears.

My only thought was of escape.

I had to escape.

Except, there was no escape. No place to run, no place to hide, no half broken down RV to whisk me away down some endless highway. I couldn't burrow beneath the couch cushions of my childhood home. I couldn't retreat to the sanctuary of my teenage bedroom.

I was trapped. Stuck on the side of the road and staring at the one person I wanted nothing more than to punch in the face. Or maybe kiss. Or maybe punch and then kiss and then punch again for making me even think about kissing him in the first place.

God, he was maddening. Utterly, infuriatingly maddening.

And he twisted everything. Every thought, every carefully constructed decision, every absolute certainty I held close, became a chaotic jumble in my already fractured mind.

"I hear you're in South Carolina for a week or two before you head further south for your next travel assignment?" Ford asked the question with such normalcy I paused in utter shock, not sure if one of those speeding cars hadn't accidentally veered off the road, struck me down, and sent me off into some parallel universe where I'd never confessed my true feelings and we were still friends.

It wasn't wrong, what he'd heard. I had told my dad just that, a fabricated narrative to justify my fleeting visit.

I'd spent the fall on a hiatus of sorts, driving down the west coast in search of something I never found and then taken the most recent assignment at Mercy on a whim just to avoid this exact scenario; coming home... But now that we were well into winter, I was supposed to be headed to another twelve-week stint on another NICU in another hospital where I prayed the mayhem of the sick would drown out the intrusive thoughts of home.

Of him.

"Emily?" His voice, laced with a sad, knowing smile, sliced through my inner turmoil, dragging me back to the agonizing present. "I asked if you're here for the next week?"

My voice was a strangled whisper. "Why are you here?"

He tilted his head as confusion flickered in his eyes. "Here as in—?"

"As in here with Anderson picking me up?"

Understanding crossed his face. "We were getting lunch when you texted him and sent your location."

I released a harsh breath, a sound that was half-laugh, half-sob.

"So, what's the plan?" he continued, oblivious to the battlefield raging within me. "You—"

"You've only made one snarky comment," I interrupted, my voice tight with barely-restrained emotion. "Aren't there supposed to be at least three more before you ask me a genuine question?"

His face fell, a visible reflection of the chasm between us.

We'd tried this, once. Or perhaps I had tried, clinging to a delusion while he... he'd simply played along, for reasons I'd never understand. It didn't matter now. Because standing here, all I could think about was the gnawing regret of how we'd ended.

My nails dug into my palms, a physical pain to eclipse the agonizing ache in my chest, and prayed that for once he wouldn't see through my carefully constructed mask.

But I'd never been able to hide anything from him. It was as if he possessed some kind of radar, honed to detect every tremor of my soul. Sometimes, I swore he knew what I was thinking before I did.

I blinked, the movement too forced, too deliberate, and prayed he wouldn't call me out on it. I was barely holding on, teetering on the precipice between my past and an uncertain future, desperately scrambling for any escape route from this unbearable present.

"Em, I just asked—"

"My name is Emily," I corrected, the words sharp and brittle. "Not EATs, not Em, not anything else your messed up sense of humor can come up with." I closed my eyes, willing every memory of him, every single delicious, amazing, horrible memory, to vanish, to be erased from the fabric of my being. "Just... Emily," I whispered, finally meeting his gaze.

To my surprise, he simply nodded in silent acceptance of my demand.

When it came to the two of us, it was simple, messy, and at times a wonderfully horrible mix.

He was woven into the very fabric of my being, a tangled, fraying thread in the tapestry of my life. Our connection was a volatile alchemy—a simmering concoction of wit laced with malice, constant humiliation, and an undercurrent of something that bordered on pure animosity. It had always been this way, a twisted ritual we'd enacted since childhood. Even after the inferno that had consumed us, a naive whisper within me still clung to the hope—or perhaps the fear—that we would inevitably gravitate back to this orbit, this strange middle ground where we could simultaneously tolerate and despise each other.

I knew, with a chilling certainty, that I could never truly rid him from my life. He was, after all, my brother's best friend. But maybe, just maybe, we could forge a silent pact, a mutual agreement to bury the laughter, the touches, the orgasms, and retreat into the familiar fortress of manufactured hatred. Perhaps that desolate landscape was the only sanctuary left to us.

I exhaled a weary sigh as every horrible insult I wanted to throw at him disappeared. "I think my next assignment is off the table," I murmured, offering no further explanation and praying he wouldn't press.

My gaze drifted to my broken down home, and I struggled to mask the crushing weight of defeat. I couldn't bear to confess my latest catastrophe, the blunder that had left me jobless for the foreseeable future, to the man who possessed everything I could only dream of. I wouldn't reveal that my nomadic existence, the constant travel, the fleeting encounters with new places and faces, were nothing more than elaborate attempts to outrun the ghosts of this town. And I certainly wouldn't dare to articulate the most painful truth of all: that he was inextricably bound to that equation. Especially not while he stood before me, an untouchable monument of devastating perfection.

I barely registered Anderson's abrupt exit from the RV, his hands clutching the only two towels I possessed.

"What are you talking about?" His voice grated against my raw nerves. "Your job doesn't start for another week. I know you only planned to stay for a day or two, but this will give us an excuse to catch up a little more. And I'm sure we'll have Ramona working by the time you need to leave." He nodded towards Mona and tossed one of the towels in my direction before taking the other to what I assumed were the pristine leather seats of Ford's sports car.

I didn't correct his inaccurate assumption of my life. Especially not in front of Mr. Perfect's twin.

While Anderson and Ford could have in no way passed for actual siblings, they were two sides of the same impossibly dazzling coin effortlessly soaring above everyone else in our small town.

Both had graduated in the top of their class while barely ever having to crack open a book.

Both had lettered in every sport they played.

Both had been accepted to multiple colleges, some offering full rides.

And both had now earned their MD's in their desired specialities, each with a beautiful wife on their arm.

And while Anderson mirrored my own features, possessing the warm brown eyes that had captivated every cheerleader in high school. Ford... Ford was a different beast altogether. Rugged muscle, dark brown hair that always seemed to fall just so, and eyes so deep blue they swallowed the light. He radiated a dangerous, rebellious aura that drove even the desperate mothers in the afternoon pickup line a little crazy.

But he drove no one as crazy as he did me.

Chapter 3

Present Day

Emily

I took twice as long in the shower as I normally would.

At first, it was a simple matter of scrubbing the grime from my hair. But then I pictured Ford leaning against poor, broken-down Ramona, arms crossed, the hint of his tattoo peeking out from beneath his sleeve and even two rounds with my favorite detachable shower head couldn't wash him from my mind.

As soon as the water shut off, I leaned back against the cool tile and cursed myself. One moment in his presence, and the months of carefully constructed self-restraint crumbled. I'd blocked him from all my socials and made Becca, Liz, Lynn, and Anderson swear to never speak his name again. It didn't matter. Ford always seemed to maneuver himself back into my orbit.

I'd just pulled on my pajamas when a knock echoed through the quiet house.

"Emmy?" Dad called and I ran to throw open the bedroom door. He hadn't been home from work when I'd arrived, meaning this was the first time I'd seen him in almost a full year—one of the longest stretches we'd ever been apart.

"Dad!" I wrapped my arms around his neck, breathing in the familiar scent of home. A tightness gripped my chest at that smell. It should have been accompanied by comforting laughter and mom's teasing remark about how, even after nine months of carrying me, I'd still come out looking like my father's twin. But that voice never came because mom was no longer there.

When Dad pulled back to look me in the eyes, I could have sworn there were tears gathering in his own. "You look damn near the same as you did fifteen years ago with that wet hair and no makeup."

I laughed, silently thanking him for the shift in the air, then crossed my arms. "You mean when y'all refused to let me wear false eyelashes or get hair extensions?"

He shrugged. "I guess things have changed a bit, huh?" He reached out and squeezed my hand, and we both knew there was more to that statement than either of us would admit. "Come on. Dinner's ready, and I have a date with the best-looking girl in town tonight."

I laughed. "I'm going to assume that date is me, and the attire is casual, because I'm way too comfy in these." I kicked out a leg, gesturing to the fuzzy pink pajamas I'd found tucked into an old dresser.

"No other girl for me!" Dad said as the microwave beeped, and he backed himself out into the hallway.

"I'll be right there!" I called out just as my phone buzzed on the nightstand.

> Becca: Thanks for the update, bitch. I had to find out from your location that you made it safely?! I'm contemplating a revocation of your maid of honor status. Consider this your one and only warning

I smiled at the text, the words practically echoing Becca's voice in my head. I could see her so clearly: brows furrowed in mock frustration, that tiny nose scrunched up in concentration. She'd be perched on the couch, knees drawn up, and a box of cereal perched beside her. One long, dark auburn ringlet would have escaped her bun, falling across her face, and there'd be far too much blush, her latest makeup obsession, dusted across her cheeks.

I also knew a litany of profanities was being hurled in FitzWilliam's direction. And that was the saddest part. Poor, innocent FitzWilliam, the black and white cat we'd shared in college and both sworn was somehow a haughty human trapped in a feline body, was now the unwilling recipient of her tirade.

> Emily: HA! And who would take my place? Jess? Mandy? Connor?

> Becca: Connor's brother owns that massive beach house in Charleston. I bet he would plan me an amazing bachelorette party.

> Emily: Ugh. Fine you win. I'm soooooorrrrryyyyy. But do me a solid and let FitzWilliam go eat his dinner so he doesn't have to listen to you rant about me anymore.

The smile that covered my face was immeasurable. It's not like we hadn't recently spoken. Hell, we'd facetimed that morning, but talking to Becca somehow always seemed to bring a smile to my face.

> Becca: FitzWilliam says to shush. He's on my side.

> Emily: FitzWilliam is a cat. He doesn't speak. Also, FitzWilliam is a victim of Stockholm syndrome.

Becca: FitzWilliam is now hurt. I'm having to comfort him from your harsh words. Also, FitzWilliam wouldn't forget to text me back.

Emily: Again, Stockholm syndrome.

Becca: Maybe, maybe not. How's your dad?

I was both relieved and apprehensive at the turn in conversation. There was a part of me that wanted to pretend I wasn't here. If others didn't acknowledge my presence in this godforsaken town, then maybe I could ignore it as well.

Emily: Fine. We're about to eat dinner. How much do you wanna bet he ordered a large pan of lasagna from Cavilla's earlier in the week and has been reheating and eating off it since…?

Becca: No bet. He definitely did. How's Anderson?

Emily: Same. Perfect. Tired. Stressed. Anderson.

Becca: Hmm . . . Sounds about right.

The three little dots indicating Becca was still typing popped up and then went away... and then popped up again.

Becca: And how's… everyone else?

I stalled as the reality of the question sunk in. Though we never verbalized the thought, we both were well aware that being back here meant I could run into someone I didn't want to.

My fingers raced across the screen as I typed, then deleted, then typed and reworded, and then deleted and retyped my response. I knew what Becca was asking, but again... maybe if I just didn't acknowledge it... I hit send before I could rethink what to say.

> Emily: All my imaginary friends from childhood have long since moved out, so I don't know who you could be speaking of.

There was a moment of absolute torturous silence where I didn't know if Becca would push harder or leave it be before the response finally came through.

> Becca: If you say so... On a more serious note. Pick a day/night this week and get your butt up here.

> Emily: Yes ma'am.

I sighed, letting the conversation die. I longed to tell Becca everything about my disastrous reunion with *him*. But I couldn't. Not yet. I needed time to process, and if there was one constant in my life, it was this: one word to my best friend about what had happened would unleash an hours-long conversational excavation, just like that morning.

I flipped my phone over, ready to leave my room and appease my now-ravenous stomach when another ping echoed, and my heart rate hitched. I closed my eyes, unwilling to tread that path with Becca tonight. I'd need at least three glasses of Pinot before that Pandora's Box was opened.

Relief washed over me when I glanced down and saw, not a reply from Becca, but a message from Anderson staring back.

> Big Bear: I can come by after my AM shift at the hospital to help out with the repairs if needed.

I had almost typed the entire response when a second message came through.

> Big Bear: I promise not to bring Ford with me this time.

I cringed at the name, but decided to ignore it. It didn't matter how long I was stuck back here, I would not let Mr. Three First Names ruin my time.

> Emily: Honestly, what were you thinking?

> Big Bear: We were at lunch.

> Emily: You'll only be forgiven IF you bring my baby with you!

> Big Bear: You do realize James is mine and Lynn's son...

> Emily: Semantics seblantics... He is MINE! BRING HIM TO ME!!! I am his most favorite aunt!

> Big Bear: You're his only aunt...

> Emily: Still his favorite.

Big Bear: But... I can probably make that work... Lynn will enjoy an hour or two of quiet as long as you promise to stop by and see her later in the week.

Emily: DEAL!

The thought of endless snuggles with a newly mobile James filled me with a warm glow as I stepped into the living room to find my father had arranged two TV trays like some bizarre, impromptu feast. Each groaned under a mountain of lasagna, enough to feed a small army, and what looked like the entire contents of a parmesan cheese factory lay scattered on top.

The logo on the discarded cardboard box overflowing the trash confirmed my suspicions: Cavilla's.

It had been almost two years since Mom died, and Dad existed solely on takeout. Ironically, it was often food he openly disliked. He'd always hated lasagna. Every single time it had appeared on the dinner table when Mom was alive, he'd cut his eyes over to Anderson, Ford and I with a grim look on his face and then would turn back to mom with an excited smile.

My heart cracked a little more as I stared at the box in the trash. I knew this was his way of keeping her alive, a desperate attempt to hold onto something that was no longer there.

I pulled my gaze away from the overflowing bin and gave Dad a quick kiss on the cheek before sinking onto the sofa to tackle the daunting meal.

"Thanks," I managed, forcing a smile. "It looks delicious."

I could do this. For a little while, at least. I could fake the happy smiles, mask the ache that throbbed beneath the surface. I could slip on this newly manufactured glass slipper and pretend I was someone else, someone who fit seamlessly into this world and not the awkward girl I truly was. I could pretend Mom was just on one of her trips with her girlfriends, and not buried six feet under on the other side of town. I could let Dad and Anderson focus on Ramona for the next few days, isolating myself with James and Lynn while avoiding all other human contact. And then, when my life was magically fixed, I could escape, only returning when absolutely necessary.

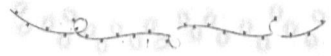

Ford

I wasn't sure how I'd even managed to speak when I saw her standing there all covered in gunk and dirt. She'd looked absolutely miserable, and there was more brown muck strung throughout her curls than there was blonde showing through, but damn if she still wasn't the most beautiful thing I'd ever seen.

And she hated me.

I could tell by the way she'd immediately crossed her arms in a defensive move forming a wall between us. A blatant declaration of her desire for absolutely no contact with the man who'd shattered her world. What she couldn't have known, in that fleeting moment, was how that defensive shift had positioned her just so, allowing the dying rays of the sun to bathe the left side of her face. The effect was devastating. She was radiant. Luminous. Sunlight itself paled in comparison to the incandescent light that emanated from Emily Ann Truse.

This woman was going to be my undoing.

Three hours had passed, and her image still burned behind my eyelids. Every blink was a futile attempt to erase the picture.

I stared blankly at my computer screen, my eyes scanning the meticulously constructed reply to my lawyer's latest email, yet the words barely registered. Something about shared debts and payouts far exceeding my expectations. But none of it mattered. I just wanted it over. I craved closure, an end to this torturous chapter. I yearned for freedom.

With a pounding heart that was still halfway broken, I shut the computer, rested my forehead against the cool surface of the table, and prayed tomorrow morning would finally end it.

I replayed our reunion in agonizing detail. My mouth constantly malfunctioned in moments of high stress, and around her, I was perpetually on edge. I'd stumbled over my words, each syllable a testament to my utter lack of composure. She'd simply stared, her eyes a mixture of hurt, anger, and something that might have been a flicker of lingering pain. A pain that mirrored my own.

Before a coherent thought could form, the stupid words were out of my mouth—something about her initials and her mother and God damn it, I was the world's biggest idiot.

I was right in the middle of trying to figure out how to dismantle years of hatred in two weeks when my phone buzzed.

> Anderson: I need to cancel lunch tomorrow. Going to dad's after my shift to help Emily with the RV.

> Ford: No problem.

> Anderson: And do me a solid . . . try to vacate the area while she's here.

I grunted, tossed my phone onto the kitchen counter, and walked down the darkened stairs into the partially completed basement my father had somehow never had the time to finish. Raw heat surged upward with the memories I'd spent years burying, and it took more than a few calming breaths to rid me of the anger that vanished man evoked.

I all but fell flat on my face and let out a string of curses when I ran straight into the stacks of boxes that contained the entirety of my life. After finding the pull cord for the light, I surveyed the area, but before I could get started with going through it all, my mom called out from the first floor that dinner was almost ready.

The frayed edge of the blanket snagged on my thumbnail as I dragged it over me, the thin fabric offering little comfort against the chill that had seeped into the bones of the makeshift bed. I stared at the ceiling, a blank canvas against which my anxieties played out in stark relief wishing I was instead staring at beautiful lights above.

How was I going to navigate the next few days?

The thought hung heavy in my chest.

My gaze drifted to the window, the pane a dark mirror reflecting the turmoil within. Beyond it, just a few feet away, lay her window, a silent witness to the tangled history between us. I wondered what thoughts lingered in her head and what conclusions she'd drawn from our brief, unexpected encounter earlier that afternoon.

A bitter taste coated my tongue as I replayed the events in my mind. If I were a better man, a man deserving of her, I would have driven Anderson back to his own car to spare her the inconvenience of seeing me. But I wasn't that man, not when Emily was involved. The thought, once a shield, now felt like a brand, seared into my very being.

I rubbed my hands roughly over my face, as if I could physically erase the memories that clawed at me from the past. It wasn't just the childish cruelties, the thoughtless jabs of our youth, that haunted me. It was the more recent wounds, the two years where I'd succumbed to my own ego and allowed my immaturity to dictate my actions. I'd hurt her then, deeply, and the knowledge of that festered, turning into a constant reminder of my failings.

A sudden realization pierced through the regret. This, I knew with a chilling certainty, might be my last chance. Not a last chance to win her back or rekindle a love that had long since turned to ash. Even I could see that the probability of that was gone. No, this was a last chance of a different kind. A chance to show her, before she left for Florida and disappeared from my life for good, how truly sorry I was.

Perhaps, just perhaps, if I could set aside my own selfish desires, and put her needs and feelings first for once, I could show her the depth of my regret, the vast emptiness that her absence had carved into my life.

Maybe, just maybe, we could end this chapter not as enemies, locked in a bitter struggle of resentment, but as something akin to friends.

I turned away from the window, choosing to face the blank wall instead. If I continued to stare out into the night, knowing she was so close, I knew I'd give in to the desperate impulse to cross the distance between us, to stand on her porch and make a complete and utter fool of myself. And I couldn't, wouldn't, risk shattering the last bit of respect she might still hold for me.

Chapter 4

11 Years Prior

Emily

It didn't matter that I was only a year younger and technically an adult in the eyes of the law. In their eyes, I would always be the annoying little sister, the one who drove Anderson and Ford to the brink of madness. From the day our families became neighbors, our lives had been a constant, chaotic collision, and no matter how hard the boys tried to pin every little mishap on me, the blame couldn't fall solely on my shoulders. They, too, had made my life a carefully orchestrated hell.

There was the time, when I was seven, that I'd accidentally toppled their precious Star Wars Lego set. The next day, every single one of my dolls was adorned with crude, drawn-on tattoos. In middle school, when I'd defied my parents and started making coffee, Ford had secretly swapped the sugar for salt and I didn't find out until well into first period when I took a huge gulp and then promptly spit it all out over my desk. And then, the daily ritual: the boys would hide, lurking, waiting to leap out and scare the living shit out of me, usually when I was carrying a drink that would then inevitably spill all over my clothes.

But the sticky note incident was the one that truly seared itself into my memory. I'd walked into my room after school one day to find the entire space – clothes, furniture, everything – plastered with them. I'd spent the afternoon watching, a smug satisfaction blooming in my chest, as my mom scolded them, then forced them to spend an hour peeling each note away, and then writing something positive about me on every single one.

Most of Anderson's notes were sarcastic jabs: "Emily's farts aren't horrible" or "Emily doesn't look like a gremlin anymore." But Ford's were different. And I still refuse to fully admit that I might have saved a few and tucked them away beneath the creaky baseboard by my bedroom door.

"Emily is smart." "Emily has good taste in music." "Emily tells good jokes." And then, the one that made my breath catch in my throat: "I like the way Emily's shampoo smells."

I'd found that one at the bottom of the stack on the table, and a hot blush stained my cheeks.

Over the years the pranks, once a constant barrage, faded into memory, just like our acknowledgment of each other. It was as if an invisible wall had risen between Ford and I, brick by silent brick, until we existed in separate, soundproofed worlds.

It was only at the end of my junior year while Anderson and Ford were prepping for college that something changed. It struck me then, with the force of a physical blow, how the past years, the years of vanishing pranks and side glances, had irrevocably altered us.

Ford and I had perfected the art of mutual nonexistence, performing Oscar-worthy displays of indifference. But then, something shifted. The ground beneath our feet trembled, and the carefully constructed facade crumbled as I began to notice his every move, every breath, every subtle shift in his posture.

Every time he walked by after a pick-up basketball game, clad in a sleeveless black tank and gym shorts, I practically melted into a steamy puddle on the scorching pavement of our driveway.

He'd always been beautiful, I supposed. A breathtaking sculpture of muscle and angst. But until that specific moment, the one where I was a prisoner behind the living room curtains, meticulously mentally tracing the sculpted dips and ridges of his perfectly defined physique, he'd been nothing more than an annoying extension of my infuriatingly perfect older brother.

I'd never understood why he spent so many nights on our couch, or crammed into the second twin bed in Anderson's room, instead of in his own bed next door. Until that year, I hadn't even cared. He was just... there. A familiar, comforting presence. An extra member of the family. He simply fit. But that year, everything changed. The irritating cadence of his laugh, the disgusting way he chewed his dinner, the acrid stench of sweat that clung to him after football practice – all of it faded into the background noise of my burgeoning obsession.

That year, I saw the alluring sheen of sweat on his flexing muscles. I became mesmerized by the confident curve of his smirk, and his laugh echoed in my ears with a newfound resonance. I watched, practically spellbound, as he mowed his front lawn, the rhythmic push and pull of the machine was a hypnotic dance. But my nights.... Oh, my nights were the best. Those were invaded by visions of his hands on my body as his imaginary touch burned a brand onto my skin.

He'd transformed. He was no longer the boy who pilfered my favorite cookies from the pantry, who drank milk straight from the carton with unapologetic disgust, who left a disordered mess on my bathroom counter on the mornings he stayed over. He'd become... something else, someone else. Someone I couldn't tear my gaze away from. Someone who consumed my every waking thought.

And the most agonizing part of it all? He knew. He knew the power he held over me. He'd caught me staring at him from across the room more times than I could bear to count, and each stolen glance was a fresh wound, a searing brand that marked me as his.

Trapped.

Captivated.

Utterly and irrevocably his.

My routine was perfected. School, snack, movie, homework—a monotonous cycle designed to drown out the relentless thrum of my own thoughts. But last year, my grades had suffered, a silent testament to the war waging within me.

Even now, I'd come home, grab my usual snack, and let the familiar cadence of Pride and Prejudice fill the suffocating silence of the house as I studied. But my attention wasn't on the textbook or the looming math problems in front of me. My eyes were instead glued to the window, stealing glances of him.

I'd lose track of time, lost in a dream that would never come true, until he'd turn, his gaze meeting mine and a maddeningly knowing smirk on his lips. Each time, I'd practically disintegrate on the couch, a molten core of shame and longing burning through me. I'd shrink behind the armrest, silently berating my obviousness, before retreating to my room.

It would have been fine if he'd simply ignored me. But Ford never made anything easy for me. He reveled in my torment, taunting me with every stolen glance, every subtle smirk. I'd try to retaliate, to wound him with words as sharp as his gaze, but I was no match for him. He knew precisely how to ignite my fury, how to further my obsession, all while weaving himself deeper into the fabric of my dreams.

He'd wink across the crowded hallway. He'd casually brush against me in the kitchen, his hand grazing my hip as he reached for something on a high shelf, sending tremors of confusion through my very core. He'd anticipate my every need, leaving the exact book I was searching for just out of reach in the school library, a cruel game designed to keep me perpetually on the edge of frustration. He'd dunk me in the pool the moment I declared my hair off-limits, and there was that time, which he vehemently denied, when he'd "accidentally" stopped the dryer, leaving my clothes damp for the agonizing ride to school.

He was a beautiful, infuriating paradox. And my foolish, teenage heart, in all its agonizing naiveté, was utterly, and completely in love with him.

But he never spoke to me. Not with words. And perhaps that was the most intoxicating part of it all—this silent, unspoken language of stolen glances and accidental touches. Our conversations were a battlefield of brooding looks and unwavering stares, a fleeting brush of skin that sent electric shocks through my veins. But it was a hell I craved, a delicious agony that kept me tethered to him, even in the crushing silence between us.

Ford, like Anderson, was the golden boy, the untouchable senior. He was destined for college, a pre-med football god in the making while I, on the other hand, was the invisible rising senior, more comfortable with my nose buried in a book or lost in the worlds of fanfiction than real life. Especially after I'd stumbled upon the reason why all the moms devoured those cheesy grocery store novels with the long-haired, shirtless men on the covers.

Perhaps it was my insatiable appetite for stories that set everything in motion. Enemies to lovers was my weakness, my favorite trope, and if Ford was anything, he was my enemy. So, instead of immersing myself within the real world, I consumed every romance novel I could find, clinging to the hope of one day turning fiction into reality. Besides, book boyfriends, with their guaranteed lack of disappointment, were a far safer bet than real friends who would inevitably stab you in the back.

Truthfully, real friends were a rare commodity when I spent so much time contorting myself to fit their ever-shifting expectations. By the time I'd finally deciphered the current ideal, there was a new one to strive for. It was as if my brain simply operated on a different frequency than everyone else's. I would reach the destination... eventually. But my journey was always peppered with a thousand and one detours, side quests I couldn't resist exploring, while everyone else sailed smoothly down the main road.

And maybe I was jealous of Ford and Anderson's relationship. They seemed to orbit each other without any need for instructions. They just understood each other. Me? I wanted that. I wanted someone who looked at me and saw past the questionable life choices and into my heart (or at least past the questionable mascara and into my general vicinity).

So, while those two were busy being disgustingly great at literally everything, I was waging my own personal war against boredom by smuggling smutty books from the county library or downloading then onto my e-reader while praying my mother, a woman with the investigative skills of a seasoned detective and the nose of a bloodhound, never found out.

And maybe those books were the reason I'd suddenly noticed Ford – and not in the "he's a human being with a pulse" way I had previously. Maybe they truly were a gateway drug...to...well, I wasn't entirely sure what the final destination was, but it definitely involved less sensible cardigan-wearing and more...well, more Ford. Or maybe, just maybe, they gave me the final nudge I needed to admit, even if only to myself, exactly why I enjoyed staring at him so damn much.

"Emily!" Mom yelled, shattering my inner fantasy.

"What?" I jumped, sending a box of gingersnaps cascading to the floor like tiny, sugary dominoes of disaster.

"I've been calling you for the last five minutes," Mom said, leaning against the door frame between the kitchen and the living room. A dish towel hung limply from her hand, and a knowing look plastered on her face.

"Okay?" I mumbled, shoving my hands into my pockets, hoping she wouldn't notice the brand-new and ridiculously long, fake nails I'd purchased and gave her an eye roll.

Mom, unfazed, smirked and mimicked the gesture. "I asked if you liked the view?"

My brows furrowed in confusion. What view? The view of the overflowing recycling bin? The view of the cat napping precariously on the windowsill?

Then, following her line of vision, I turned back to the window to find Ford standing mere feet away, his muscular back facing me. He was holding a basketball, cradling it between his hip and arm in a way that was...well, let's just say it was effective.

"Ugh!" I groaned, stalking back to my bedroom with the dramatic flair of a tragic Shakespearean heroine and pretended I couldn't hear Mom's laugh echoing in the hallway, a sound that could only be described as pure, unadulterated amusement at my expense.

"Dinner will be ready in about ten!" she called.

"Got it!"

"When your face turns back to a normal shade – I swear, you look like a tomato – go grab the boys and tell them to wash up!"

I rolled my eyes again. "I hate you!" I called back, but with absolutely no sincerity as I crossed into my room, fully expecting the door to shut behind me, but then I heard a familiar sigh.

"Emily."

I turned to find her leaning against the doorframe, a dish towel drooping from her hand like a defeated flag.

"Mom." I matched her tone, a perfectly flat monotone honed from years of teenage negotiations

"He's a good kid."

"He's not a kid," I countered.

"He'll always be a kid in my eyes." Mom sighed, a dramatic, world-weary sigh that suggested she'd personally witnessed the fall of Rome.

I flopped onto my bed, and hurled a shimmering pink pillow over my face. It muffled my voice, turning it into a deep, underwater rumble. "What's your point?"

"Does he know you like him?"

"Ugh! Mom!" I could have spontaneously combusted. It would have been a far more dignified exit than having this conversation.

"I think he likes you, too." Mom chirped, completely oblivious to my internal meltdown.

I balked.

"Emily, I think he–"

"Absolutely not," I interrupted, a swift, decisive end to what I knew was coming. "First of all. His parents hate me. They probably have a dartboard with my picture on it."

"They do not hate you." Mom countered as she tried to hold in her laugh.

I threw the pillow off my face and stared her down, a laser beam of indignation. "I heard what his mom said last week. I'm practically on their enemy list. Right below the squirrels who keep raiding their bird feeder."

Mom gave me a curious look. "What did she–"

"Last week," I paused, willing the rising tide of emotion to recede. I was giving a better performance than Mr. Wickham ever did. "I was walking home from the bus and I overheard her talking to Mrs. Mills next door. Mrs. Mills, bless her heart, said she liked my entry into the art festival and that I had true talent and then started on about how cute of a couple Ford and I would make. She's basically a walking, talking romance novel subplot."

"She isn't wrong." Mom agreed, completely undermining my carefully constructed misery. Then she added, "On both accounts."

I rolled my eyes. For some reason, taking compliments, even from my own parents, had always been hard for me. I was clearly destined for a life of self-deprecation and awkward pauses.

"Well Mrs. Thomas didn't agree. She balked as soon as the words left Mrs. Mills' mouth. She actually balked. Like a startled horse. She said there was absolutely no way Ford and I would get together. I was headed nowhere. Apparently, I'm on a one-way train to Lonelyville. But he was going to make it out of this town and meet a nice girl with a good stable job and a head that was firmly placed on her shoulders and not high in the clouds. You know, someone sensible."

Mom tilted her head to the side with a questioning look in her eye. "Did she now?"

"Yes." I fell back and placed the pillow over my face again. "Besides, he has every girl in school after him. He could literally have anyone he wants. He's practically drowning in them."

"So why doesn't he want them?" Mom countered, delivering the killer blow with a perfectly timed, perfectly innocent question.

"What do you mean?" I mumbled from under the pillow.

"You said it. He has every girl after him and yet he's never brought a girl to his house or ours while your brother seems to be on track for breaking the Guinness world record for how many girlfriends he can have in a year."

I laughed, a snorting, pillow-muffled laugh that threatened to give me a nosebleed.

Okay, so she wasn't wrong. Anderson did cycle through girlfriends faster than a Tour de France hopeful on performance enhancers. Ford, though? Ford barely registered them.

"He's just being defiant. You know how Mrs. Thomas is."

From my vantage point, I couldn't actually see the eye roll Mom launched across the room, but I could feel it. It radiated across the space like a low-grade electromagnetic pulse.

"Mrs. Thomas," Mom stated, as if delivering a crucial piece of intel, "has her own personal brand of demons she is desperate to put down and not hand off to Ford."

"That's... cryptic," I offered, squinting. I craned my neck and discovered Mom had materialized in my desk chair by the door.

"You'll understand when you have kids," Mom sighed. "All we want is for you to have a life that doesn't resemble the train wreck we call our own."

"I don't want kids," I stated. "What I do want is for you to just say what you mean."

The chair squeaked in protest as Mom stood. "Fine," she huffed. "You don't want cryptic? Here's non-cryptic. That boy likes you, you like him, and I don't give a flying fig what that—that cunt next door says–"

I practically levitated. "Mom!" The word, so unexpected, hung in the air like a rogue firework.

"No," Mom insisted. "You two would be spectacular together. End of discussion."

"I can't believe you just called her a—a—" I stammered, lost for words. It was like trying to describe a particularly vivid dream to someone who spoke a different language.

Mom rolled her eyes. "You can say it," she drawled.

"You called her a *cunt*," I whispered, like I was sharing top-secret intel. I was newly eighteen, yes, but there's nothing quite as awkward as intentionally uttering a curse word in front of your mother. It was as if I was breaking a fundamental law of the universe.

"Because she is one," Mom declared. "Nobody talks about my kids like that. Especially when I'm basically single-handedly raising her only child as well."

I leaned back on my elbows, trying to look nonchalant, like I wasn't about to spontaneously combust from sheer embarrassment. "Why do you think we'd be good together?"

I shifted my gaze from the wall, which had suddenly become the most fascinating object in the room, to Mom. She was smiling, and then she just... shrugged. "I'm an expert at my kids."

"Ford's not your kid," I pointed out.

She scoffed. "Not by blood. But he's mine. He's mine, and he's your dad's, and he's Anderson's. Might as well be yours, too."

"You're so weird," I blurted and mom laughed.

"One day," Mom said, with a dramatic pause for effect, "one day you're going to have to stop hiding all those feelings behind the makeup and the clothes and the hair, and start actually using all that hard-earned knowledge you've accumulated." She turned to leave the room.

"What are you talking about?" I called out just as she leaned back into the doorway, tilting her head.

"Emily," she said, her voice dripping with sarcasm, "you're a straight-A student and you still haven't figured out we share a Kindle library."

My face, which had been a kaleidoscope of colors for the past few minutes, settled on a particularly vibrant shade of crimson.

Chapter 5

PRESENT DAY

Emily

T he cramped quarters of Ramona, my B-Class camper, were a constant reminder of my hasty, impulsive life. Every inch was accounted for, every possession a carefully curated necessity. Yet, within these limitations, I'd found a strange sort of peace. Some days, I resented Mona for this imposed minimalism, the constant awareness of boundaries. But on others, I reveled in the lack of clutter and freedom from unnecessary things.

Despite the frustrations, I'd fallen deeply in love with that little camper. When inside the driver and passenger seats swiveled to meet a small pop-up table, creating a cozy workspace where I'd spent countless hours lost in thought. Behind it, the surprisingly efficient toilet and shower combo offered a welcome sense of normalcy (and good water pressure). To the left of the side entry door, my miniature kitchenette held almost everything I needed—a two-burner stove, microwave, a sliver of counter space big enough to chop a vegetable or two, a tiny sink, and a mini fridge. I still regretted not considering a dishwasher in my impulsive purchase, a minor imperfection in an otherwise perfect arrangement.

Beyond the kitchen and bath, nestled against the back double doors, and a whopping five feet from the driver seat, was a surprisingly spacious bed that concealed a wealth of storage beneath. It was a small sanctuary.

But my true obsession, the feature that had sealed my immediate purchase on that horrendous day, was the hidden gem in the ceiling. Above the small table, a hatch disguised itself as access to the roof, but it was so much more. Unlatching it revealed a second, tent-like ceiling that could be pushed upwards, creating a soft-top loft. A small ladder hidden under my bed when not in use led to this magical space, where I'd retreated countless times, escaping the confines of the camper and transporting myself to imagined worlds.

Up there, surrounded by my favorite pillows, I'd stretch out, lost in books or simply gazing through the plastic window-covered walls. The world outside faded away, and within that canvas-walled haven, I felt truly, utterly free. It was in that intimate space, beneath the soft glow of the setting sun that I felt most connected to myself, to the vastness of the world, and to the quiet promise of unexpected adventures.

Ramona offered a peculiar kind of freedom, one that demanded a slight tempering of my more extravagant tendencies. Fewer impulse buys and a significantly smaller shoe collection—my bank account offered a silent thanks for the reduced expenditure on all things sparkly. But mostly living in Ramona had honed my meal planning. The only hitch? My newfound expertise was geared toward cooking for one, not five.

I'd envisioned a serene grocery shopping experience. Me, a list, and unwavering focus. Instead, I was reenacting a scene from a disaster movie, except this time with crustaceans.

My mission was simple. Acquire the ingredients for a family feast so dad didn't have to live off Cavilla's for the foreseeable future. My problem was massive. My complete inability to navigate a grocery store without triggering an apocalypse.

Feeding my dad, Anderson, Lynn, baby James, and myself—while generating leftovers—felt like a logistical nightmare. I'd envisioned my dad finally breaking free from his takeout addiction, lured by the call of a home-cooked meal.

I'd unearthed a promising chicken casserole recipe online, but the small-town store's Wi-Fi was about as reliable as my ability to actually follow through with completing a task. Instead of consulting the culinary wisdom I found on a random blog post, I was locked in mortal combat with a loading bar that refused to load. My brow furrowed. My jaw tightened.

Then, seemingly out of nowhere, came the voice. Smooth, familiar, undeniably... Ford.

"If you scowl a little more I'm sure whoever pissed you off is sure to apologize."

My internal monologue went something like this: Ford? Here? Now? When I'm operating on approximately zero brain cells, no caffiene, and a rapidly dwindling supply of patience? This is a cosmic joke.

My brain promptly short-circuited in shock and in a move that would surely land me on an ESPN "Worst Throwing Arm Ever" compilation, I hurled my phone. My intended target: absolutely no one. My actual target: a giant, glass tank full of lobsters.

Ford, being the D1 athlete he was, dodged that ill-fated throw with ease. My phone, however, had no such agility. It careened into the tank, triggering a watery explosion and a cascade of clawed creatures onto the linoleum.

Cue the screaming.

Mostly mine.

I shrieked. I jumped. I performed an impromptu hopscotch routine across the aisle, dodging rogue lobsters like a contestant on a bizarre game show. I even scaled a shelf of bread, clinging to the loaves like a shipwreck survivor clinging to driftwood.

Ford, meanwhile, was doubled over with laughter. Genuine, tear-inducing, belly-shaking laughter. It was infuriating. And also, strangely... endearing?

No, Emily. Focus. Crustacean catastrophe.

"Oh my god! Oh my god!"

"Emily!" Ford gasped between guffaws, his face a mixture of shock and amusement.

"Holy—!" I scrambled higher onto the shelf.

By the time the store employees arrived, I was perched precariously amongst the whole wheat, a soggy, slightly hysterical mess.

"I'm sorry," I squeaked from my perch. "It was me. I'm so sorry."

"You've said that already," a bewildered manager pointed out.

"I think I startled her," Ford offered, still chuckling as he retrieved my now-soaked phone from an empty tank.

The manager's gaze narrowed. "Do you know this man?"

I rolled my eyes as I stepped down.

"Yeah. I know him. It's fine. Everything's fine. I'm sorry. I wasn't paying attention and...listen, I'm sorry and I...I don't know what to do," I babbled, my voice rising in pitch.

The earth swallowing me whole was starting to look like an attractive option. Dealing with embarrassment was one thing. Dealing with this level of absurdity, in front of Ford, was a whole different species of mortification.

I ran a hand through my hair. "Do you need me to pay for the tank? I definitely can pay for it. I just–" I rubbed the exhaustion from my face. "What normally happens when you know..." I gestured vaguely at the aquatic carnage, "...when someone breaks the tank?"

The manager smirked, then outright laughed. "To be honest, this is a first."

"I can take care of the tank," Ford offered, stepping forward.

"No! No, you can't. I can pay for it," I insisted, yanking my water-logged phone from his hand.

"It's not a big deal," the manager interjected. "We have insurance. We'll take care of this. I just wanted to make sure you were okay. You're welcome to finish your shopping."

I mumbled another apology and retreated, my cart trailing behind me like a wounded soldier. I'd come for casserole ingredients; I'd left with a lobster-induced trauma and a renewed sense of my own clumsiness. It was official: I was the undisputed queen of grocery store disasters. And of course, Ford had to be there to witness my crowning achievement.

"You wanna wait up?"

I groaned. "So I can throw something else at you?" I stopped the cart, a metallic beast groaning in protest, but refused to turn. If I didn't see him, maybe he'd cease to exist.

"Your shoes are soaked." Ford stated as he materialized beside me. We both looked down at my shoes, the same shoes I'd just spent a solid fifteen minutes de-mudding yesterday.

"Apparently, that's my new thing," I mumbled, shoulders slumping in defeat.

"Soaked shoes?" He actually sounded confused.

"Yeah," I swallowed. "You haven't heard? I like to split my time between shoes covered in newborn vomit, coffee, mud, and now, apparently, lobster water." I gestured vaguely at the offending footwear. It was a masterpiece of disaster.

"Hmm." Ford mumbled, and out the corner of my eye I could see a small smile tugging at his mouth. "Which one is your favorite?"

I couldn't help the laugh that bubbled up. "Probably the coffee. At least it smelled good."

"Good choice," he added before nudging my cart, sending it careening forward a few inches. "What's all this? You feeding a small village tonight?" He gestured to the overflowing cart. In truth it did look like I was prepping for a zombie apocalypse, but with more family-friendly snacks.

"I'm making a meal for my family this week," I cringed the second the words were out. Too loaded. Too much history. "Dad, Anderson, Lynn, James, and me," I amended quickly, hoping he wouldn't pick up on the unspoken name that used to belong on that list. The one that haunted my dreams and apparently my local grocery store.

"Chicken?" He asked, eyes scanning the four packs of poultry like he was inspecting them for flaws. "Are you cooking for a night or the month?"

That's what finally made me turn. Really turn and look at him. And when I did, I almost choked. Because of course, *of course*, he was wearing a three-piece suit. In a grocery store. How had I not noticed it earlier during the lobster fiasco? What was this, Legally Blonde meets Supermarket Sweep?

"What are we doing?"

Ford swallowed, looking adorably uncomfortable. "I think we're talking. Specifically talking about dinner and—"

"No," I cut him off. "You and I. What are we doing? Why are we standing here like two old neighbors just catching up? I don't want to fake a conversation with you. And honestly, I have no idea how to even fake one to begin with." I leaned against the cart, which wobbled precariously, and finally met his stare. Then scoffed as I really looked him over. "And who in the absolute hell goes grocery shopping in a fucking suit?" I paused, remembering how much that last therapy session cost, and reeled in the torrent of angry, hurtful words I wanted to unleash. "I'm not good at faking being friends," I finished lamely, feeling like a petulant child.

He swallowed, looking pained. "I'm not faking anything. We're just catching up."

I shook my head as I rubbed my temples. "I'm tired. I drove halfway across the country yesterday only to make it within ten miles of my dad's house and break down. Then, I see you." My voice was low, exhausted.

Ford opened his mouth, probably to say something soothing and infuriating, but I lifted my hand.

"And no offense, but I had absolutely no plans of seeing you. And then after I found out that my dad is still living off Cavilla's, I come to the store to fix him some meals, only to, once again, see you. And well, then there were lobsters and," I paused as his previously dejected expression morphed into something suspiciously like amusement. "And well, honestly, the lobster aspect of this just kind of sucked."

Ford grinned, a genuine, heart-melting grin that made my stomach do a little flip. "You thought they were going to pinch you, didn't you?"

"Yeah," I admitted, because admitting ridiculous things seemed to be my theme for the day.

"They have rubber bands on the pinchers," he said, crossing his arms, looking infuriatingly charming.

"Yeah. I know," I replied, because of course I knew. I was a rational adult. Mostly. I turned to leave, because lingering felt like poking a bruise. "Listen," I paused. "I was going to say it was good to see you, but that would have been a lie. So I'm just going to say I hope you have a good day." And then I walked away, leaving him standing there in his suit, surrounded by the ghost of lobsters.

"Emily?" Ford called out.

"What?"

"How are you paying for that?"

I twisted to meet his stare. "What?" My confusion was swiftly turning to rage. "You think I can't—"

"You still use Apple Pay for most everything?"

I rolled my eyes in response. Leave it to Ford to remember every little detail I just wished he would forget. "Why does that matter?"

"Cause your phone isn't really working at the moment." He added as we both looked down to the broken contraption in my hand.

"Mother Fucker!" I called out as I stomped my foot and heard a gasp from a nearby woman. I scoffed in response.

"I can—," Ford started.

"No. You can't." I pushed the cart forward and made my way to customer service.

The next hour ticked by in agonizing slowness as I waited for my dad, stranded at the grocery store without a penny to my name. Then, I looked up in surprise to find Anderson, his gaze fixed on me. The only comfort in the situation was the small boy nestled in his arms.

I'd half-expected him to rush straight to Ramona the moment we had all the groceries packed away, but Anderson was always several steps ahead. He settled James back into his car seat and gave me a questioning look when I didn't immediately follow.

"You coming?"

"I thought you were going to look at Ramona. Where are we going?"

He chuckled, circling around to the driver's side of his truck. "Emily," he said, his voice laced with amusement, "that broken phone is practically one of your vital organs. No way you last more than an hour without checking some feed. Get in. You've got to get a new phone."

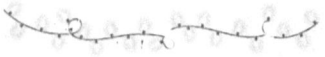

"That's not fair! You're such a little cheat!" I called out in jest, chasing a chubby-legged James across the driveway and through the front yard, desperately trying to outrun the morning. My mood had taken a nosedive when Anderson and Dad spent the last hour surgically dissecting the engine of poor Ramona. Sadly, Anderson's impressive bedside manner didn't translate to things with engines instead of hearts. It was a mechanical tragedy.

But then, salvation arrived in the form of a very fast, very adorable one year old. I was too busy trying to wrangle a tiny human tornado to wallow in the frustration of my broken-down home. For the first time in ages, I actually smiled at something that wasn't the glimpse of a memory.

"Give me that back!" I pleaded in a sing-songy voice, rounding the corner of the garage in pursuit of the little scoundrel who'd stolen my new phone. But instead of finding a mess of blonde curls mirroring my own, I collided with something solid. Very solid and covered in hard muscles and tanned skin.

You've got to be fucking kidding me.

"Hey. Again." Ford had me by the upper arms, catching me before I could become intimately acquainted with the unforgiving concrete which would have ensured another crop of impressive bruises I'd discover later.

I yanked free, but it felt like his hand had left a brand on my skin. Turning away, I called out for James, who promptly hurled himself into the arms of Ford's mom.

Having lived next door to the woman for most of my life, I barely knew her. Mrs. Thomas rarely ventured outside. No one ever talked about why, but we all knew what plagued her nightmares. And seeing her there, holding James, and with a genuine smile gracing her face? It threw every preconceived notion I had about the day out the window.

"Emily!" Mrs. Thomas chirped, a smile plastered on her face as she ruffled James's perpetually messy hair.

This woman, a barely-there presence for most of our childhood, was now standing outside, dressed in something other than pajamas, playing with my James like they were old pals.

"Hi!" I squeaked, way too enthusiastic, waving like a game show contestant before awkwardly yanking my hand back.

"Ford said you were here for a few days. It's so good to see you again! And all grown up! You're a nurse now, right?" Her smile was dazzling, but underneath, I sensed a hidden agenda.

I managed a strained smile. But when I glanced at Ford, a flicker of apprehension danced in his eyes. What was his deal?

"Yes, ma'am," I mumbled, just as Ford interrupted.

"She's a nurse practitioner." He puffed out his chest, practically glowing with pride. I shot him a look of pure, unadulterated confusion. How did he even know that? My social media presence was all about picturesque RV life in the middle of nowhere. The average person wouldn't even know I had a job, let alone its fancy title.

"Only technically," I corrected, trying to sound nonchalant. "I just passed my boards, so I'll start looking for a job once my next rotation is over." I smiled with the bold-faced lie. In reality, I had no clue when I'd be applying for that fancy NP job. I didn't even know what I'd be doing next week, let alone next year.

"That's such an accomplishment," Mrs. Thomas gushed, her eyes sparkling. "I always knew you were going places."

I bit back the first thing that popped into my head: *That's hilarious, considering you used to tell everyone I was a space cadet who'd never amount to anything.* Instead, I forced a gracious, "Thank you."

The door to Ramona clicked shut, and I whipped around to find Anderson, the picture of sophistication, shaking his head, and a smirk playing on his lips as he fixed Ford with a pointed look.

"All those fancy letters behind your name, and you still don't know what the meaning of vacate is?" he drawled, as if Ford had just committed some grave social faux pas.

I furrowed my brow, utterly confused, and then nearly jumped out of my skin when a loud laugh boomed from behind me. I spun around to see Ford, head thrown back, a hand dramatically clutched to his chest as if he'd been mortally wounded by Anderson's jab.

"You know I have no self-control," Ford gasped between bouts of laughter. I turned back to find my brother, still sporting that bewildered expression, now at the tail end of an epic eye-roll.

"Are we still on for tonight?" Ford asked, his laughter subsiding slightly as he smoothly plucked *my* James from his mother's arms and sauntered over to Anderson, completely unfazed.

Anderson, recovering quickly, simply smirked. "Yeah. I need to change though."

The scene unfolded around me – Mrs. Thomas asking my dad something I didn't quite catch, Ford engrossed in a lively conversation with Anderson about last night's game, James giggling at the ridiculous faces they were both making. It was this warm, familiar moment. And suddenly, I realized I had nothing to say.

I stood there, rooted to the spot with a strange ache in my chest.

This was *my* house. *My* driveway. *My* brother. *My* father. *My* James. *My* Ramona. And yet, I felt like an outsider, watching it all from a distance, as if I were separated from them by some invisible barrier. I was on the outside looking in.

This wasn't my life anymore. This was the life I'd run from, the life I'd convinced myself I no longer belonged to. This was a moment in time that wasn't supposed to exist, a scene from a past I thought I'd left behind. And yet, it was happening right in front of me.

Minutes ticked by as those around me chatted and laughed, oblivious to the turmoil brewing inside me. And for the first time in years, I felt a pull to be a part of the very thing I'd spent so long fleeing from. I wanted to be on the inside, surrounded by the warmth and chaos, the love and laughter. I wanted to be home.

"What's going on tonight?" I blurted, the words echoing a little too loudly, silencing the laughter and chatter that had filled the space moments before. Five pairs of eyes, each reflecting a flicker of confusion, turned my way.

"Tonight?" Anderson's arms crossed over his chest. "We were just talking about the game last weekend."

I mirrored his stance. "No. He"—I nodded in Ford's direction—"just asked you if tonight was still on, and you said yes."

A flicker of recognition dawned in their eyes.

"Oh." A low laugh escaped Anderson. "That was four topics ago, Emily. Keep up."

Ford took a hasty step forward. "We're going to Jake's Bar for a few beers. It's really nothing, just—"

"Nothing?" Anderson interrupted. "We are cele—"

But Ford's voice cut him off.

"I made a bet that I can get Lynn singing karaoke by the end of the month." The words tumbled out in a rush as Ford nervously rubbed the back of his neck.

At that precise moment, Mrs. Thomas and my dad chose to engage in a sudden, hushed conversation about the weather.

I eyed the group warily as the ease of conversation from earlier abruptly shifted. But that wasn't completely abnormal. Sometimes the entire world felt off around me.

Anderson's gaze flicked between Ford and me, then, as if catching a private joke, he let out a bark of laughter. "Doubtful. Lynn isn't singing anytime soon."

A fleeting impulse to question the awkwardness crossed my mind, but I reined it in, a familiar thought surfaced: maybe it was me, not the moment, that felt out of place.

"Lynn loves singing karaoke," I countered, a desperate urge to bridge the growing divide. "Why did you need to make a bet?"

Ford laughed. He and Anderson were so close that anyone important to one became important to the other. When Lynn had captured Anderson's heart, she'd become a surrogate sister to both Ford and myself.

It was the one thing I couldn't fault him for: his fierce loyalty and ferocious protectiveness. Despite the hell we'd been through, I knew, deep down, that if push came to shove, he'd have my back. Maybe not for who I was, or because our strange, once-relationship had crashed and burned, but because I was his best friend's little sister.

"Lynn loves singing karaoke when she's drunk," Anderson corrected. "But that hasn't happened in a while, what with nursing, so... no tequila, no karaoke."

I rolled my eyes, glancing between the two. "I bet if I come, I can get her on the mic within the first hour."

Ford raised an eyebrow. "Wanna bet?"

Ford

I stood in my childhood bedroom—the one I'd practically ghosted as a kid— wondering how in the absolute hell I was supposed to make it through the night.

Drinks at Jake's was our weekly ritual—a sacred ceremony, if you will—one that had been going on for ages. So long, in fact, that Emily used to be a regular. It also happened to be the one place where my entire life had fallen to pieces years ago.

But tonight was different. Tonight was a long-overdue celebration of... well, freedom. Sweet, glorious, slightly terrifying freedom.

I was officially single. The bang of the gavel signifying my sudden independence had occurred at exactly 8:47 a.m, two hours before the lobster debacle, and now all I wanted to do was get drunk. I wanted to drown out every single hidden, complicated emotion I'd never had the first clue how to deal with.

Even after a year of separation—and let's be real, a practically non-existent relationship since, oh, the honeymoon—I kinda expected a twinge of something when I saw her signature on that dotted line. Remorse? Sadness? Nope. All I felt was... relief.

Caroline wasn't a bad person. Not really. She just wasn't *my* person. She wanted a life I now realized was not for me. A life I couldn't even begin to imagine.

I couldn't even blame her for the actual divorce. I'd sold her a fantasy, a carefully curated image of "us" knowing deep down it wasn't my real dream. I didn't go to medical school to become a doctor with a walk-in closet full of designer clothes destined only for stuffy fundraisers. I went to med school because I actually want to help people.

And beyond that? I craved adventure.

I wanted to float down a river, play endless hours of ultimate frisbee until I'm sporting a sunburn that could rival a tomato, then spend the next two days slathered in aloe watching the same movie six times. I wanted to chase fireflies on the beach and burn marshmallows while making smores after a long hike in a surprise thunderstorm. I wanted to spend all day on the slopes, freezing my ass off so badly I could barely hold my cup of hot chocolate.

I didn't want predictable, boring peace. I wanted glorious, unpredictable chaos.

My first call after walking out of the court room had been to Anderson. The laugh that escaped me was hollow, dissolving quickly into a sob that clawed its way from the depths of my chest. Unwelcome tears streamed down my face in a deluge I rarely experienced. I could count on one hand the times I'd allowed such vulnerability to surface. Yet here I was, a dam broken, weeping into a silent phone while my best friend waited patiently on the other end. But even more perplexing than the tears themselves was the realization of why they'd come. They weren't for myself, but for the choices I'd made, the intricate web I'd woven that had landed me in this bewildering in-between.

My feelings for Emily had never been a secret between Anderson and me. I'd tried, desperately, to conceal the depth of those feelings, to build walls around my heart, but I'd failed miserably. And now, I stood, staring at a packed suitcase overflowing with unironed shirts and the weight of my mistakes pressing down on me wondering how in the hell I was going to fix what I had broken.

Normally, I paid little mind to punctuality or attire, but tonight was different. Tonight, I would be sharing an Uber with Emily. I'd offered her a ride, and when she'd met my offer with a questioning glance, I'd stammered out a half-truth about helping my mother with renovations. It wasn't a complete lie; I was assisting her with moving boxes. What I'd conveniently omitted was the fact that those boxes contained the entirety of my life, and the "renovations" were simply me assembling furniture in an empty space while I desperately searched for an apartment.

I'd also neglected to mention that the fruitless apartment hunt was a carefully constructed charade. I had no intention of signing a lease. I merely needed to fulfill my residency contract with the hospital.

Afterward, I would retreat north, to the secluded cabin I'd purchased the previous year.

I leaned against my bedroom wall as a vivid image painted itself in my mind: dark wood panels, a backyard shimmering under a blanket of stars, a scene Emily would never witness.

When the elderly woman had pressed the keys into my hand, her wrinkled fingers had brushed against mine, and she'd made me swear a solemn promise.

Fill it with laughter.

That was her wish, her legacy. So far, fulfilling that promise felt impossibly distant. Aside from the music that reverberated through the walls at all hours, the cabin mostly echoed with the sharp sting of my curses as I repaired a crumbling wall or mended a leaky pipe.

In the past year, between endless shifts at the hospital and countless meetings with my lawyers, I'd driven the agonizingly long trip up to North Carolina, pouring my energy into salvaging the dilapidated home that had become my sole distraction. Even Anderson remained oblivious to the secret I was hiding in plain sight.

My cabin nestled just outside of Boone and clinging to the side of a ski mountain we'd once frequented was a place I'd never imagined owning. The morning Caroline and I had officially parted ways, I'd driven straight to that small ski resort and spent the next eight hours careening down the slopes, desperately trying to erase the memories of the preceding months. On my final run, I'd abruptly veered to the side, the sharp screech of my snowboard against the ice echoing as I stopped beside an old woman struggling to maintain her balance on the icy porch of a house hidden amongst the trees. I was at her side before I'd even processed the movement.

She'd offered the polite thank you one might expect, her voice warm and trembling, and then invited me in for a cup of steaming cocoa, an invitation I'd gratefully accepted. And then, miraculously, as I'd made sure she didn't need anything else, a conversation had begun. Two hours later, I was on the phone with my favorite anesthesiologist, who happened to be married to a realtor.

The cabin had been on the market for over a year, its neglected state deterring any potential buyers. But the sweet old woman was just weeks away from moving to the Florida Keys to be with her daughter, and was forced to sell the home and land she and her late husband had poured their hearts into. And for some inexplicable reason, even though I barely knew her name, I couldn't bear the thought of her losing something she cherished so deeply to some developer who would inevitably transform the peaceful haven into a sterile hotel or bustling restaurant.

And so, without fully understanding how I'd arrived at this point, I was now the weary, yet inexplicably proud, owner of a once-ramshackle cabin nestled within *her* beloved woods, clinging to the side of *her* favorite ski mountain.

I blinked, forcing the image out of my head, and glanced at my watch. Soon, Emily and I would be confined in a car for fifteen long minutes without Anderson as a shield with no idea how it would unfold.

I snatched a shirt, hoping it conveyed at least a semblance of composure, and swallowed hard against the rising nausea that threatened to explode when my phone buzzed, announcing the Uber's arrival. Then, I nearly fainted as I peered through the curtains to find Emily strolling across her lawn, a vision in the most captivating black jeans that embraced every curve, paired with a silky white top that would have looked great on my bedroom floor. Her hair cascaded in perfect curls, and even from this distance, her thick, beautiful eyelashes were strikingly visible. I drew slow, deliberate breaths, willing the sudden tightness in my pants to recede and silently vowing to behave.

S poiler alert . . . I did in fact *not* behave.

The silence of the car was a physical weight. Each mile was a fresh wound, a reminder of the chasm that had opened between us. My thoughts were a frantic, endless loop: a thousand apologies for the night everything shattered, a hundred ways to mend what I'd broken. But the words remained unspoken.

I knew there was a chance forgiveness was never going to be in our cards. And the possibility that no amount of groveling on my part would shatter the barrier I'd built between us was a bitter pill I refused to swallow. Maybe, just maybe, if I could prove I wasn't the monster she remembered, my apology wouldn't fall on deaf ears? Maybe she'd accept it... accept me?

We walked into Jake's, mere feet apart, yet oceans separated us. It wasn't until Lynn and Anderson materialized that I could finally draw a ragged breath.

The bar was a blur of noise and color... drunk college kids, grizzled old-timers on stage, a cacophony of sound I barely registered. My focus was a laser beam, trained on Emily. On the way her eyes shifted and darkened on her bar stool, on the fleeting strobe light that painted her face gold, turning her deep brown gaze incandescent. On her smile and how she lit up everytime a favorite song of hers played.

"I hope you brought your shiny credit card." Her voice, sharp and sudden, yanked me from my thoughts. Was it real, or a cruel trick of my mind?

"And why would I need that?" I returned, a playful jab masking the confusion that clawed at me. Had she finally decided I was worthy of her attention? Perhaps the alcohol had loosened her tongue and she would regret acknowledging my existence when she sobered up? But then, her fingers brushed my chin, and my world tilted on its axis as her touch sent a jolt of longing through me.

Then I saw it: the purpose behind the touch. She turned my face towards the stage, where Lynn had seized the microphone, butchering some pop song I'd never heard.

"Time to pay up!" Emily shrieked over the music with a triumphant tap on my cheek before she threw her hands up and vanished onto the dance floor.

I swallowed, willing the lingering heat of her touch to fade and smiled when I saw the familiar smattering of bruises on her elbow. For Emily, such injuries were the norm, a constant reminder of the chaos that clung to her. The world saw the truth behind the bruises, but Emily seemed perpetually surprised by them, oblivious to the tables, rugs, and walls she'd seemingly tripped over or collided with. She was a beautiful, broken storm.

"Fuck," I whispered as Anderson clapped me on the shoulder.

"Leave it to Emily. Twenty-four hours back, and she's already a whirlwind."

"Leave it to Emily," I echoed in a barely audible tone. Then, without a second thought, I yanked out my card and stormed to the bar, settling the tab before they could order another round.

I had to escape. To find the space where the relentless *what if*s could finally quiet, where I could face the agonizing truth: she would never be mine. Even if my heart refused to accept it.

I signed the bill, leaving a generous tip to atone for the havoc Lynn and Emily had unleashed over the last few hours. I was turning to leave when Anderson found me.

"Ford! Screw the bet!" he yelled over the music. "I was supposed to pay. Tonight's for you!"

I only shrugged and turned back to our table as Anderson trailed in my wake.

When he'd proposed this celebration that morning, I'd agreed without hesitation. It wasn't until later that the hollowness of it struck me. What was there to celebrate? A failed marriage? The loss of time? This wasn't a celebration; it was a wake for a future that would never exist and only I was grieving.

As the night continued, the bar's clamor faded, replaced by the thrum of my own pulse. Anderson and Lynn, mere blurs in my peripheral vision, were all but forgotten until he made me promise to escort a drunken Emily home as he did the same for Lynn.

My hand instinctively found Emily's elbow, a silent offering of support as we navigated the uneven pavement towards the awaiting Uber.

"You okay?" The question escaped my lips, laced with a Southern drawl I hadn't realized was still there.

"I'm fine," she laughed, and for the first time since our unwelcome reunion it was a warm sound that resonated in my chest. "Haven't had that much fun in a looooooooong time." The last syllable stretched out, punctuated by a stumble that sent her tilting. I reacted without thought, my arm encircled her waist to draw her into safety. To my astonishment, she didn't pull away. No flinch, no stiffening. Just her body against mine.

"I'm glad we could oblige."

Her laughter deepened and she tilted her head back, exposing the delicate curve of her neck. A place I'd once worshipped with my lips, a place my fingertips now ached to touch. The memory, sharp and visceral, tightened my pants and prickled my palms with a nervous sweat.

This close, her jasmine scent intensified, mingling with the subtle sweetness of her shampoo. It was the same scent she'd worn in high school, a potent trigger that unlocked a flood of memories I hadn't dared to revisit, until now.

"Oblige?" She tilted her head up. Her eyes, luminous in the dim light, held a teasing glint. "So now that you're a fancy doctor, you use fancy words?"

I laughed, the sound a little shaky, and tightened my hold. "I don't think we can blame medical school for my proper English. If I blame anyone, it's you and your constant replaying of Pride and Prejudice during my formative years."

She gasped, feigning offense. "Pride and Prejudice, circa 2005, is a masterpiece, and Keira Knightley deserved an Oscar for that role!"

A slow smile spread across my face.

"Of course you would only take away a few fancy words from possibly the most important film for feminism of our high school years. Jane Austen knew that the real problem with society was stuffy dinner parties, guests showing up unannounced, and men. If you were a true feminist, you would have—"

"If your feelings are still what they were last April," I interrupted, the words tumbling out before I could stop them. A nervous smile tugged at my lips as her expression stilled, then, "Tell me so at once. My affections and wishes are unchanged, but one word from you will silence me on this subject forever. If, however, your feelings have changed, I need to tell you: you have bewitched me, body and soul, and I..." I paused as the next words clinging to the back of my throat, "I never wish to be parted from you from this day on."

"You didn't!" she whispered with a mixture of laughter and disbelief in her voice.

"I did." My cheeks burned, a heat I prayed the dim street light concealed.

"You mixed up the lines between the book and the movie."

I shrugged, unwilling to confess the countless hours I'd spent immersed in Austen and Dickinson, a secret homage to her literary passions.

"You missed a few words," she murmured, and the air between us crackled with unspoken meaning. When I remained silent, she tilted her head, a mischievous glint in her eyes. "How did you remember all that?"

Relief washed over me, a wave strong enough to almost buckle my knees. "You drilled it into my head."

I didn't add that it had become my refuge, a constant companion in moments of darkness. At first, I'd convinced myself it was because

I knew every line, could let it play in the background, a soothing white noise against the hell of my life. But somewhere along the line, the truth had surfaced: it wasn't background noise at all. It was her. It reminded me of her laughter, the way she'd draped herself upside down on the couch as her golden curls cascaded like a fallen crown.

Her expression shifted, the giddy light replaced by a flicker of something darker, something akin to fear and my stomach clenched.

"Why that line?" she whispered.

"I don't know," I lied.

But I did know. It was a coward's way out. A way to voice the truth without truly confessing it. A way to protect myself from the vulnerability that threatened to consume me. I, who could navigate the horrors of the ER, who could perform emergency surgery with a steady hand, was rendered helpless by this woman, by the weight of the feelings I'd buried for so long.

"Ford?" Her voice, barely a whisper, broke the spell. It was the breaking point. I could endure my own self-loathing, but the thought of her suffering, of hearing the pain in her voice, was unbearable.

"I'm sorry," I blurted, the pitiful apology was my desperate offering into the void. I didn't know which atrocity I was apologizing for, but I hoped she would somehow understand.

"You throwing that line at me was cheesy as hell."

Our eyes met, and the carefully constructed apologies crumbled into dust.

"I'm sorry," I repeated, the words now stripped bare, raw and honest.

She shook her head as a faint, forced smile graced her lips. "Nothing to apologize for." She remained within the circle of my arms. A long, charged silence stretched between us, a silent negotiation, a desperate attempt to decipher the unspoken. Then, she whispered, "It was almost two years ago."

"Em," I breathed her name, a prayer on my lips, and leaned in, desperate to—

"Emily," she corrected, and the world shifted, the magic shattered as the sharp and unforgiving reality crashed down. She pulled away, breaking the connection and my heart. "I need to get home." She turned to leave.

"We can still share an Uber."

She shook her head. "You live across town. I know you came from your mom's house and that's why we rode together, but there's no point in—"

"I live there now."

Her head snapped up. "You what?"

"I live there... temporarily," I stammered, "until I can find a new place, I'm living with my mom."

"Y'all live with your mom?" Confusion clouded her features, and I knew she meant Caroline.

I shook my head as my breath caught in my throat. "Not us. Just me."

"Where is Caroline? And why wasn't she here tonight?" A flicker of fear, raw and vulnerable, shone in her eyes.

"She's still at the old house across town. It was one of the conditions of the divorce," I confessed, omitting the fact that giving her the house was the only way she'd agreed to let me keep the cabin. I rubbed the back of my neck as the awkwardness became a physical weight pressing down on me. This wasn't the conversation I'd envisioned.

"Divorce?" She stepped back, then forward, then back again, her movements mirroring the turmoil within me. "You're getting divorced?" The shock reverberated between us, a tangible presence.

"As of this morning, I am divorced."

Chapter 6

10 Years Prior

Emily

It wasn't entirely my fault, this sudden, dizzying fall. Had fate allowed, we would have continued in our separate orbits, never colliding, never exchanging a single word. But then Ford Edward Thomas, and his annoying three first names, had to open his impossibly handsome mouth and speak.

It was two weeks before summer that would mark my final days at home when the universe decided to orchestrate a seismic shift. I was hunched over the kitchen table, wrestling with my final high school project for the most tyrannical English teacher ever to grace the planet, when he walked past and toward the pantry in search of a late-afternoon snack.

On the surface, I played the role of the exasperated younger sibling, feigning annoyance at his return from his freshman year of college. But in the secret chambers of my heart, I savored every stolen glance, every fleeting glimpse of his profile. Except for that particular moment.

I was so deeply immersed in my work that I hadn't fully registered his presence. When a low voice drifted from behind, I dismissed it as a phantom, a trick of the light. We hadn't exchanged a genuine word, one untainted by the sharp sting of childhood rivalry, since elementary school.

Then he did the unthinkable, something so utterly out of character it threatened to unravel the very fabric of my composure. From the corner of my eye, I watched as he moved closer, so close I could almost feel the warmth radiating from his skin. And then, as if the stars had realigned themselves just for this singular instant, Ford Edward Thomas offered a comment about my project.

And it wasn't even mean. It was... kind. And in that single, unexpected word, the foundation of my carefully constructed indifference crumbled.

I must be hallucinating. There could be no other explanation. After years of icy silence, there was no possible way he'd spoken directly to me. But when I finally dared to lift my gaze, he stood there, a nervous smile playing on his lips, shifting his weight from one foot to the other.

"What?" I breathed, the word barely a whisper of disbelief.

"I said that looks good. I'm sure Mrs. Causen will give you one of her rare A's," he repeated, taking another bite of the fruit bar he held in his hand.

I stared, speechless.

He returned my stare, his eyes holding a flicker of something I couldn't quite decipher.

I stared a moment longer, the air between us thick with unspoken tension.

And then I wondered if I'd somehow stumbled into an alternate reality. Perhaps I'd conjured the entire encounter in my mind? Was I suddenly unwell?

I must have held his gaze for far longer than conventional social interaction would allow, because just as suddenly as it had begun, the fragile connection was broken. He turned and walked away, leaving me in a state of utter disorientation. I couldn't even be certain what year it was, if I was still anchored to this earth, or if some otherworldly being had taken up residence in his body.

"What in the absolute hell?" escaped my lips, the only coherent phrase I could manage for the next four hours.

Later that same week, Ford's *Hey* echoed in the hallway four separate times as he passed on his way to Anderson's room, each one a small tremor in the carefully constructed walls around my heart. Then, on the last Monday before finals, the same day Mrs. Causen did in fact give me one of her rare A's, he left a snack pack of snickerdoodle cookies on my desk. I promptly discarded them as my mind raced with suspicions of foul play.

That summer unfolded in the space between what had been and what was becoming. We hovered in the rift between the comfortable silence and mutual dislike of the past and the unsettling new territory of polite exchanges and heart-stoppingly beautiful smirks and my foolish, inexperienced teenage self found herself falling, tumbling head over heels, for the hot college guy who just happened to be my brother's best friend and my sworn enemy.

I traded the secret world of smutty grocery store novels in my bedroom for stolen moments by the pool. What started out as being curled in a pool chair became stretched out on a float, then the forgotten book found itself on the ground as I found myself perched on Ford's shoulders for a game of chicken. His hand would graze my thigh, skin meeting skin, and I knew, with a terrifying certainty, that I was on the precipice of something life-altering. I was going to die right there and then, consumed by this unexpected, overwhelming connection.

The humid summer night air clung to me as I slipped out of the quiet house. Tonight was the official senior farewell party, usually reserved for the polished elite and the few returning college freshman wanting to flaunt their new independent status. Mostly, it was somewhere I would never have been caught dead. But I had a plan.

I knew he would be there and I was going to confess it all. I was going to tell him how I felt.

I tossed my current read in the corner of my room, put on my favorite outfit, and snuck out of the house and into my first real party.

Tonight, I wasn't just going to be Anderson Truse's invisible younger sister. Tonight, I was a woman with a purpose, armed with borrowed confidence and a dash of shimmering rebellion in the form of sparkly clothes and perfectly applied false eyelashes.

I held in the laugh at my silly brain that planned out exactly what I would say and how I would act in order to cross into the party house when, in reality, no one even seemed to notice I'd arrived. Once again, I was invisible.

The vibrant energy of the party swirled and yet, beneath the thrill of what I was about to do, a familiar ache resonated. Spending my teenage years nose-deep in books had left me an outsider, a silent observer in the theater of high school social life. I'm not even sure if some of the people in my grade knew I existed. The only familiarity connected to my name was my older brother and even then people seemed shocked to know we came from the same family.

I could read the minds of each person the second they put it together.

How in the world did the perfect outgoing jock that seemed to ace everything he attempted without ever lifting a finger have a younger sister that was so average she practically melted into the beige walls of the classroom?

Truthfully, those confused looks were the catalyst that caused my boring personality to shift into something a little more chaotic. Maybe wearing the sparkly clothes, the false eyelashes and the bright pink nail polish was a silent promise to never let myself blend into boring normalcy again.

Unfortunately, putting on those eyelashes did not give me the lifetime's worth of social skills needed to know what to do while attending my first party and I soon discovered that alcohol and my brain's well made plans did not mix as I found myself on one of the most promising college recruit's lap, letting him murmur sweet nothings into my ear.

It's not like I hadn't caught Chase looking at me from across the classroom the last few weeks. If anything he wanted it made known he was checking me out. I just didn't know how to process the attention.

And I certainly had no expectations of him pulling me down into his lap the last night before everyone ventured off to their new lives.

But maybe this was exactly what I needed. I'd spent the last year so wrapped up in my own head and those stupidly delicious dreams of Ford that I thought of barely anything else. Maybe I didn't need to say a thing to Ford at all? Maybe I just needed to get over him all together?

And this was my opportunity.

I leaned into Chase as he switched between nuzzling my ear and saying exactly what every girl wanted to hear. Except, I wasn't every girl and I truly couldn't care less how many passing yards he racked up over the previous season. I sure as hell didn't care to know how well connected his family was.

By the time my alcohol rattled brain was desperate to escape his wandering hands, my problem solving skills were completely depleted.

Those sweet nothings and football stats turned into touches I didn't want or ask for and before I could comprehend what was happening, I was causing a scene as I screamed at the boy with the wandering hands who didn't seem to care for the word no.

But that alcohol had a stronger hold than I realized and I lost my footing as I moved to stand and get away from the creep.

I'd just hit the floor, angry tears springing to my eyes when two strong arms lifted me up and cradled me into a warm, familiar chest.

Ford's face, usually a mask of easygoing charm, was now a storm of fury. His eyes, dark and intense, burned with a protective fire I'd never seen before. The sight sent a jolt of electricity through me.

Why was he so mad at me? Surely he wasn't thinking of running off to my home three houses away to tattle on me like I was still a little kid? Yeah, I technically wasn't supposed to be here, but hell, this party was on my street for Christ's sake! I would be off to college and on my own in a few weeks! Why was he so—

His gaze shot from mine to somewhere behind me.

"She said no. And though we both know math isn't your strong suit, she said 'no' four separate times. That's three more than is needed."

"Dude–," Chase scoffed. "Come on I–"

"Touch her again and I'll make sure you never run another play. In fact, I'll make sure you never touch the field again. You understand me?" Ford's voice was thick and his chest rattled with every spoken word.

I know Chase replied but at that moment I had no clue what he said.

All I could focus on was the fact that Ford's anger wasn't directed at me but *for* me. He was sticking up for me. He was damn near royalty in our small town, and he was protecting me.

I thought about fainting at the shock of it all. Every nerve ending was firing off, every hair was standing on end. This was it. This was the moment Ford finally–

"You're going home," Ford urged under his breath, snapping me out of that lust-filled haze, as he guided me to the side door and out of view of everyone else.

I yanked my arm from his grip. "What?"

"Go home, Emily. This party isn't for you." He sighed but the words were lost in the haze of alcohol swimming through my veins.

Ford had to have been at least a foot taller than me, and I'd never really paid attention to exactly how his square jaw tensed when he was angry, but with him so close my chest was practically pushing into his, I could no longer ignore it.

Neither could I ignore the way his full lips moved when he said my name. And damn . . . the sound of those five letters strung together on his lips was positively sinful... Positively Sinful? Seriously? I really needed to stop rewatching those old romance movies every afternoon. Now I was even thinking in that–

"Emily!" Ford urged as his hand grabbed the side of my face, and fuck, I was going to melt into him.

"W– what?" I stammered as I leaned my face further into his touch.

"I said go home."

I recoiled as realization dawned. "I'm not going home. I just got here!"

Okay, that was a lie. I had no idea how long I'd been there but numbers and clocks and time were a really hard concept to manage while standing in the arms of the one guy I let fill my every dream.

"You shouldn't be here." His hand latched around my upper arm to pull me closer to the back door.

"And why not?" I countered.

He took a deep breath and said, "You're too young?" It sounded as though he was trying to convince himself more than me.

I thought I might throw up. "I'm an adult. By law I'm–"

Ford rolled his eyes. "Go home. Go turn on your silly romance movie, eat your cookies, and go to bed."

Is that what he really thought of me? Were all those touches and teases just built from a man who only saw me as a sister? Had I made the entire summer up in my head?

"Is that really how you see me?" My voice quivered, and I couldn't tell if it was more from anger or sadness at the realization of the truth between us.

In his defense, he had the gall to look a little regretful at his words. "Come on, Em. Don't look at me like that."

"Go to hell, Ford," I whispered as I pushed against his chest and stormed out the door.

Chapter 7

PRESENT DAY

Emily

The ceiling fan spun, a hypnotic blur against the dim light of the room. I stared at it, willing its rhythmic whir to pull me under, to drag me down into the oblivion of sleep. But sleep was a stubborn beast. I'd walked out of that bar definitely drunk, but somehow, by the time I'd slumped into the waiting Uber, the fog had cleared and I was stone-cold sober.

Ford was divorced.

Ford was single.

Ford was... *oh, shit.*

I wouldn't. I couldn't fall for him again. Absolutely not. Just because the shackles of marriage had been broken didn't mean anything. It couldn't mean anything.

My mind raced, replaying the night, each blurry frame snapping into sharp focus now that the alcohol had evaporated. Eight hours. Eight hours that now felt utterly alien.

I thought it had been Lynn's night, a celebration for her, but a strange, unsettling undercurrent had pulsed beneath the surface. Something to do with Ford. But as usual, I'd played the fool. I feigned ignorance to the strange looks Lynn and Anderson exchanged, barely registered the awkward hug a strange couple had given Ford, and tuned out the ache of heartbreak that seemed to surround us.

I'd deliberately glossed over those veiled moments, shoving them into the dark corners of my mind. But now, everything was different. I couldn't ignore it anymore.

With a sickening clarity, the meaning of those glances, those hushed comments, slammed into me. I cursed myself for the amount I'd drunk. The plan had been simple: stay away from him. But with every glass, I'd drifted closer, drawn by an invisible thread. I couldn't even remember why, but at one point, I think I touched his face.

What was I doing?

The path to Ford was a road I'd traveled once, a journey I had no desire to repeat. I didn't ever want to hear his laugh again. I certainly didn't want to feel the heat of his skin against mine. Most of all, I didn't want to want something I couldn't have.

Before tonight, he'd been untouchable.

He'd been married.

He'd been happy.

In my mind, the image was complete. Every piece of the Ford Edward Thomas puzzle fit perfectly, forming a beautiful, flawless, agonizing design. A design I was, and always would be, outside of. But tonight had shattered everything. The pieces of the happy life I'd convinced myself he lived had splintered, one by one, until the whole picture had burst into flames.

T he clock ticked by and the desire to drive three hours north to Becca was almost overwhelming. Only the lingering effects of alcohol held me back. I reminded myself that with the sunrise I could call her and explain everything, and my best friend could remind me why Ford and I were a terrible match.

But I wasn't known for my patience and fifteen minutes later, I made the call.

"Emily?" A groggy and slightly scared voice answered. "Are you–"

"He got a divorce!"

"What?" Becca's sleepiness vanished.

A familiar groan echoed in the background, making me wince.

"Shit. I'm sorry. Are you staying with Liz tonight?"

"Technically, she's staying with me," Becca replied.

"I'm sorry. Call me in the morning."

"No!" Liz called out. "If you're calling this late—or early—then something happened, and I'm a nosey bitch."

Becca groaned, "Heads up, you're on speaker."

I laughed. "Obviously."

"And what do you mean divorced? Who are you–," Becca paused, realizing the truth in my words. "Oh. Shit."

"Yeah," I breathed.

"Emily, this doesn't change–"

"I know that." I rolled my eyes. "I just don't know what to do. Should I do anything? Maybe I should just act like nothing's changed?"

"So Mr. Three First Names is on the market again?"

"Don't call him that," I groaned.

Becca balked. "Don't call him that? What do you mean 'Don't call him that'? Babe, you call him that."

Liz laughed, and I groaned again.

"I know, but–"

"Oh, fuck," Becca's whisper crackled through the phone, and even without seeing her, I pictured her sitting bolt upright, mind already racing, dissecting the problem. We spoke our own language, Becca and I. No explanation was ever needed.

"Yeah," I managed as the rustling of her bed covers confirmed she was now awake.

"Does this mean I'm fixing coffee?" Liz's voice, thick with mock annoyance, sounded muffled, as if she were still burrowed under the covers.

Becca didn't answer, but another shift of the covers was followed by Liz's grumbled lament about how even after coming out, men still found ways to screw with her sleep schedule.

"Tell Liz I love her and thank her for letting me borrow you," I pleaded, and Becca let out a short laugh.

"Yeah, yeah, yeah. Besides, you're still paying for my bachelorette party, so she owes you."

"So true," I agreed as a knot of unease tightened in my stomach. I wasn't sure I was ready for this conversation and half regretted making the call in the first place.

Before the regret fully blossomed, Becca cleared her throat. "Back to the matter at hand. At exactly what point in your return to the middle of nowhere, South Carolina did you decide to fully accept that you still love him?"

I tensed. "I don't–"

"Yes, you do," Becca countered, her voice firm.

I shook my head violently, as if she could see me through the phone. "I don't. I didn't. I hadn't even thought of him in years."

"Really?" The skepticism in Becca's voice was palpable.

"I swear!"

"You lie," Liz chimed in, and Becca whispered a quick thank you before taking a sip of whatever Liz had offered her.

"I'm not lying. I'm just–"

But the words died in my throat. I didn't love him. I couldn't love him. How could I love someone I hadn't seen or spoken to in years? Ford was a memory... a distant, faded memory. He might not even be the same man he was back then.

Maybe his divorce was because he was a horrible snorer? Or maybe he'd become a slob, his house perpetually a disaster? Maybe he'd forgotten how to find the clit? No, impossible. That man had been a god in the bedroom. What if he didn't take the trash out every week, and flies swarmed in the garage, leading to some kind of infestation and–

"Emily!" Becca's voice cracked through the phone, sharp enough to cut glass.

"What?" I mumbled.

"You zoned out again."

"I'm sorry!" I rubbed my face.

Becca's voice softened as it morphed into that perfect mom-voice she only used when I was on the verge of completely falling apart. "It's fine. It's practically morning, that adderall has definitely worn off. At this point you might as well just take another one to get your day started right."

"Thanks for the advice... Mom." The word came out in a drawn-out jest, a pathetic attempt at lightheartedness. But the moment it left my lips, a cold dagger twisted in my chest.

I'd called Becca 'mom' for so many years, all through college and even after. It had become second nature, like breathing. Becca was the responsible one, the steady anchor in my storm. I was pretty sure I would have flunked out of college if she hadn't been there, a constant reminder of every exam, every event, every doctor's appointment I'd inevitably forget.

I hadn't realized how brutal the transition from home, where my actual mom managed most things, to the chaotic free-for-all of college life would be. Especially being undiagnosed ADHD back then. But somehow, by some miracle of the universe, I'd ended up with Becca as a freshman roommate.

Becca was organized, meticulous, a master of color-coded calendars and perfectly aligned sticky notes. I was... not. I was a whirlwind of chaos and tangled headphone cords. Becca had it all together while I could barely keep a consistent sleep schedule. Becca was, as I'd once eloquently put it to Anderson during a phone call, "the literal shit." It was even Becca who'd practically dragged me to the doctor to get on the medication I'd so desperately needed.

It had taken six months and two rescheduled appointments before I actually went. And that wasn't because of my usual lack of organization or talent for procrastination – Becca made sure I stayed on a schedule, bless her soul. It was because having a doctor confirm what I'd always known, deep down, was a whole other level of terrifying. A whole other level of real I hadn't been ready to face.

I knew I was different. Always had been. In elementary school, the teacher's voice was a drone, a background hum easily drowned out by the insistent tick of the clock on the wall behind me. It hammered in my ears, each tick a physical blow, scattering my thoughts until I could barely remember my own name, let alone the answer the teacher was demanding. Middle school was a blur of sideways glances and whispers behind cupped hands. I was the odd one out, the girl who didn't quite fit. So I escaped, dove headfirst into the quiet world of books, where the chaotic jumble in my head felt... okay. Acceptable. Even praised. But in the real world, that same jumble was an obstacle, a wall between me and every single goal I'd ever set.

High school offered a brief respite in the form of art class. Finally, a place where mess wasn't a liability, where mistakes didn't exist, only happy accidents waiting to be transformed into swirling colors and vibrant shapes. I could lose myself in the process, creating something beautiful from nothing. There were other obsessions too, fleeting flames of interest that flared brightly and then died just as quickly: old movies, crocheting, nutrition, even a brief, intense affair with gardening but two weeks after my dad had finished putting together the raised gardening beds, I'd decided gardening wasn't really my thing, and maybe I should try out yoga.

It was a relentless cycle—new crafts, boundless enthusiasm, and then, the inevitable crash, the crushing weight of unfinished projects and wasted money gathering dust in my closet.

College was supposed to be different, a fresh start. But no matter how hard I tried to impose order on my life, it remained a mess. Then there was Becca. Sweet, patient, amazing Becca, who somehow managed to untangle the knots in my brain, who helped me see that my "neurospiciness," as she called it, wasn't a curse but a different kind of brilliance. For four years of college, and then three after, Becca became more than a friend, almost a mother figure, a steady presence in my ever-shifting world. But then, my real mother died, and the familiar joke, the easy label, suddenly became a raw, painful wound.

"The barrier is officially gone," Becca stated, her voice ringing through the phone.

"What barrier?"

"The ring on his finger. As long as he had that, he was untouchable, not even a possibility. But it's gone. And with that barrier goes all your self-control."

"I still have self-control," I balked, the word sounding weak even to my own ears.

Becca mirrored the sound. "Babe, listen. I love you. I love you so much my heart could burst. But just because he gave you endless orgasms doesn't mean he's the one."

"Hey!" Liz chimed in from the background. "I give you endless orgasms and I'm definitely the one," she teased with a voice full of laughter.

"Shut up." From the playful tone in Becca's voice, I knew she was rolling her eyes at her fiancé. We all three burst out laughing.

Maybe talking to Becca was exactly what I needed. We hadn't necessarily come to any life-changing conclusions, but hearing her voice somehow calmed the noise in my brain. "It's okay. You give her the orgasms and I'll be the best friend who spoils your babies."

"Deal!" Liz screamed from the background with an infectious enthusiasm.

"Oh my god!" Becca groaned, and I could hear her fall back against the plethora of pillows I knew were stacked behind her on her bed. "Would you two stop talking about babies?"

"I like babies," I countered, trying to hide the smile that was beginning to grow. "I just don't want any of my own. I want to give them back to my favorite people when I'm done."

"I can work with that," Liz chimed in. I chuckled as she added with an exuberant yell, "I promise to supply you with an endless number of little heathens to corrupt."

By the laugh that erupted from Liz, I knew Becca was shooting daggers at her fiancé.

Becca wanted kids, she just didn't want them anytime soon. If it had been up to Liz, I was sure they would've been at the clinic by date number three.

"Emily," Becca cut in between her two favorite people, her tone shifting, becoming serious, a tone she kept for only the most intense moments.

"Fine," Liz whined, the playful edge still there. "Go back to fixing."

"As I was stating before you two derailed the conversation... I love you," Becca added and the sound of a door shut in the background, "but Ford somehow has this ability to break down every barrier you build up."

"I thought I'd worked through him." I confessed.

"You mean in therapy?"

"Yeah." I sighed. "I thought I'd accepted what happened and moved on."

Becca scoffed. "Emily, you may have accepted what happened between you two but we both know you never moved on."

I laid the phone down by my head as I took in what I knew were truthful words and said, "You know how in Grey's Anatomy there is that scene between Christina and Meredith when they're like 'You're my person?'"

"He's your person," Becca answered.

A beat of silence hung in the air. "He was." I swallowed as the emotion threatened to overtake me.

Becca gave a knowing sigh.

"Don't be mad," I pleaded and Becca laughed.

"I'm not mad. I may be your best friend, but I can't be your everything."

I sighed in relief. "He just got me. We fit so well together. It was like I didn't have to think around him. He knew what I needed before I did. It made me feel..."

"Calm," Becca stated. "He makes you calm."

I closed my eyes, the sadness and brutal reality of our situation washed over me. "Ugh! I wish I hadn't done all that freaking therapy. Now I can rationalize what actually happened tonight, and I hate it."

"Explain." Becca commanded with a hint of a laugh.

"I fucked up." I admitted. "I keep saying I've grown up and I'm mature and I'm figuring my life out but the second I get handed something that scares me I freak and run. He told me he was divorced and I ran. I mean technically I had to ride with him in the Uber but it was so painfully silent and then I practically bolted as soon as the car turned onto the street."

"You can still fix it, you know."

"What should I do, just show up at his front door tomorrow with coffee?" I rolled over and buried my face in the covers hoping to hide from my own embarrassment.

"That would depend on how you want to fix it and where you want it to lead."

"There was a time when he was there for me whenever I needed him. He never even questioned it. He was always there for me, and in the moment he needed me, I completely shut down."

"Babe?" Becca sighed at the notion of regret in my voice.

"I think in order to close that chapter and really move on from him I need to face it head on. I need to show him that though we didn't work out, I can still be there as a friend." Tears sprang to my eyes.

"I'm proud of you."

Ford

Relief washed over me when her bedroom light finally clicked off at 4:42 a.m. I could only imagine what she'd been doing for the past four and a half hours, though a dark suspicion lingered that it involved plotting my prompt demise.

She'd practically flung herself from the Uber, a desperate escape from the barely-stopped car. It was as if the vehicle itself were ablaze, and staying inside a moment longer would cause her to burst into flames.

But that wasn't the most agonizing part of the night. No, the true torture lay in knowing her escape wasn't from a metaphorical burning car, but from me. I'd told her about the divorce, and she'd turned to ice. I'd apologized, albeit very indirectly, and she'd brushed the words away like dust.

There was nothing left I could do. It was over. I'd broken us. So completely that no matter how diligently I tried to piece us back together, we would never be anything but shards of glass, sharp and forever fractured.

The sudden noise ripped through me like an exploding bomb, scattering the remnants of sleep. I jolted, tumbling off the pathetic excuse for an inflatable mattress and onto the unforgiving hardwood. Before I could even register the noise, the telltale creak of the front door announced that someone was here.

It was the doorbell.

I rolled over and tapped my phone, finding it to be well into the morning. In fact, it was almost noon. I groaned when the slight bit of lingering nausea swayed my insides and then used every bit of restraint

I had not to vomit when my bedroom door swung open to Emily standing in the hallway.

"Good morning," she offered, a perfectly sculpted eyebrow arched in amusement.

"Good afternoon," I corrected, the words thick with the residue of a restless night and promptly retreated back to the mattress.

A nervous laugh escaped her lips. "I brought coffee."

A flicker of something akin to gratitude sparked within me. "You read my mind."

"Boring and black still?"

"Why tamper with perfection?"

She rolled her eyes, a familiar gesture that sent a bittersweet pang through my chest as she stepped into the room, her gaze sweeping over the desolate scene. "Where's your bed?"

"Right here." I rubbed the sleep from my eyes, desperately trying to mask the turmoil that her sudden presence had ignited.

She recoiled slightly, extending the offering of coffee like a peace treaty. "You know what I mean. Your actual bed. The one you've had since—"

"Mom junked most of that broken shit after I moved out." I finally met her eyes. She was breathtaking. Leggings that clung to her enviable curves, a fitted shirt that left little to the imagination. As if I needed to imagine anything. After all these years, I knew every contour of her body like the back of my hand. "What are you doing here?"

She shifted from foot to foot, her mouth opening and closing as if searching for the right words, before finally settling on, "I was kind of a terrible friend last night."

A hollow laugh clawed its way from my throat. "How did you come to that conclusion?" I scooted back against the bare wall, seeking some semblance of composure.

Without hesitation, she sank to the floor beside me.

"You could sit up here," I gestured to the small space beside me on the mattress, cursing my awkwardness. I wanted to fix this, yet I couldn't even manage a simple gesture of courtesy. I started to rise. "Or I could sit on the floor, and you could—"

"I'm fine here." She wiggled slightly on the unforgiving wood, a timid smile gracing her lips, as if to reassure me of her nonexistent comfort. I slowly lowered myself back down, and in the silence that followed, the world seemed to hold its breath as our gazes locked.

The air hung thick between us, heavy with unspoken words.

"Okay." My voice was a strained whisper, barely audible over the frantic pounding of my heart. "What's going on? If I remember correctly, you made it glaringly clear that we were not friends during the lobster debacle." The memory stung, a fresh wound reopened. I paused, desperate for her to hear the vulnerability beneath my carefully constructed facade, feeling like a pathetic, insecure boy instead of the confident man I usually was.

Her breath hitched, a ragged, shuddering sound that tore at me, and she finally turned to face me. "I shouldn't have said that."

I swallowed, the silence amplifying the frantic drumming in my chest, waiting, agonizingly, for her to elaborate.

"You told me you were getting divorced... were already divorced," she corrected, her voice a hollow echo, "and I... I completely freaked out. I didn't even ask if you were okay. I didn't ask what happened, or what–"

"Wouldn't that have made it even more awkward?" I tilted my head as I forced a brittle, self-deprecating smile and caught her hesitant, wounded gaze.

"We were once friends," she whispered the words like fragile relics, as if speaking them too loudly would shatter the delicate, precarious foundation we'd once built.

"We were once... so much more than friends." I stared down at the cup clutched in my hands, lost and unsure what to do, what to say, how to even breathe. This—her being here, in my childhood bedroom, the air thick with memories—this was not how this morning was supposed to unfold.

"Can I admit something... and you promise not to make it weird?" She offered up a fragile smile as if even forcing the request scared her.

I shook my head, a mirror of her own broken gesture. "That's a terrifyingly vague statement."

Emily rolled her eyes and a flicker of her old fire ignited within her as she nudged her shoulder against mine, a ghost of the easy intimacy we'd once shared. "I went to therapy."

"That's amazing." I offered her the praise, praying that her therapy had more to do with the loss of her mother and nothing to do with the wreckage I'd left in my wake.

"I wanted to forget... everything that happened here. But I think I realized... I'll never truly be able to forget it. I know that in theory. It's just... sometimes, it's so hard to actually live that."

I nodded, lost for words, the weight of our shared history pressing down on us.

"I think what I'm trying to say is... I tried to forget you. And," she paused, her breath catching in her throat, "I tried to forget this town, and how... how invisible and inadequate it always made me feel. And that's not fair. To anyone. I miss being your friend. I know we royally screwed it–"

"I royally screwed it up." I cut her off, the confession a strangled sob caught in my throat. "And for the record," I drew a shuddering breath, "You were never invisible. Not to me."

Emily swallowed hard, her eyes glistened, and I knew she was struggling, desperately, to find the right response. I was right. I had shattered us.

"But I was never... *enough*." Her voice broke, cracking with the force of her suppressed pain, and with it, something inside me shattered, too.

"Emily, I need–"

"Can we... have a do-over?" She quickly wiped at her eyes before the evidence of emotion became visible.

My eyes snapped to hers as raw surprise and a flicker of desperate hope warred within me.

She shifted awkwardly, and I wondered if she felt as lost and out of place as I did in this room, steeped in the memories of our shared past.

"I mean... the friend thing. I'm only going to be in town for a few more days, and I... I want to spend it with my family, and my friends. Not tiptoeing around a guy I once had a thing with."

"Are we... calling a truce?" I nudged her shoulder with my own, and a weak, watery laugh escaped her lips.

"That is my last name." She whispered with a ghost of a smirk playing on her lips as she finally turned to face me. "But no more pranks."

"Pranks?" I scoffed in jest, though I knew exactly what she was referring to.

"If we're going back to being friends, then that means friends who don't switch out the salt and sugar, or–"

I groaned in mock frustration. "But those... those were the good ole days."

She recoiled with a look of pained disbelief on her face. "Fun for you. Not for me."

I nudged her shoulder again, grateful for this sudden, fragile shift, but knowing, with a crushing certainty, that I was too much of a coward to seize this moment, to say what I truly wanted to say. "Oh, please. You gave it right back to us."

"Nowhere near what you two did. It was two against one. You had a distinct advantage."

"Fine. I'll... I'll concede." I murmured, as if the very thought caused me physical pain.

Emily laughed, a genuine, heartfelt sound that pierced the suffocating tension, and nudged me back. "Can I admit... one more thing?"

"I'm not stopping you."

"For a while there... you were one of my best friends."

I met her gaze with a sad, bittersweet smile tugging at my lips. "Becca is your best friend."

She mimicked my shrug with glistening eyes. "You... you were once, as well. And last night... I wasn't a friend. I wasn't there for you. I'm... I'm sorry."

"You don't need–"

"And I'm sorry," she whispered, trying not to laugh, "about the grocery store. About throwing my phone. About the lobsters. It was...a disaster." Her face twisted in a grimace.

I laughed. "You don't have to apologize."

Her eyes, full of all that attitude I loved, rolled upward. "Just accept the damn apology. Stop being so... noble."

A bitter laugh escaped my lips. "Fine. You're sorry. I'm sorry. We're all drowning in apologies." I raised my hands in mock surrender, a hollow gesture. "What if we made a pact?"

A single, wary eyebrow arched. "We've tried that. Remember?" Her voice was laced with a painful reminder of past failures.

"We were young then." My voice dropped, heavy with the weight of the years. "Foolish. Reckless."

A brittle laugh escaped her. "Ha! I'm still young! On the contrary, you're ancient, practically thirty. I'm still...mid-twenties." A flash of defiance sparked in her eyes.

"Twenty-eight is," I countered as a ghost of a smile played on my lips. "Late twenties. You're practically...withering." I broke off as her hand connected with my head in a teasing blow.

"Chivalry is dead," she muttered with a faint attempt at a British accent faltering on her lips. "Especially from...ruffians like you." Her crossed arms were a vulnerable shield against the world and I couldn't help the answering smile that tugged at my lips.

"Fine, fine," I conceded, "you're only just starting to enter spinsterho–" I winced as her elbow found my ribs. "Jesus woman this is bordering on... torture."

"Dramatic," she sighed as her softening gaze met mine. "What's the new deal?"

"Just what you said. A clean slate."

Her eyes narrowed, distrust flickering within them. "In what capacity?"

"Friends." The word felt foreign, yet desperately necessary. "We were friends. And I need a friend." The admission felt raw, exposing a vulnerable part of myself I rarely showed.

"What about Anderson?"

My laugh was harsh and humorless. "He's married with a baby, up to his elbows in... domestic bliss and blenderized food. I can't burden him with my... failures when he's living... the dream."

Her brow furrowed. "So, you'll burden me instead? Because my life is... also a train wreck?"

"No," I protested, throwing my hands up in exasperation. "That's not... I just..."

"It's alright," she interrupted, her voice low, understanding. "If you must know, my life is also in shambles. I might need someone to talk to as well."

"What about Becca?"

She rolled her eyes. "Becca's planning a fairytale wedding to her dream girl. She doesn't have room for my chaos."

A genuine smile spread across my face. "Sounds like we're kindred spirits."

"Yeah."

"Okay." I reached out a hand, then hesitated, pulling back. "Only if you promise me an invitation to Becca's wedding."

She laughed, a sound that resonated deep within me. "Still?"

"Always," I said, my gaze unwavering as I pictured what finally meeting Liz's dad, a football hall-of-famer, would be like. "I'm aiming for... lifetime membership to all the games. Or maybe... adoption."

"You're delusional. Her parents can't legally adopt you."

I rolled my eyes but we both knew nothing would stop me from trying everything I could to enter that family.

"Deal." Our hands met, a stark, brief contact in the hushed air. "I'll go first." My voice was rough. "I got divorced." The words hung between us, a ghost of what had been. "What's your wreckage?"

A heartbeat of silence stretched, thick with her unspoken hesitation. Then, a whisper. "I got fired." Her hands lifted in a preemptive surrender. "I know it's not the same, not even close, but..."

"Emily." My hand rose to stop her. "Just because I'm drowning in fifty feet of water and you're only drowning in thirty doesn't mean we aren't both drowning."

"I thought you were an ER doctor, not a psychiatrist." A brittle, humorless laugh escaped her.

"You'd be surprised how often those lines blur."

Her gaze drifted to the wall. "And... I had a boyfriend."

A raw, unexpected heat flared in my chest.

Married. I'd been married. I had no right to this sudden, possessive sting.

"Had?" I tested the word, needing the explanation, craving it.

"Yeah. Turns out he was sleeping with another nurse on my unit."

"Did you at least cover his room in dick confetti?"

A cracked, broken laugh burst from her. "God. I'd forgotten. I should have."

"We still could, if you—"

"No. He's not worth the effort."

"Okay." I cleared my throat, the sound too loud in the quiet. "So. You're home for a week before Florida?"

"Supposed to be. Actually, that's not correct. Florida's off the table."

My brow furrowed. "Part of the drowning?"

"Part of the '*Emily got fired*' drowning, yes."

"Does Anderson—"

"No." Her reply was sharp and quick. "No one knows. Not even Becca. Becca knows about the assignment ending and about my ex, but not about... this. The travel company. Florida. Everything."

"Why not?" I took another slow drink, turning to face her fully, holding her gaze.

"I don't want their pity. I'm drowning in it already."

"Everyone gets fired at some point. No one will pity you."

She gave me a harsh, disbelieving scoff. "They already do."

"You're a damn Nurse Practitioner. Who the hell is pitying you?"

"I don't know. My dad. Anderson. You." Her voice dropped to a whisper.

"I don't—"

"I know. I know. I just... I don't want anyone to know."

I nodded. "So. What now? Start the NP job early?"

"If I even had one." She mimed blowing on her cold coffee.

"Have you applied anywhere?" An image of her tucked away in that small mountain hospital, coming home to warmth and safety every night, filled my mind.

She gave me a humorless laugh. "Not yet."

"Why?"

She finally met my eyes, and the raw, desolate truth in them made my breath catch. "There aren't as many travel NP positions." The laugh came again, empty and hollow.

"What else?"

She just...stared at her lap as a fragile silence hung between us.

"Are we friends?"

She looked down at her watch. "As of three minutes ago, yeah," she laughed.

A brittle smile touched my lips. "Then, as your friend," I declared, the word tasting like ash, "I'm going to be brutally honest."

Her dark and weary eyes met mine. "Okay," she whispered.

"You're lost. You're still running, but the road's ending. You're tired of..." I trailed off, unable to voice the unspoken: tired of running from me.

"But I don't know who I am when I'm here."

"Just be you," I murmured, hoping to provide some comfort.

A harsh laugh escaped her. "Easy for you to say. I've spent years twisting myself into what everyone else wanted, I've forgotten the real me."

"Emily Ann Truse," I began, my voice thick with unshed tears, "you love vibrant colors. Your music's always too loud, and you devour scandalous books when no one's watching." A faint smile tugged at her lips, and I pressed on, each word a precious offering. "You're clumsy, you bump into walls and trip over thin air causing a constellation of bruises you never remember acquiring."

"Hey!"

"Eh!" I cut her off. "We both know that is probably the most accurate statement in this entire little speech so shut it and let me finish."

She playfully rolled her eyes and I had to swallow at the idea that we were doing this. We had somehow, and with extreme ease, fallen back into that friendship we'd once had.

"You pretend to be indifferent to animals, but I know you're destined to be the ultimate cat lady." A genuine laugh finally broke through the gloom, and I felt a flicker of hope. "You swear like a sailor, ski like a goddess. You're selfless, fiercely loyal, and..." My voice dropped to a husky whisper, "a breathtakingly great lay."

Her laughter faltered, my words hanging in the air between us, charged with unspoken longing.

"You're a painter, an artist," I continued, forcing myself to meet her gaze, "and even veiled behind this facade, you see right through everyone."

I swallowed, the coffee tasting bitter on my tongue.

"Not you," she whispered, her voice barely a breath against the silence.

My throat tightened. "I know you don't need me to fix this," I stammered.

"I don't know what I need anymore," she interrupted, the despair in her voice was a knife to my heart.

"But," I persisted, refusing to be silenced, "if you'd let me... I want to help."

"Help how?" she asked with eyes filled with a desperate skepticism.

"Let's just... get through this week. We can drown in our shared misery, watch the world move on without us. And maybe," I added, my voice trembling slightly, "I can help you find your next job."

She lifted her empty cup in a mock toast to the unknown.

"Okay," she breathed. "Let's drown."

Chapter 8

9 Years Prior

Emily

"I hate him!" I shrieked, flinging my unfolded laundry from the hamper to the drawers with the grace of a snail. Tears threatened to erupt but I batted them away.

"He's an idiot," Becca concurred as she paced our dorm room. "Honestly, he's a complete waste of a human. This is the type of man the song 'Goodbye Earl' was written for!"

"Exactly! We should bury him! I can buy a shovel, and we could–"

Becca burst out laughing. "You wouldn't make it three inches into the ground with those press-on nails. You'd probably break a nail and then sue the dirt."

"I could hire someone to do the dirty work for me," I countered, puffing out my chest. "I know a guy. No questions asked. Cash only. He specializes in... uh... landscaping."

Becca feigned contemplation, stroking her chin. "Hmmm... but we would inevitably get caught, and let's be honest, I don't think either of us would make it behind bars. I'd probably try to organize a prison talent show and accidentally start a riot with my interpretive dance." She spun across the floor.

I scrunched up my nose in agreement. "You're right. And orange isn't my color. Plus, I hear the food is terrible. They don't even serve avocado toast."

I fell back onto my bed, the springs groaning in protest, as Becca continued her frantic pacing. We both devolved into silent contemplation.

"I got it!" Becca yelled, practically bouncing on top of me, which, considering my already precarious position on the squeaky bed, was a risky maneuver. "Exploding dicks."

I blinked in confusion. "I'm sorry, what?"

"Exploding dicks." She confirmed as if those two words in that precise order were the most normal phrase one could say. "We order a massive box of sparkly dick confetti and then we buy those birthday cards that when you open them up the butterflies burst out but we replace the butterflies with glittery dick confetti and he spends the next ten years having dicks explode into his face on his birthday."

I burst out laughing at the image. "Exploding dicks?"

She fell onto the bed beside me as we both stared up at the ceiling with a smile plastered onto our faces. "Exploding dicks." She confirmed.

I stared at her for a moment, then slowly grinned. "You're a genius. A devious, diabolical genius. But a genius nonetheless."

"I'm sorry," Anderson choked, his eyes bugging out so far I half-expected them to do a little boing. "You did what?"

We were crammed into his living room, which smelled faintly of stale pizza and questionable laundry. Ford, naturally, was already doubled over, wheezing with laughter.

"Well," I explained, with the air of someone discussing the weather, "it was just supposed to be a letter. A letter filled with exploding glittery dick confetti."

Ford's wheezing escalated into full-blown honking. I didn't usually trek up to Clemson—a ninety-mile drive from USC, but this was an emergency of epic proportions.

"Supposed to be...?" Anderson gasped.

"We went to slip the dick-bomb under his door," I continued, adopting a slightly more heroic tone, "and discovered he'd left it unlocked! Opportunity knocked. And we, naturally, took the opportunity that was handed."

"So," Anderson swallowed hard, "you covered his entire dorm room with..." He paused, as if the words themselves were too horrific to utter, "...glittery dicks?"

"Glittery dick confetti," I corrected with pride. "And it's not my fault he left the windows open and the heat decided to throw a little melting party. Honestly, the humidity practically liquefied the poor little glittery ding dongs."

"They melted?" Anderson rubbed his temples, his expression conveying profound despair. "Are you fucking serious?"

"This," Ford managed to gasp between gasps of air, "is solid gold! He cheated on you, and you...you covered his entire life in glittery dicks?"

"Glittery dick confetti," I corrected again, flashing him a dazzling smile. Ford beamed back, looking as proud as if I'd just won a Nobel Prize for this glitter-based warfare.

"Remind me never to cross you, EATs," Ford said, shaking his head and giving me a high five.

Anderson cut through the celebratory atmosphere like a buzzsaw through butter. "How much is this costing Mom and Dad?"

"Nothing!" I declared, with a perfectly innocent smile.

"Emily," Anderson sighed. "How much is—"

"I drove home," I interrupted smoothly, "and grabbed the letter from the mailbox while they were at work. They know nothing!"

"They know nothing?!" Anderson's voice squeaked.

I threw my hands up in exasperation. "Of course they don't know! I can't tell Mom! She'd have a conniption! An absolute conniption!"

"Do they even know you're here?" Anderson asked, crossing his arms.

My shoulders slumped. "No. I turned off my location and texted Mom that my phone was 'glitching.'"

Anderson took a deep breath. "How much?!"

"It's really not that much," I said, giving him my most sincere smile. "I promise."

"Emily Ann—"

"Woah there," Ford interrupted, turning to me with a smirk I instantly mirrored. "He's using your full name, EATs. Better answer. And if you value your life, I'd make it snappy."

I shoved his shoulder before turning back to my brother, swallowing my rising panic. "It's...$1,200 to replace the...damaged belongings. And I need help. I only have $600 in my account and..."

"Fuck," Anderson groaned, burying his head in his hands. "Emily. You cannot hide this from them."

"And," I added, for the final, devastating blow, "I'm on some kind of behavior probation plan."

"What?!" He lunged towards me, looking like he was about to spontaneously combust. "Probation?!"

For the first time in years, I felt the urge to shrink into a tiny ball.

"Let up, man," Ford said, stepping between us. "She's nineteen, and she got revenge on some douchebag. If anything, we should be building a statue in her honor! If his stuff wasn't already ruined, you know we'd be down there...probably ruining his face and ending up in jail for what he put her through."

"Thank you," I mouthed, as he turned back to face me.

"I get it," Anderson said, his voice softer now. "It's just not like you and..." He paused. "You can't lose your scholarship. Mom and Dad have no money to help out."

"I know," I whispered.

Anderson pulled me into a hug. "And for the record," he mumbled into my hair, "you know I'll help you with the money."

"We both will," Ford added.

I pulled back to look at Ford. "You don't have—"

He held up a hand. "Emily," he said, his eyes shining with laughter, "you covered your cheating ex's room in glittery dicks. I promise you, this is the best money I've ever spent."

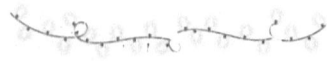

"W hat's the plan?" I asked, adjusting my slightly-too-tight dress as we shuffled forward in the line snaking towards the velvet rope.

Sneaking into a bar was definitely not on my usual Friday night agenda. Though, then again, neither was the epic fallout with my ex that had landed me here.

"No plan," Ford whispered, his breath warm against my ear. "Just act cool. Don't forget to breathe." He paused with a playful glint in his eyes. "You remember your name?"

I inhaled deeply, wincing internally as I glanced down at the fake ID. "Jessica Beans," I mumbled.

Ford snorted. "You know, I feel like Jessica is the perfect name for someone who decorates their ex's room in dick confetti."

I shoved his shoulder, a grin tugging at my lips. "You're never going to let me live this down, are you?"

"Never," he said, shaking his head. "This has probably been one of the greatest afternoons of my life." He paused, his expression shifting to something softer. "So much better than what we thought was happening when you showed up on our Ring doorbell."

"Y'all really need to get me a key," I rolled my eyes. "Wait, what did you think was happening?"

"You were pregnant," he deadpanned.

"Pregnant?!" I hissed, shrinking back as the line lurched forward. "You thought I was pregnant?"

"Not really," he admitted. "We just saw you on the app looking scared stiff with your arms wrapped around your stomach. First thing Anderson said was how he was going to lose his scholarship for murdering the guy that knocked you up."

"Knocked me up?" I winced. "First of all, that is patriarchal as sh–"

"Whoa there, Shakespeare," Ford cut in as a smirk played on his lips. "I was just relaying the information. And for the record, Anderson would totally do it. We both would, and you know it."

I met his gaze with a surprised flutter in my chest. "You'd... kill someone for me?" I whispered, and he just shrugged, like it was no big deal.

He rolled his eyes in answer.

"Awe," I teased, playfully bumping his shoulder. "Somehow you went from absolutely hating my guts five years ago to being willing to,

97

like, take it up the ass in a jail shower for me. Thanks for the love." I winked.

"Is your mind always in the gutter?" he asked as a faint blush crept up his neck. "Or is it just the natural consequence of all the smut you devour?"

"That smut is very educational," I defended myself.

Ford practically recoiled. "In what way?"

"Seriously? Smutty romance novels are like a textbook for learning how to take three dicks at once".

"Emily!" Ford clamped a hand over my mouth as I burst out laughing.

"Oh my god. You should see your face right now," I gasped when he removed his hand.

"Don't say stuff like that," he muttered, clearly mortified.

"Don't question the importance of a well-placed forbidden romance," I countered.

Ford rolled his eyes. "Getting back to reality. What about the address?" He whispered, shielding the ID from prying eyes.

"Ugh... Fine. Ummmmm. 436 Billingways Drive. Houston, TX. 77003?"

"77006," he corrected, lifting his hand. "But close enough. I doubt they'll ask you for a zip code."

"Lucky me," I muttered.

I leaned over to peek at the ID in his hands. "Who are you?"

He barely contained his laughter. "FitzWilliam Rothschild."

"Are you kidding me?" I tilted my head. "No one in their right mind will believe that." We inched forward, finally close enough to see the bouncer.

Ford gasped in mock offense. "Are you, Miss Jessica Beans, trying to imply that I don't look like a rich trust fund kid named Fitzwilliam from the wonderful city of New York?"

I burst out laughing and gave him a playful once-over. "Well," I began, ruffling his messy hair, "your hair is pretty amazing."

"Agreed," he said with mock seriousness.

I cupped his chin, tilting his face from side to side. "And you aren't really a pretty boy, but..."

"I think I'm very pretty," he interrupted, swatting my hand away with a grin.

"But what's really going to give you away is this," I said, gesturing to the sleeve of his shirt, which did a terrible job of hiding a freshly inked tattoo.

"Fancy people get tattoos, too," he insisted.

I rolled my eyes. "Sure they do, pretty boy," I teased. "Where did y'all get these anyway?" I waved the license in his face.

"Some guys on the team know a guy who knows a guy," Anderson answered, stepping back into line beside us.

"Where have you been?" I scoffed, only now noticing his absence.

"Nowhere," he replied with a devious smile.

Ford laughed. "Nowhere is code for fingering a girl against the—"

"Ew! Stop. I don't want to know about that!"

T hree weeks.

Exactly twenty-one days of mastering the art of deception, of wielding my newly forged identity like a shield and I was a pro at being the one and only Jessica Beans. What I hadn't yet conquered was the volatile cocktail of cheap vodka and my own inherent gracelessness. Apparently, my two left feet had a vendetta against smooth surfaces.

Everything would have been tragically, beautifully, disastrously fine if fate hadn't intervened in the form of a dorm-wide fire drill. Thirsty Thursday had barely begun, yet the world already tilted precariously on its axis. Becca and I had almost made it to the lobby when my vision blurred, the floor shifting violently to the right as my feet betrayed me, veering sharply left. The laws of physics had clearly abandoned me.

By the time Becca wrestled me into her car at three in the morning, the alcohol's deceptive comfort had evaporated, leaving only a throbbing, insistent pain. The thought of the ER and the inevitable mountain of debt a visit would create made me sick. Instead, we haunted the urgent care parking lot for what felt like an eternity as we waited for the doors to open.

My heart plummeted when Anderson's name flashed across my phone's screen just as they wheeled me back for x-rays. By the time

I returned, four missed calls stared back at me. Becca gave me a look heavy with worry, but I made her swear—a desperate, whispered promise—not to breathe a word to Anderson or my parents.

"They'll freak," I pleaded, my voice a broken whisper.

"How are you going to hide this?" she whispered back, her eyes wide with concern, as we limped out of the sterile, brightly lit lobby.

"Easy," I lied. "I'm not going home for a few weeks, and there's no reason for Anderson to even see me. They'll never know."

Becca rolled her eyes as a weary sigh escaped her lips. "They'll know once your insurance is billed."

My shoulders slumped. "I didn't think of that."

She shook her head. "It's fine. You're sober now. Just... don't mention the alcohol. Say it was a freak accident."

I looked down, my phone vibrating incessantly in my hand.

> Big Bear: Why the hell is your location at an urgent care by the hospital? You're not answering my calls. ANSWER MY DAMN CALLS OR I'M HEADED DOWN THERE!!

"Shit," I breathed, turning the phone to Becca. Her eyes went wide.

"Well," she murmured with a strained voice, "I guess there's no time like the present."

"No," I shook my head vehemently which almost resulted in another fall.

A sprained ankle wasn't the worst thing I could have done, not by a long shot. But facing my family, having to explain yet another injury, another testament to my inherent clumsiness, was a conversation I desperately wanted to avoid. My life was a tapestry woven with sprains, cuts, and bruises, a running joke that echoed around me, a joke I was always on the outside of.

"Let's get breakfast," I murmured, silencing my phone with a trembling hand, "and then I'll call him back." We pulled out of the parking lot, the rising sun a cruel reminder of the day that stretched out before me.

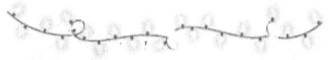

"W hat are you doing here?" I gave Ford my best "incredulous" stare, which mostly involved widening my eyes and tilting my head, as he leaned against the entrance to our dorm like he owned the place.

"You wanna sign me in?" He gestured with a nod to the front desk where a student—definitely a senior, probably regretting all her life choices that led her to phone-staring duty—sat slumped over.

"What are you doing here?" I repeated, because my brain was short-circuiting. Sure, I'd been to their apartment multiple times but he had never been here.

He leaned down and picked up four shopping bags that seemed to appear out of thin air at his side. "And what are those?"

Ford glanced at Becca. "You wanna tell her, or should I?" he asked with a charmingly crooked grin.

Becca groaned dramatically. "Anderson called me while you were using the bathroom at Waffle House. He was terrified something terrible happened, and I couldn't exactly lie to him."

I nodded. That was totally logical and I was too tired to argue. Plus, I was on crutches, and maintaining proper balance while being dramatic was a skill I hadn't quite mastered yet. "Still doesn't explain why you're here." I nodded towards Ford.

"Anderson had an exam this morning. I didn't." Ford shrugged, as if that explained everything. Which, in his world, it probably did. "Are we going to continue standing out here in the hallway or are you going to sign me in?"

"What's that?" I leaned forward, momentarily forgetting I was on crutches and nearly face-planted into the doorframe. Two hours. That's how long I'd been navigating this new, wobbly reality. Two hours and I could already write a thesis on crutch-induced near-death experiences.

"You're so frustrating," Ford said as he caught me, but there was a smile tugging at the corner of his mouth as he steadied me then leaned down to open a few of the bags at his feet.

I furrowed my brow. Inside, I saw a small mountain of frozen meals, my favorite kind of cookies, two pints of ice cream, and several packs of bottled water. Clearly, this was a man who did his research. The research being ... me.

"I know you," Ford said, like that was the only explanation needed.

"You brought... food? I didn't die. This isn't a wake. I just sprained my ankle." I leaned heavily against the doorframe as Becca finally, finally, walked over to sign him in. "We have a—"

Ford shook his head. "You shouldn't be walking to the student lounge. You're stuck here for the next two weeks unless you're at class." He held the door open as we hobbled—me on crutches, Becca trailing behind—towards the elevator. "And," he drew the word out. "I know you. If you get out of your routine, you will forget to eat. And you definitely will forget to drink water. And if you don't have read-ily-available, ready-made, idiot-proof sustenance at your fingertips, you're going to live off snacks for the next week and get completely dehydrated. Your body can't heal properly if you're—"

"Okay, okay, okay, Dr. Three First Names," I conceded, a grin spreading across my face as we finally stepped onto our floor.

Unknown Number: How's the healing process?

Emily: Who in the year of our lord and savior Taylor Alison Swift is texting me at this un-godly hour?

Unknown Number: It's Mr. Darcy. You know, of Pemberley fame? Though, I'm slumming it these days. Budget cuts, you see.

Emily: Wait, seriously? Are you trying to tell me you're a fictional character? Because my therapist specifically warned me about these kinds of relationships. I may need to block you…

Unknown Number: Relax, it's Ford.

Emily: Ah. That makes more sense. Thought I was getting more FitzWilliam or Wickham vibes when you first text. Though, I don't know if 'relax' is the appropriate term when seeing your name on my screen…

Ford: Damn … knife straight to the heart.

Ford: WAIT! Why is seeing my name not relaxing…?

Emily: Ahh…it's just Ford and not my long lost Darcy. Of course! Turns out, it's just another guy with a cell phone. My disappointment is immeasurable. And no reason…What's up?

Ford: Just checking in. Seeing how the foot is feeling and also wondering if you, by any chance, decorated any other rooms with… anatomical things in the last few weeks? You know, the usual artistic expression.

Emily: Foot is doing well. But sadly, no on the anatomical things. My muse has deserted me.

Ford: Serious, life altering question incoming...

Emily: I'm enthralled.

Ford: Pineapple on pizza? A question that divides nations.

Emily: You'll never know.

Ford: It's not nice to keep secrets.

Emily: I did tend to always wind up on the naughty list. Guess things havent changed much.

Ford: Ummmm.

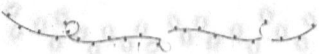

Ford: If I were to, hypothetically, punch your brother, would you, hypothetically, maybe sort of possibly keep it a secret? Asking for a friend.

Emily: Scouts honor. But I need the juicy details. What heinous crime has Mr. Perfect committed now? Did he use all the good shampoo?

Ford: Sorry, top-secret clearance only. Decorate a few more rooms with, you know, "art," and we'll talk about a promotion. Maybe then you'll be privy to the full extent of his offenses.

Emily: Ha! Out of morbid curiosity, what's my current clearance level? Is it "sees all the memes"?

Ford: Can't say. It's classified. But let's just say you're not quite at "knows the government's secret pizza toppings" yet. But with hard work and copious amounts of glitter, you'll get there.

Chapter 9

Emily

"So, are you still nursing a hangover?" Lynn's gaze snagged on the monitor, where James lay sprawled, utterly unconscious.

"Nah. I'm good." I lied.

A soft "Hmmmm" rumbled in Lynn's throat as she turned, her eyes searching mine. "It was just like old times. I miss you being here."

"It was." I echoed, deliberately sidestepping her second comment.

A beat of silence stretched between us. Then, she swallowed hard, the movement a visible struggle. "And how was seeing Ford?"

"It was good." I cleared my throat, the sound echoing in the sudden quiet. "I wish someone had given me a heads up that he was divorced." The words tumbled out, carrying a weight I hadn't fully realized until they were spoken.

Lynn's eyes widened, a flicker of shock mirroring my own surprise from the night before. "How did you–"

"He told me after we left the bar. Actually, I just left his house." The confession hung heavy in the air, charged with unspoken meaning.

"I'm sorry. I—" Confusion clouded her features. "You just left his house?"

"Not like that." I shook my head, a weary smile tugged at the corners of my mouth. "I went over to apologize for how I acted when he told me. We just talked." The explanation felt inadequate, failing to capture the complex swirl of emotions that had filled the night and the morning. "But it still would have been nice if I'd had a heads up on the matter." A bitter edge crept into my voice.

A flicker of something akin to shame crossed her face. "I promised you I would never speak of him again."

"It's okay. You kept your promise." I offered a small, strained smile, trying to diffuse the tension.

She placed her glass on the table, the action deliberate, as if bracing herself. "How do you feel about the divorce?"

I shook my head. "There's nothing to feel. They didn't work out and I hope the best for him." The words felt hollow, devoid of the conviction I tried to inject into them.

"They didn't work out because she isn't you."

I took a steadying breath, a desperate attempt to maintain control. "Please don't go there."

"Look. I know I haven't been in y'alls family as long as Ford has, but everyone knows that you two had something." The words echoed the unspoken truth that had haunted me for years.

"'*Had*' is the appropriate word. We *had* something. And now we don't." My voice was low, strained with the effort of containing the emotions threatening to spill over. "I'm not just going to fall weak at the knees because a guy I used to fuck got a divorce." The words were harsh, defensive, a shield against the vulnerability I felt cracking within me.

Lynn offered a sad smile, a fragile thing, as she drifted over to the bookshelf and gently lifted her wedding album. "You know," she said, her voice a soft whisper, "next week is our anniversary."

A knot formed in my throat. "I completely forgot."

"It's okay." Lynn's smile was timid, hesitant, but she drew a steadying breath, her eyes fixed on some distant point. "I always thought I would have a huge wedding, you know? Ten bridesmaids, a train that would put Princess Diana's to shame."

I moved closer, my gaze drawn to the cover photo, and had to fight back the wave of emotion that threatened to break over me.

Lynn had been breathtaking. Truly beautiful. Her dress, a last-minute find at a local shop, wasn't the grand, sweeping gown of her dreams, and there was no fifty-foot train. But there was a beautiful family surrounding her. She and Anderson were perched on the edge of Mom's hospice bed in the living room, my dad, Ford, and I standing on one side, her parents on the other.

"I'm so sorry. Maybe y'all can have a redo," I managed as my voice cracked. I swiped at the tears that sprang to my eyes and turned back to the couch, silently begging the universe to erase the image seared into my mind.

I'd wasted so much time, so much precious mental energy, desperately trying—and failing—to forget what Mom looked like lying in that bed. Seeing a picture of her smiling face, knowing the pain she was hiding in that moment, felt like a knife twisting in my heart.

Their wedding had been thrown together in a matter of weeks after the diagnosis was confirmed. No one had anticipated Mom's rapid decline, and by the time they were ready to exchange vows, she was barely holding on. Their dream of a beautiful ceremony by the lake had turned into a tearful, whispered exchange in the corner of our living room.

That picture... it was one of the few tangible reminders we had.

"I miss her," Lynn breathed, her fingers tracing the figures in the photos. "And you know what Anderson pointed out? I always felt so sad that we never got a picture with James and your mom. But it turns out he was there all along." She touched the picture, right over her stomach.

A heavy weight pressed down on my chest. I forced myself to swallow. I didn't want to talk about Mom. I didn't want to think about her. That wasn't why I was here.

"She was such a good cook, too," Lynn continued, a small, wistful smile playing on her lips. My mouth went dry. "I'd hoped Anderson had inherited some of her knowledge, but that man only knows how to cook if charcoal is involved." She gave a watery laugh, but a bitter taste rose in my mouth. "Emily?"

I stared down at my phone, willing my trembling hand to still.

I wanted to call her.

The contacts list was open, my thumb hovering over her name.

It was a ridiculous impulse. She never answered. But I needed her to answer. Just once. I needed to hear her voice.

"Emily?"

I needed to tell her about Ford, about my graduation, about James. Oh, God, she would never meet James. My vision blurred with tears.

"Emily?"

I jolted as Lynn's fingers gently cupped my chin and lifted my face.

"What's wrong?" Her brow furrowed in concern, and then, in an instant, confusion gave way to understanding. "Oh, Emily. I'm so sorry. I didn't—"

"It's okay," I choked out, wiping my eyes with the back of my hand. "I'm kind of a mess right now." I shoved my phone into my pocket. "I should probably go."

"You don't have to. We haven't even had lunch yet?" she pleaded, her voice laced with worry, as we walked to the door.

"I'm tired," I mumbled, trying to force a light laugh. "We were all out late last night, so I think I'm in need of a nap." I'd just reached for the door handle when she touched my shoulder. "Honestly, I have no idea how you're even functioning, knowing how drunk you were when you left." I managed a weak, brittle laugh.

"Babies don't really care how late you're up," she murmured, her own smile strained. "They still want their breakfast." A heavy silence hung between us.

"Thanks for inviting me over," I finally said, reaching out and pulling her into a tight hug.

"You never need an invitation," she whispered, cupping my face in her hands. "You're family."

I 'd barely parked my dad's truck—a beast in beige that smelled vaguely of mothballs and regret—when my phone vibrated. The screen lit up with a message:

> DON'T EVER ANSWER THIS: Wanna get lunch and drown in our sorrows?

Emily: Will the food be laced with a laxative?

DON'T EVER ANSWER THIS: I really should apologize for that. In my defense, Anderson did it, and it was meant as a joke for the rival team. We had no idea you were coming home early and would grab a piece before we could leave.

Emily: Ahhhh. So, you're saying it was a targeted attack on someone else, but I became unfortunate collateral damage? Excellent.

DON'T EVER ANSWER THIS: I'm sorry.

Emily: I'll accept only because you were a dumb 13-year-old at the time. Though, let's be real, that's a low bar for forgiveness. Like, if I robbed a bank at 13, I doubt the judge would be like, "Eh, kids will be kids. Case dismissed."

DON'T EVER ANSWER THIS: I kinda still am a dumb 13-year-old.

Emily: Most honest thing I've heard in years lol…

DON'T EVER ANSWER THIS: Sooooooo, lunch?

Emily: Only if we can order enough food to compensate for the trauma. And you're paying. Because therapy is expensive.

"Aren't you ever scared, galavanting around the country all by yourself?" Ford asked, wrestling with a burger the size of his head.

"Used to be," I admitted, taking a sip of sweet tea as if this was the most normal situation I could be found in. The problem was, sitting with Ford felt like playing with a live grenade.

"But no more?" he prodded.

"Took some self-defense classes back in Seattle. Bought a taser. It's pink. Very stylish."

Ford's eyes widened as a smirk bloomed across his face. "Self-defense, huh? How fast could you rearrange my dental work?"

"Let's just say, if you value your...assets...it's best not to cross me." I teased.

He nodded, chewing thoughtfully. Then a truly mischievous glint appeared. "Duly noted. Just promise not to mail any glitter-bombed anatomical surprises to my office and we're golden."

I snorted, nearly launching a rogue ketchup projectile across the table. "You know, I stalked him on social media a while back."

Ford's brow furrowed. "And what's the slimy weasel up to? Still breaking hearts faster than a teenage boy playing Call of Duty?"

I rolled my eyes. "He's a pastor now."

Ford froze in utter, comical stillness.

"And he cheated on his wife with the youth pastor's wife."

Ford practically inhaled his burger. It was a near-choking experience. I considered performing the Heimlich, but decided against interrupting the comedic timing.

I grinned. "So, yeah. Still an Earl."

"An Earl?" Ford tilted his head. "Like... with a fancy title and a sprawling estate? Do I need to address him as 'Your Lordship'?"

I burst out laughing. "No, not that. Just a silly little joke between Becca and me. But speaking of not bringing confetti dicks to your office... how is doctor life treating you?"

Ford's smile faltered, a deep breath escaping him. "It's... good. Normal. There are good days and bad days and—"

"I thought you wanted to drown in sorrow?" I interrupted. "Don't give me the politically correct bullshit. How is it, really?"

He paused, leaning forward, obviously choosing his next words carefully. "Not what I thought it would be."

"Healthcare never is," I agreed. "In what way is it different for you?"

He swallowed as he ran a hand through his hair. "I don't know. I think I spend more time fighting insurance companies, charting, and going to meetings than I do actually helping people."

I nodded in understanding as he continued. "I think I had this idea that I would come home feeling like a superhero every day, but instead I just come home so tired I can barely function, and so frustrated at the system I don't want to go back."

I pushed my plate to the side, mirroring his posture. "You and Anderson are both contracted at Baptist for your residencies, right?"

Ford nodded.

Baptist was a behemoth, one of the largest hospital systems in the southeast, perhaps even the country. I knew the compensation was generous, but the obstacles one had to navigate were staggeringly overwhelming. "Not to intrude," I began softly, "but I gather Anderson barely has a moment to himself. How is it that you seem to have these past few days free?"

"The divorce," He sighed. "My director went through a nasty one last year and is still dealing with the fallout, so when mine came through, I think she had some sympathy and offered me a few days off. Which is completely unheard of, by the way. But I snatched up the opportunity. I think she thought I was going to need some time to grieve, but that time has long passed."

I shifted awkwardly, debating my next words. Thankfully, Ford, ever the charming escape route, jumped in.

"You don't need to apologize for the divorce." He tapped my hand. "I'm not faking the idea of not grieving it. I think we both knew it was never going to work, even before she walked down the aisle. But her parents had already sunk a fortune into the wedding." He rolled his eyes playfully.

I gave him a sad smile just as the waitress slipped our bill onto the table.

"Your turn. Tell me all the horrible details of your drowning." He said with a grin, fishing out a card.

I'd spent the last hour expertly dodging the topic of my own personal disaster zone, but apparently, he wasn't going to let me off the hook that easily.

"I accidentally injected someone with a tetanus vaccine instead of giving them a TB test." I blurted out, bracing myself for his reaction.

Ford's eyes widened so dramatically, I half-expected them to pop out. He dropped the card like it was burning his fingers.

"I'm sorry," he stammered, shaking his head in disbelief. "Did you just say you–"

"Yep. I did." I confirmed with a wry smile

"Fuck." He breathed the word like it was a revelation.

"Fuck." I echoed.

"I'm assuming they're okay?" He tentatively asked, like he didn't really want to know the answer.

"Yeah. Had a nasty rash, but I texted one of the other nurses yesterday, and it went down with a heavy dose of Benadryl." I explained with a shrug.

"Ah. It was another nurse?" He raised an eyebrow, a playful glint in his eyes.

"A new hire. I was doing the TB tests for the week," I clarified.

He smirked, a slow, charming smile spreading across his face. "So that's why you're not in jail."

"Precisely," I said, returning the grin.

"You know that doesn't make you a bad nurse, right?" He said in a softer tone.

I shrugged, but a tiny smile tugged at my lips.

"Maybe a tired one. But definitely not a bad one," he insisted as his eyes meet mine.

"Maybe," I conceded, feeling a warmth spread through me.

"Is that why you haven't applied for another job? Or are you worried about them finding out and–"

"No," I cut in, shaking my head. "I haven't applied because I don't know where to go." I looked down at my hands, suddenly feeling vulnerable.

Ford reached across the table and gently took my hand. "Well," he said, his voice low and reassuring, "maybe I can help you with that." He paused, a mischievous glint in his eye. "I happen to know a few places."

Ford

The air hung heavy and still as I stepped into the house. The only sound was the faint rustling of photos, a sound that grew louder as I rounded the corner into the dining room. There, under the harsh glare of the overhead light, was my mother; hunched over the table, her shoulders slumped, surrounded by a sea of photographs. They were scattered across the wood like fallen leaves, a chaotic mosaic of moments frozen in time.

A knot tightened in my chest. "What are those?" I asked softly, my voice barely a whisper as I leaned against the cool surface of the kitchen counter, the words catching in my throat.

Her response was a broken, almost painful sound. "I don't remember." The words cracked as the final syllable dissolved into a sob.

A wave of confusion washed over me, quickly followed by a sharp pang of fear. "You don't remember?" I repeated, my voice laced with disbelief. How could she not remember? These were her memories, her life.

She lifted her head slowly, her eyes glistening with unshed tears. Her gaze met mine, and in that instant, I saw a depth of sorrow I had never witnessed before. "I keep trying to picture everything," she choked out with a trembling voice, "but I can't remember."

My breath hitched in my throat but I didn't hesitate. I was at her side in an instant, my heart pounding in my chest. I reached out, my hand hovering over her trembling shoulder, unsure what to say, what comfort I could possibly offer. "Mom, it's–" I began, but she cut me off.

"You were—are my greatest accomplishment," she sobbed, the words wrenched from her soul, "and I don't even remember it. I spent so much time either making him happy or worrying about making him mad that I don't remember raising you." The confession hung in the air, heavy with the weight of her regret.

A lump formed in my throat, choking back the tears that threatened to spill. "It's okay," I murmured, my voice barely audible, as I wrapped my arm around her shoulder, pulling her close. But even as the words left my lips, I knew they weren't true. It wasn't okay. Not even close.

"It's not," she insisted, pulling away slightly. Her eyes, red and swollen, were filled with a desperate plea. She stood taller, her shoulders squaring, a flicker of defiance in her eyes. "I was so consumed with trying to be the perfect wife and keep the peace that I completely failed at being your mom." The self-reproach in her voice was like a knife twisting in my heart.

"You didn't fail at anything," I insisted, my voice rising with conviction. "You're still my mom." But even as I said the words, I could feel the fragility of the moment, the precarious balance we teetered on.

She shook her head slowly, her gaze drifting to the window. Outside, the world was a blur of muted colors, mirroring the turmoil within her. "I realized something," she whispered, wiping her nose with the back of her hand.

"And what is that?"

"I never really knew you," she confessed. "I spent so much time worrying about your future and doing everything to make sure you didn't turn out like him that I never lived in your present. I never knew you." The words hit me like a physical blow.

I swallowed hard, the air thick with unspoken emotions. A thousand feelings surged, threatening to overwhelm me: sadness, anger, confusion, and above all, a profound sense of loss.

"I pushed you towards Caroline," she continued, her voice barely above a whisper, "even when I knew she wasn't right for you. And I selfishly knew you would do anything to make me happy after he left." The admission hung in the air, heavy with the weight of her regret and my own unspoken pain.

"Mom—," I tried to interrupt, but she held up a hand, cutting me off.

"No," she said firmly, turning back to face me. Her eyes, though still tearful, held a newfound resolve. "I've needed to say this for a while, and with Emily back in town, I think I—" She shook her head as a bitter laugh escaped her lips. "I was jealous of them."

"Of who? Caroline's parents?" I scoffed, a hollow laugh escaping my own lips. "Just because they're wealthy doesn't mean they're happy. They barely ever see each other, and—"

"No," she interrupted, her voice gaining strength. "I was jealous of the Truse's. And I think I pushed those feelings onto Emily. I knew you loved her. I've always known." A genuine laugh escaped her lips then, a sound of surprised amusement that made my own heart lighten slightly. Her gaze found mine, and she fell back into the chair, the weight of her confession finally lifting. "Hell, Ford. Do you remember when they moved in? You hid in the garage for a week, staring out the side window towards their backyard swingset. Then, out of nowhere, you became hell-bent on learning how to make snickerdoodle cookies."

I pulled up a seat and stared at my hands, a smile tugged at the corners of my lips as the memories came rushing back.

"The day after they moved in, I saw her and Anderson at school. She was sitting by herself at lunch and eating those cookies with the biggest smile on her face." I paused with a bittersweet ache in my chest, not sure how to articulate the next thought. "She had on a red dress and these sparkly shoes that reminded me of The Wizard of Oz movie." I laughed softly at the memory. "I remember thinking she looked funny, and I couldn't figure out why she was so happy. She was the new kid, and she was supposed to be nervous or scared or something, but she wasn't. She was as happy as could be, reading a book and eating her cookies. The next day, another kid took the cookies out of her lunchbox, and she didn't smile at lunch that day." I swallowed hard as a lump formed in my throat. "I don't know why, but I just wanted to make her smile."

She reached out and grabbed my hand. "We made a mess out of the kitchen making those twelve cookies for you to take over there. I didn't realize till later that they were for her."

"I don't remember making the cookies," I admitted with a low voice. "I just remember what happened afterward." I squeezed her hand gently.

"It wasn't all bad," she whispered as her eyes closed. "He did love me in his own way."

I shook my head firmly, my voice laced with conviction. "You don't beat your wife because you come home to find flour on the kitchen counter. That's not love."

"Maybe you're right," she murmured, wiping her eyes with the back of her hand. "But that was all I knew."

Chapter 10

8 Years Prior

Emily

"Why's he texting your phone again?" Becca groaned.

"He's just being silly. I think our glittery dick debacle last semester kinda blew his mind. He's probably still processing the sheer genius."

Becca balked. "You know, you only started tagging along on these weekend trips to see your brother once Mr. Three First Names started noticing you existed."

"That's a lie!" I protested, feigning outrage. "I wanna see Amanda and—"

"You loathe Amanda." Becca interrupted, a master of dramatic timing.

"I don't loathe her. I just don't understand why she can't grace us with her presence sometimes. Relationships are a two-way street, you know. You shouldn't have to always be the one making the trip up to see her."

"This isn't about Amanda, this is about... him." Becca said, her voice dropping to a conspiratorial whisper, and I knew that avenue of conversation had just been closed for construction.

I didn't really loathe Amanda. I was sure she was a perfectly respectable human being. She just treated Becca like a doormat. Okay, maybe I did kinda loathe her. But only a smidge. Like, a polite, passive-aggressive smidge.

And maybe I did have ulterior motives for these bi-weekly expeditions, but who cared? I was making sure I was there when her girlfriend inevitably shattered her heart into a million tiny pieces, and that just so happened to mean I also had to endure the company of Anderson and... Ford. I couldn't help it that most of these visits devolved into quality time with just Ford and me since Anderson had discovered the joys of serial dating.

"Listen," Becca said, interrupting my mental rambling, "I've only encountered Mr. Three First Names a few times, but aside from the whole bringing you juice boxes when you dramatically twisted your ankle last year, he's kinda a Grade-A numbskull."

"He's a total numbskull." I agreed. "But he's like... the brother I never wanted, and—"

Becca recoiled as if I'd sprouted tentacles. "Most people don't have secret, inappropriate fantasies about their brother."

"I do not have fantasies about him. Besides, we're not actually related. We're just neighbors, and he basically grew up in our house. It's like... accidental sibling adjacent status."

Becca swiveled to face me as she killed the engine. "Let me rephrase. I've only met Mr. GQ a few times, and he was a total dimwit, which is why I'm utterly bamboozled as to why you spent every single interaction practically drooling over him."

"I did not drool."

"Honey, you practically laser-beamed him with your eyeballs. I was half-expecting immaculate conception to occur."

"Becca!" I shoved her shoulder playfully. "I did not."

"Oh, you totally did. And now here we are back in Clemson after a non-stop text-a-thon, and I'm wagering our drive home Sunday will consist of you providing a detailed anatomical breakdown of his... physique."

"I'm not going to—"

"And don't get me wrong," she cut in, "I have zero desire to get within ten feet of a dick, but even I can see the man is... aesthetically pleasing. I'm not going to judge you if you do the horizontal mambo with him, but just... don't hurt yourself in the process."

I swallowed, trying to maintain a semblance of composure. "How would I... hurt myself?"

"From what I gather, he's going to be a fixture in your life for a long time. Don't do anything you'll later regret. Like, accidentally super-gluing yourself to him."

"Fine... Mom... I won't... engage in any inappropriate behavior with him." I rolled my eyes, but we both knew I never kept my promises.

The hours that followed were a blur of nervous energy and meticulously planned contingency escape routes – just in case this whole 'promise' thing went south. Spoiler alert: it didn't. Much to my own surprise, I'd actually pulled it off. Though a small, rebellious part of me still mapped out exactly how spectacularly I could have failed.

A week and one swig of the illicit liquor later, and my throat promptly staged a rebellion. I sputtered, coughed, and momentarily questioned all my life choices. It was only when I dared to lift my gaze from the blessed safety of the stable ground that I saw it: Ford's face, a perfect cocktail of worry and genuine surprise.

"I'm not entirely sure whether I should be filing a missing person report or handing you a medal," he drawled, crossing his arms in that way that screamed, 'Look at my biceps.'

He'd just gotten a new tattoo – a shiny, attention-grabbing piece – and this was his grand reveal. I rolled my eyes. Other girls might fall for the flexing routine, but I'd seen this play a thousand times.

"If you strain any harder, I'm pretty sure you'll single-handedly impress the entire freshman class with that new ink," I deadpanned.

A smirk played on Ford's lips as he looked down at his arm. He gave a small, almost imperceptible flex – a move he'd clearly perfected in front of a mirror. "It is rather captivating, isn't it?" he teased, wiggling his eyebrows with exaggerated flair.

"You have absolutely no shame, do you?"

"Zero," he confirmed with a grin.

Just then, Anderson's voice cut through the air. "Everything okay here?" He wasn't looking at me; his gaze was fixed on Ford.

Ford rolled his eyes. "She's fine. Stop hovering."

"She's not exactly twenty-one yet, you know," Anderson countered, closing the distance between us with an almost protective air.

Ford let out a bark of laughter, handing me a bottle of water as if it were the cure for all my woes. "She will be in a few months. Besides, didn't we sneak her into O'Malley's last year? Remember that time—?"

Anderson scoffed, clearly unimpressed with the trip down memory lane. "This is different."

"Is it?" Ford challenged. "Remind me when you and I started sneaking into places we weren't supposed to be?"

"It's not about that!" Anderson's voice was rising in exasperation. "She's taking her upper-class nursing entrance exam next—"

"Hey, newsflash!" I interrupted, waving my hand in front of Anderson's face. "I'm actually right here. Feel free to address me directly."

Anderson just scoffed again. Typical.

"And just so you're aware," I added before he could retreat, "I took the entrance exam last week. And... I passed."

The two of them stared, their mouths hanging open in perfect unison.

"You... passed?"

"Yeah," I said, rolling my eyes. "I know, it's practically earth-shattering, isn't it?"

But then a slow smile spread across Anderson's face. It was so bright, it could have powered a small city. "Get over here, you little genius," he said, pulling me into a hug. "Why didn't you tell us? Do Mom and Dad know?"

"Of course they know," I mumbled into his chest but pulled back as soon as he loosened his grip. "And I did tell you in the form of a message. You've just been too busy in "Lynnland" to actually pick up the phone when I call."

"Sorry," he said, cupping my face in his hands. "I'm so proud of you, little bear," he whispered, placing a gentle kiss on my forehead.

"It's okay. I forgive you," I said, giving him a playful punch on the arm.

Anderson turned to Ford, his expression now one of mock disapproval. "I'm not proud of you. Stop supplying minors with alcohol. She's about to be a nurse, for fucks sake." He shot Ford a pointed look before turning and heading back to Lynn.

"So," Ford said, turning back to me with a genuine smile, "it's official?"

I huffed. "I still have to finish classes, graduate, and pass my national boards. You know, the small stuff."

Ford just grinned, his eyes sparkling. "Emily Ann Truse," he declared, "you are going to be the best damn nurse this world has ever seen."

By the time we were floating down the river, I couldn't take my eyes off him.

"You okay?" Becca bumped her ridiculously oversized unicorn float into my equally ridiculous flamingo. We were supposed to be relaxing, but all I could think about was him.

"Yeah," I sighed, which, judging by Becca's unimpressed expression, was about as convincing as a cat in a dog show.

She laughed as she reached out to secure my tube to hers. "You're shit at lying."

"I know."

"What happened? What did he do?"

"He didn't do anything."

Becca closed her eyes as she tossed her head back to take in the sun. "Again, you're shit at lying."

I splashed some water her way. "I'm being serious. He hasn't done anything. That's the problem."

"Care to elaborate?" She turned and whispered as another couple floated past us.

"I don't get it. We went from practically despising each other to texting every day and hanging out whenever one of us is in the other's town?"

"Okay?" Becca laid her head back on the float.

"Why? Why is he being so nice to me?"

"Are you an idiot?" Becca balked.

"He doesn't like me." I stated before she repeated what had been her go to phrase for the last few months.

"He definitely likes you."

I reached over and swiped Becca's much stronger drink out of her hand. I took a swig causing the coughing from earlier to re-emerge with a vengeance and Ford to swing his head backwards to find me. I lifted up the bottle in a mock toast he mirrored.

"Holy shit," I whispered between a second bout of sputtering, "What the fuck is in this?"

"I don't know. I think moonshine." Becca answered as I stared, wide-eyed, at the drink and then back to her. "Go ahead, you take it. I think you need it more than I do. Anyway, back to Ford."

"You know his mom hates me."

Becca hummed as she thought over my words. "So you've said."

"And he's like my brother."

Becca rolled her eyes. "So you've said."

"He could get any girl he wants."

"So you've said." She repeated for the third time.

"Seriously. He could get anyone."

"Not me." Becca added with a smile and I laughed.

"Shut up. We all know you're way out of his league anyway."

"Truer words have never been spoken." Becca reached over and swiped the moonshine from my hand and took a swig.

"Are they still coming over later?" Becca asked.

I nodded. "Yeah. I told them they could crash at our place, but it looks like Anderson and Lynn are ditching us for a high school reunion of some sort."

"So Ford is staying with us?" Becca's eyebrows did this little dance of suspicion.

"I don't know, maybe?" I shrugged, playing it cool, even though my heart did a little flip-flop at the very idea.

"Is he going to be exiled to the couch, or will he be invited into your–."

I nearly choked on air. "I have a twin bed."

Becca gave me that look. "Have you never heard of the 'one bed in an inn' trope?"

I burst out laughing. "This is not that. We're just friends."

"Yeah. Yeah. Yeah." Becca rolled her eyes. "Friends that practically set off fireworks with their eye contact every chance they get."

I chose to ignore this blatant truth. "I'm going to head up. I'll see you when we reach the bridge." I pushed off from her tube, letting mine drift aimlessly ahead, just like my thoughts.

The idea of Ford and I actually becoming something more than friends, something that existed outside the realm of daydreams, was my ultimate fantasy. I wanted, with every fiber of my being, to confess my feelings. But the fear of his rejection – the gut-wrenching, soul-crushing fear – always slammed the door shut on my courage, turning my words to lead before they could escape.

I would have given anything to evict him from my every waking thought, but nothing seemed powerful enough to break the hold he had on me. It was as if there was this invisible thread connecting us, one that even distance couldn't sever. Even the weeks we were separated – by miles, football practice, and college classes – were no match for the pull. He'd flicker across my mind, and then my phone would light up with a text from him, or a package containing my favorite gum, or cookies, or that ridiculously embarrassing pair of socks with his face plastered all over them –which I, naturally, wore for a week straight– would magically appear in the mail.

The absolute best thing, the thing that made me feel like I could actually breathe again, was when he'd pushed me to pick up my paint brushes. I'd initially resisted, balked at the idea of baring my soul on canvas again. But he hadn't given up, hadn't let me retreat into my shell. And before long, mine and Becca's small campus apartment had become a glorious explosion of art supplies, a chaotic swirl of works-in-progress. It was a testament to the fact that maybe, just maybe, this thing between us was worth fighting for. Even if it was just a friendship...for now.

Ford: So, how's the… new boy toy? It doing well?

Emily: It has a name.

Ford: Oh, does it? Is it… like… Kevin? Or… Brenda? I'm terrible with names. Unless they're, like, spectacularly terrible. Then I remember them. Like, "Bartholomew Buttsmeller the Third." Now that's a name.

Emily: You're ridiculous.

Ford: And apparently the new boy toy is un-reMarkable.

Emily: Is that a joke?

Ford: I mean kinda, but I seriously can't remember his name.

Emily: It's Mark. His name is Mark.

Ford: Mark. Right. Of course. Mark. Classic Mark. I'm dying here. I'm a comedic genius. Should I take this on the road?

Emily: Please don't. I would hate for your precious ego to suffer a hit.

Ford: We will see... Second question.... So... no... uh... miniature, glittery anatomical oddities planned for his foreseeable future?

Emily: Not presently. How's your girl ..... You know there isn't really a word that rhymes like boy toy.

Ford: Eh. Also unremarkable. Too boring. Not chaotic enough for my liking.

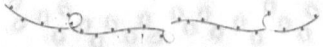

Emily: What cologne does Anderson wear?

Ford: Hey! Great to hear from you. I just became a TA for organic chem. Life's pretty good, minus the chicken salad I had for lunch, that shit was disgusting but thanks for asking. What's up with you?

Emily: We talked about this already...this morning...

Ford: Oh, right.

Emily: So… cologne?

Ford: How am I supposed to know?! Also, why do you care?

Emily: Duh, you live with him. Mom's getting him some for his birthday, you weirdo.

Ford: Fine. I'll tell you after practice.

Emily: See? That wasn't hard.

Ford: You didn't ask about my cologne, and my birthday's a week after his…

Emily: Okay, fine. What cologne do you wear?

Ford: I don't need cologne. I have a natural scent that drives everyone wild.

Emily: Jesus, please save me.

Ford: Anderson told me about Mark. Sorry (kinda - he wasn't worth it though, I promise). If you wanna cover his room in dicks I'll expedite the materials to your apartment.

Emily: Thanks but I think I'm good. Just gonna drown my sorrows in tequila.

Ford: Text me if you need to talk.

Emily: Sounds good.

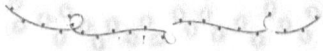

Emily: I hear your girl toy turned out to be a cunt.

Ford: You have no idea.

Emily: Do they make glittery vagina confetti? If so I can send some your way.

Ford: What's the point of electives? To make us well rounded?

Emily: Maybe? What elective are you currently hating?

Ford: Astronomy

Emily: I officially can no longer be your friend. I love astronomy.

Ford: Come take my midterm then. I'm hopeless.

Emily: This reminds me....What's your astrological sign?

Ford: You know astronomy and astrology aren't the same thing?

Emily: Aw. Look at you. You're definitely going to pass that midterm. Now answer my question.

Chapter 11

Emily

T hough no one but little James seemed to acknowledge the truth, we all knew the chicken casserole tasted like absolute shit.

It was an utter, inedible catastrophe. I watched, a knot tightening in my stomach, as Anderson finally rose and began clearing the still-full plates. Each scrape of fork against ceramic was a tiny stab of failure. All that effort, all that meticulous preparation, wasted.

"I'm so sorry." The words were muffled, my face buried in my hands as Anderson scraped the last, congealed mess from the dish into the trash.

"Not a big deal," he said with a hollow laugh that made me cringe. "Kinda expected, really."

"I hate when you say things like that." My voice was sharp and laced with a bitterness I hadn't meant to reveal.

He scoffed. "Come on, I'm not trying to be mean. But seriously," his gaze held a strange mix of amusement and exasperation, "did you really think you could pull off an entire meal without something going wrong?"

I met his stare with a glare. "Yeah. Actually, I did." I crossed my arms as a stubborn defiance rose within me. "And the last thing I need is you throwing my inadequacies in my face."

"Emily—" he drew out my name in exasperation. "You picked a hugely complicated meal. Four side dishes, for God's sake."

"So?" I snapped.

"You can't just..." he trailed off, shaking his head.

"Yes, I can."

"Obviously not." He set the dish on the counter, holding up a hand to silence my inevitable protest. "Just stop trying to do it all. Just stop. You don't have to come in here like some kind of superwoman, making enough food to feed an army. It's ridiculous."

"I just wanted to help." My words were a whisper as the fight drained out of me.

Anderson's demeanor shifted as his eyes hardened. "You wanted to help?" he echoed with a dark edge to his voice.

"Why is that such a hard concept for you to grasp? I just—"

"Helping would have been not running away the second our life went to shit."

I recoiled as if struck. "Excuse me?"

His shoulders tensed. "You want to help?" He finally turned to face me, his voice low and trembling with barely restrained fury. "Then be here. Stay here. At least work somewhere within driving distance so Dad can actually see you. It's been over a year, Emily, a fucking year. One shitty chicken casserole isn't going to make up for all that missed time. Fuck, you even missed Christmas. Why was it so damn important to say yes to a shift at a hospital that only sees you as a number and not yes to your family?" He turned and stormed out of the house, leaving me stunned.

"I'm so sorry," Lynn murmured in mortification. "He shouldn't ha—"

"No," I interrupted. "He shouldn't have." I turned and walked away.

T he bed shifted, jarring me from the edges of sleep. A sliver of
light cut in from the hallway, and for a disoriented moment,
I was lost. New York? Montana, last year's disastrous inn stay while
Ramona was in the shop? Or L.A., a blur of too many nights with—

"Big bear?" I mumbled as Anderson's face swam into focus and I
buried my face in the pillow.

"You haven't called me that in years," he said, brushing
drool-dampened hair from my cheek.

I turned to the window. "It's still dark."

"I'm headed into work."

I dove back under the pillow. "Mmhmm."

"Emmy?" His voice, the perfect big brother tone, hung in the air.
When I didn't answer, he repeated it, shaking my shoulder.

"What?!" The touch seemed to unlock a flood of memories from
just hours before.

"I only have a moment. I wanted to stop by on my way in."

"It seems you accomplished what you set out to do." Graciousness,
niceness before coffee—those weren't my strengths. Especially not
after the way he'd been acting.

"I wanted to apologize for last night."

He swallowed audibly.

"He's..." Anderson trailed off and I sat up a little. "He's fragile right
now?"

"What?" I pulled my hand from the warm space under the pillow,
rubbed sleep from my eyes, and flipped on the lamp. "James?" If
something was wrong with James, I'd—

"Ford," he corrected, cutting off my thoughts before they could
spiral.

But instead of spiraling down that road, the whispered name sent
me careening in a different direction. My heart hammered and I wasn't
sure if I was about to faint. At least there was a cardiologist within
arm's reach.

"Did you hear me?" Anderson's voice, laced with a hint of annoyance, broke through my thoughts.

"That isn't an apology."

"Just hear me out," he pleaded.

"What about him?"

Anderson rolled his eyes and nudged my thigh in a silent command to move. He settled himself against the mountain of pillows and turned to face me. "He told me y'all grabbed lunch yesterday."

"And?"

"The ink is barely even dry."

"Anderson." My voice held a warning and I threw an arm over my face.

"I get it. You had a thing and then you didn't, but I'm...nervous. I don't—"

"I'm twenty-eight," I snapped, dropping my arm and turning to him. "I'm not a child, not even a college kid. I have a career, a life. I'm an adult. No offense, Anderson, but please don't start sticking your nose into my business. He came to me to vent, as a friend. That's all."

He buried his face in his hands. "I feel like I've gone crazy. Am I seriously the only one who remembers what happened last time y'all—"

"This isn't like last time. We're adults now, just friends."

He scoffed. "You were adults last time, too. Don't pretend you were silly, lovesick teenagers. It was just a few years ago."

"It doesn't matter. We've both grown, moved on. We were friends before we were..." I paused, searching for the right words. "...before that, so it's fine."

"Jesus, I swear to God you never learn."

"Anderson." I sat up straighter, facing him. "The sun isn't even up. Did you really come all the way over here to wake me up and lecture me about something that hasn't even happened yet?"

"Yet," he said, his voice rising. "Yet is the key word, Emily."

"Anderson, this isn't an apol—"

"You know we both lost a mom that day." He scoffed, and I went still. "But I lost a sister as well. I stayed here and held Dad together while you drove off into the sunset, popping in when you felt like it. When are you going to learn that the world doesn't revolve around you? We suffered, too. Me, Dad," he paused. "Even Ford."

I swallowed hard as a wave of embarrassment washed over me.

"I stayed and fixed the mess as best I could while you ran away from everything. You have no idea what those months were like for us. You—"

"For you? For you?" I repeated, throwing off the covers and scrambling to my knees. "She was my best friend. Mom was my best friend." Tears streamed down my face. "But Ford...Ford understood me in a way no one else did. No one ever has. So what if I fell in love with him? So what if we had this stupid fling? At least Mom died thinking I was happy. Maybe that was the entire point. Maybe the whole fucked-up situation happened so Mom would believe I was happy before she died. And I'm so sorry I left, okay? I didn't know what else to do. We both lost a mom that day, but I also lost the person I loved—" My voice caught, the words dying on her tongue. "He was my person. He was the person who was supposed to hold me through that, and he chose someone else. He chose someone else when I needed him. You had Lynn and I'm so happy that you did but I didn't have that, okay. I had no one."

Anderson closed his eyes, his voice softening. "Well, I needed you."

"Anderson, please leave."

He stood, running a hand through his hair. "I didn't come here for this. I didn't come here to fight with you."

"Then why? Because this sure isn't an apology."

"I'm scared," he admitted as the fight drained from his face. "Emily, it's been almost two years, and I feel like we're just now entering into something resembling normalcy. I came to tell you that I want you to be a part of that normalcy. I want you to stop running away and move back here, where you can see James grow up, where you can come to family dinners, where you and Lynn can go out for drinks whenever you want. But I know none of that will happen if you and Ford start this up again."

I shook my head. "It will never be normal again."

"Have you ever even been to the gravesite since the funeral?"

My lips trembled.

"Have you really accepted the fact that the past two years have even happened, or are you stuck still at twenty-six, pretending Mom just ran to the grocery store and Ford is busy with medical school? Where are you?"

I turned to the window, knowing the only answer I could give would confirm his every fear.

"Emily," he leaned down and kissed my temple. "Come back to us. Finish up in Florida and then come back. We need you here."

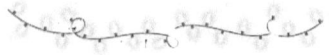

Ford

The mostly tidy basement had become a chaotic scene. Boxes were overturned, their contents strewn across the floor in a frantic search. It simply had to be in the very last box. As the top layer of items was pulled back, a wave of relief washed over me. Hidden beneath an old, worn-out, and moth-eaten blanket, a glimpse of it could be seen.

Some of the pages were torn and I cringed. I should have put it in a protective casing years ago. But after everything that had happened, after it had erupted, all that was left was a strong desire to throw this into a dark hole and never see it again.

My hand shook as I lifted it from the box, blew off the layer of dust and clutched it tightly to my chest before walking up the darkened stairs.

"You don't need to worry about the basement." Mom stated as I shut the door behind me.

"I know, just looking for something."

She nodded toward the precious item in my hands. "Did you find it?"

"Yeah."

"Hmmmm." She turned to walk toward the kitchen. "Well it looks special. Better take good care of it."

Chapter 12

7 Years Prior

Emily

The unstoppable laughter bubbled up, until tears blurred my vision.

"Stop!" I squealed, collapsing against the fireplace, Ford right beside me, his own laughter shaking his frame.

Two years. Two years of this strange orbit we'd found ourselves in during our visits. He still teased, still called me out, still drove me crazy—sometimes from across the living room, sometimes from halfway across the state. But between what would forever be etched in my memory as 'glittery dick gate' and now, something had shifted. We'd become...friends.

Which is how I found myself pressed against a wall, thigh to thigh with him, our breaths mingling in the frosty air.

"We should get out of here," he whispered, his gaze fixed on the window.

"And go where? It's almost midnight," I countered, bumping my hip against his.

His face lit up and a boyish grin spread across his features. "Do you wanna build a snowman."

I laughed. "Are you Anna? Am I Elsa?"

"Whatever works." He stood, yanking me from the warmth of the fireplace before I could protest.

I grunted as I wrestled with my layers and slipped on my boots. Our group's impromptu mountain weekend had just begun, and we hadn't yet braved the slopes.

"Be careful," Ford warned as we stepped onto the porch. "I think it's slippery."

As if fate were listening, my feet chose that precise moment to betray me. I twisted, grabbing at his arm as I fell, pulling him down with me. We tumbled down the three steps, landing in a heap on the snow-covered ground.

"Ow!"

"Seriously?" He propped himself up on his elbows.

"I can't help it," I gasped, throwing my head back into the soft snow, closing my eyes as laughter shook me. "I'm a mess."

A comfortable silence settled between us, broken only by the sound of our breathing and the gentle crunch of snow. After a few deep breaths, the cold finally seeping through my clothes, I opened my eyes to find him lying on his stomach beside me.

"Hi."

"Hi," he replied with a subtle smirk playing on his lips.

I quirked an eyebrow. "Are you assessing me for injuries?"

He licked his lips. "You have two rows of eyelashes."

"What?"

"You always wear those ridiculous false eyelashes, but you don't need to. You have a double row."

"I like the false lashes."

He scoffed softly. "I like your real ones."

My breath hitched. "Is having a double row a good thing?" I asked, trying to mask the sudden thrumming of my heart.

"It's called distichiasis. I learned about it in genetics class. It's a genetic abnormality." He gave me a wicked smile, then reached out to brush a finger down my nose.

I feigned offense. "So, there's something wrong with me?"

He shook his head as his eyes locked with mine. "Not a thing."

My breath caught in my throat as his fingers traced the line of my cheek, then gently brushed my lips.

"What are you doing?" I whispered, unsure if I was imagining the moment but desperate for it not to end.

"You have a dimple, right here," he murmured, gently poking my right cheek. I couldn't help but smile.

"Yeah?"

He nodded, his eyes fixed on my face, his own lips parting.

"What are you doing?" I asked again, my voice barely audible as his finger lingered on my cheek.

"I honestly don't know." He drew in a sharp breath of the frigid air.

"I think you might be drunk," I laughed nervously, trying to diffuse the charged atmosphere.

He shook his head. "I'm not drunk. At least, not on alcohol."

My eyes widened in question.

"Ford?"

"Eats?"

I smiled and shook my head.

"Do you want to build a snowman?" I finally whispered, knowing that if this moment continued, my carefully constructed walls would crumble.

A soft laugh escaped his lips as he stood, pulling me up with him.

I skidded to a stop at the bottom of the slope, catching my breath. Of course, Ford had to screech to a halt right behind me causing a plume of snow to momentarily blind me. I hopped to the side just as his board grazed my ski.

"You could have killed me," I said, feigning annoyance as I lifted my goggles and pulled out my earbud.

"Nah. Maybe a mildly broken leg."

I scoffed. "Oh, joy."

"What was the smile for?"

I furrowed my brow. "What smile?"

"You were standing here with this lovesick smile on your face."

I suppressed a laugh. "I think this is my favorite place in the entire world."

"The ski lodge?"

"The mountains. I think I might want to live here someday. Can you imagine it? A house hidden in the woods, skiing whenever I wanted, making hot chocolate every day, and..."

"You know it still gets warm here in the summer, right?" he interrupted.

"Shh, you're ruining the vision. I'd drink hot chocolate every day and spend my nights curled up by the fireplace with a book."

"Sounds like you have it all planned out."

I smiled. "Yeah. Now I just need to figure out how to make it a reality."

"What are you listening to?" he asked, unhooking his board and leaning against the rail separating the bottom of the slope from the kiddie area.

"Music," I said flatly.

He rolled his eyes.

"Have you seen Anderson or anyone else?" We both turned to scan the surrounding skiers and snowboarders, trying to locate the rest of our group.

The last time I'd seen Lynn and Anderson was at breakfast, and their teammate Josh had spent the entire morning showing off on the trick slopes.

"No. Honestly, I haven't seen anyone but you in a while."

Ford pulled out his phone, sending a text with shaking hands.

"You cold?" I nudged his shoulder.

"Freezing." He looked up with a smirk.

"Wanna get some hot chocolate?" I tilted my head toward the ski lodge and Ford laughed.

"All you think about is food."

"All I think about is chocolate," I countered, and he laughed harder.

"Fine, but not until you do one last run with me."

"You beat me every time," I huffed, but even the prospect of defeat couldn't stop me from another run with him.

"Come on, EATs... don't let me down," he pleaded, glancing at the lift.

"Fine. One more, then lunch," I conceded.

But before he could grab his board, I nudged it down the small embankment toward the parking lot. He scoffed as it hit the bottom, knowing he'd have to walk around to get it. I raced toward the lift as I heard him playfully call me a cheater from behind.

The lift lurched forward just as his snow-covered head popped back up from the embankment. I stuck my tongue out, our eyes met, and I couldn't stifle the laugh that burst out at his playful sneer. For some reason, I knew I'd be paying for that later.

"What has you smiling like that?" the guy beside me on the lift asked.

"Oh. Nothing." I replied as we lowered the bar onto our laps. "Just made a bet to make it back down before my friend, and for the first time, it seems like I might win."

He turned to look behind me, and though his face was obscured by layers of warmth, I could tell he was smiling. "I'm Henry." He reached out and scooted to the middle of the bench.

"Emily." Though we shook hands, between the biting cold and our thick gloves, I doubted either of us felt it.

"You live around here?"

I shook my head, hoping to signal my desire to avoid a random conversation. "No."

"I go to App State, and whenever I get a break, I like to come up here to get away."

I awkwardly laughed, counting the seconds until we reached the top. "That's nice."

"You'd think that. But then you'll inevitably end up taking a skiing instructor job, thinking it'll be the perfect way to make some extra money, but end up corralling little heathens all morning on the bunny slope while their rich parents sneak away."

"Ahhh." I smiled, replacing my earbud, hoping he'd get the hint. Unfortunately, he didn't.

"It's my first and only break of the day. I should be eating or warming up, but I can't turn away another pass down the slopes." He reached out to swipe a loose strand of hair from my face.

"No, thank you." I pulled back, unsure how to tell the creep not to touch me in a way that wouldn't make the next two minutes stuck on a lift together even more awkward.

"What?" His smile was so big I couldn't tell if he was truly oblivious to my discomfort or if he simply didn't care.

"I have a boyfriend," I lied, hoping he couldn't tell.

"I have a girlfriend," he replied, and I instantly felt sorry for whoever she was.

"That's nice."

"There's a bar at the top."

"What?" I blurted, confused.

"Wanna get a shot?"

"Of alcohol?"

He furrowed his brow. "Well, yeah. Unless there are other kinds of shots I'm unaware of." He wiggled his brow, and though I couldn't see my reflection in his goggles, I was pretty sure utter disgust was plastered on my face.

"Uh. No."

"You sure?"

"I'm sorry, I'm confused. Didn't you just say you had a girlfriend?"

"So." He gave me a bewildered stare.

"Why are you asking me to get a drink with you?"

He chuckled. "Because." He winked, and it was all I could do not to vomit in his face.

I turned and searched for Ford, desperate to escape. A sigh of relief bubbled up as soon as I spotted him five chairs back. "My boyfriend is behind us."

"I thought you said he was a friend?"

"Well, he's my boy*friend*, so…"

He rolled his eyes. "Ready?"

I furrowed my brow. "Ready for—"

In one swift second, he'd lifted the bar and catapulted himself forward. By the time I registered we'd reached the top, I was half a second from not making it off the lift. I swung forward on instinct, looking like it was my first time on skis, and proceeded to roll down the small hill until I landed face-first in a plume of snow.

I flipped over and coughed away the wet snow.

"You weren't ready," the creeper with a girlfriend said, and I peeked one eye open to find him blocking the sun.

"Obviously." I sat up, still desperate to escape.

"Where's that boyfriend?" He took a step closer, further invading my space.

I looked up just as Ford made his way to us, and from his face, I could tell he'd heard the question. "Right behind you."

Henry turned to find Ford standing over us with a menacing expression and I was more than thankful my ski goggles hid what I was sure would be a face flush with embarrassment at that title.

"You okay?" he asked me, his gaze never leaving the creep.

"I am now." I moved to sit up.

Neither of us voiced the words we longed to speak, yet after that weekend in the mountains, an unspoken shift settled between us.

Ford, having helped me to my feet, then forwent his own competitive urge, staying close as we descended the slope. The creeper with a girlfriend appeared only a handful more times during the trip, but with each sighting, Ford's arm would find my shoulder, pulling me close, sheltering me against his chest.

We never discussed those forty-eight hours spent pretending, but the silence held weight. That weekend had irrevocably changed something within me. I could only pray it had done the same for Ford.

Our contact intensified. Daily texts became hourly exchanges. Most were memes or links shared from social media.

Ford sauntered into my dorm room a month later as the first breath of spring teased through the open window. He'd somehow become a fixture as he and Anderson turned those infrequent visits into a more common occurrence.

"Are these—" he began, his voice a low rumble that vibrated through the quiet room as he gestured towards the canvas propped against the wall where I'd recently finished painting.

"Indian Ghost Pipes," I murmured, moving to stand beside him with the faint scent of paint still clinging to my fingers.

A flicker of curiosity lit his eyes. "Indian Ghost Pipes? I've never heard of them. They're... beautiful." His long fingers, calloused from countless hours on the football field and in the gym, traced the delicate, dried petals of the flowers I'd painstakingly rendered.

"They were Emily Dickinson's favorite flower," I explained, stepping closer and subtly mirroring the path his fingers had just taken across the canvas. "She even put them on the cover of her first poetry book."

A low hum rumbled in his chest, and his left arm snaked around my shoulder, the casual contact sending a jolt of electricity through me as his fingers brushed against my collarbone. He'd been touching me more freely lately, a casual brush of his hand against my arm, a lingering touch on my back and every time his skin met mine, it felt like a small explosion, a chaotic flurry of butterflies trapped in my chest.

"And what do they mean?" he whispered against my hair. I smiled as a secret understanding passed between us.

No one else would understand the weight of his question. To most, things were just things, devoid of deeper meaning. But for me, for us, there was power in meaning, in symbolism, in the stories woven into the fabric of everything.

"They were used as medicinal herbs," I explained with my gaze fixed on the intricate details of the painting. "Thought to help cure ailments related to mental health. Grief, stress, sensory overload, trauma, overstimulation, anxiety—"

"ADHD," he interrupted in quiet observation.

I abruptly turned to face him with a pounding heart . "What?" I whispered, bracing myself for the inevitable.

"ADHD. ADD. Whatever they're calling it now," he continued with a wry smile playing on his lips. "Though none of those names quite fit. I think it should be renamed," he paused as if taking a moment to think, "TMUAFATWT. Too Much Unneeded Attention For All The Wrong Things." He let out a short laugh at his own joke. "Is that why you chose to paint this flower?"

My stomach dropped as a cold knot of panic tightened in my chest. "Why would you think that?" I stammered, my voice barely above a whisper.

He looked at me, his blue eyes searching mine, as if he were carefully choosing his next words.

I did have ADHD. I'd been officially diagnosed last year, and for the past nine months, I'd been medicated. The first time the medication kicked in, silencing the relentless chatter in my mind, it had been a revelation. I'd cried with tears of relief. Nothing had ever truly helped before, but finally... *finally*, I could focus. I could read a book without my mind racing in a thousand different directions. I could keep my emotions in check when the world felt like it was spinning out of control. Most importantly, I didn't feel the constant, agonizing overstimulation that always left me on edge. For the first time, I felt peace.

But that peace was a secret. A tightly guarded secret shared only with Becca. The little orange bottle of pills I kept tucked away in my bag was a hidden part of myself.

"Emily," he said softly, his voice laced with a gentle understanding. "I know you have that."

"No, you don't," I insisted and hoped he couldn't hear the trembling in my own voice.

He let out a soft laugh. "Yes, I do. Something's changed. I just assumed you'd always been diagnosed. But when I mentioned it to Anderson—"

My eyes widened in horror. "You asked Anderson about my mental health?" I practically hissed, shoving him back.

"It wasn't like that," he pleaded, running a hand through his tousled brown hair. He moved to close the distance between us, but I instinctively stepped back.

"We have a circle of trust," I rambled and my words tumbled out in a rush. "You can't break the circle. If you break the circle, there's just a line, and lines have beginnings and ends, and that's not a circle!"

"Emily, it's okay," he soothed. "I saw the pill bottle when you stayed with us last month. It's not a big deal."

My breath hitched. "Did you tell Anderson?"

"About the pills?"

"About any of it?" I clarified..

"No," he answered immediately. "He didn't even know what I was talking about at first. And I never brought it up again."

I turned to leave, but Ford reached out and gently grasped my arm, pulling me back.

"Hey," he said softly, turning me to face him. "What's the big deal? What did I do?"

I sucked in a shuddering breath as I pulled away from his grasp and covered my face with my hands. "Nothing," I choked out, my throat tight with unshed tears. "I just... I don't want anyone to see me differently. What if people think I'm weird because I have a diagnosis? What if you think I'm weird?"

He started to laugh as he pulled my hands away from my face. But the laughter died in his throat when he saw the raw pain in my eyes.

"Full disclosure," he said softly. "I already think you're weird."

I punched him lightly in the arm.

"Ow!" he exclaimed, feigning pain.

"Oh, shut up, Mr. Big-Time Football Star," I retorted with a small smile finally breaking through my tears. "We both know that didn't hurt."

He rubbed his arm. "For clarification, it did actually hurt. You're stronger than you look. And for further clarification... we're all weird. I like weird. Be weird. Why would you want to be like everyone else? And besides, who the heck cares if you take Adderall? I'm pretty sure half the people out there also take it, and half of them probably have four other diagnoses you don't even know about." He gestured towards the door, indicating the gathering of friends that always seemed to gravitate towards our apartment.

"You don't know that," I countered.

"I do," he said with a knowing glint in his eyes. "But that's beside the point. You're a nursing student. You can't balk on mental health. Meds are good. Therapy is good. We have to stop this negative narrative surrounding our mental health."

The knot of anger and embarrassment slowly began to unravel. "I'm sorry," I whispered.

He reached out and pulled me close, burying his face in my hair. "Don't be," he murmured, his voice warm against my scalp. "I like your chaos."

The next morning I walked into our living room expecting to find a sun kissed face but instead walked in on Ford slumped on our couch and looking like a rejected tomato.

"I feel like shit," he mumbled with a low groan.

"You look like shit," I agreed.

He feigned offense. "That's not very nice."

I strolled closer as I inspected the damage. "What was that crack about me going as a lobster for Halloween again?"

"Fine. Your burn turned to tan, you win," he conceded, though his tone suggested he was far from victorious.

"I didn't burn because I used sunscreen. This"—I gestured to his fiery complexion—"is what happens when you're a stubborn man who ignores all reason and refuses sun protection during an all-day ultimate frisbee session. Just because it's a little chilly doesn't mean the sun won't turn you into a human fireball."

"Ugh," he groaned as he rolled over on the couch and winced. "Well, maybe I'll be the lobster. But you're definitely rocking a nice shade of pink. Maybe you should go as a shrimp?"

I laughed as I headed to the kitchen to grab him some water. "Halloween's months away. I'm sure we'll both be back to our normal, non-crustacean hues by then."

I nudged his shoulder when I returned, and he whined from under the blanket. "Drink up. Wouldn't want you getting dehydrated on top of everything else."

He raised a questioning eyebrow. "Yes, ma'am."

"I'm ordering some pharmacy reinforcements."

Ford yelped as he attempted to sit up. "My skin feels like it's on fire!"

"Good thing Anderson is spending all day with Lynn and we have nothing to do but sit covered in aloe and recover before he heads this way to pick you up," I said, a hint of mischief in my voice.

He gave me a knowing look. "You have a very devilish grin right now. What are you plotting?"

I batted my eyelashes, then flicked on the television. The opening score of Pride and Prejudice swelled into the room. "I've been waiting for you to wake up."

"Oh, god!" He groaned, retreating under the blanket and burying his face in the pillows.

"Come on! It's my favorite!" I yanked the covers away, revealing those adorable, albeit currently pink, cheeks.

Emily: Ugh, I'm SO bored. I wish something, ANYTHING exciting would happen.

Ford: Like what? You wanna see a mountain lion riding a unicycle while juggling bowls of goldfish?

Emily: No, something realistic. Like winning the lottery.

Ford: Yeah, right. You're more likely to trip over a snail while walking backwards.

Emily: True. But at least then I'd have a funny story and a slightly bruised tailbone.

Ford: Plus snail slime. Excellent for facials.

Emily: ...You're the worst. lol

Ford: I aim to please. So, what's new in your exciting life of... breathing?

Emily: Groundbreaking stuff, really. I mastered exhaling today.

Ford: Woah, slow down, Einstein. Don't wanna peak too early.

Emily: If you ever find a cure for boredom, hit me up. I'll be first in line.

Ford: I am the cure for boredom. Clearly.

Emily: Yeah, okay. Whatever you say, Mr. Overconfident.

Ford: You know you love it. ha

Chapter 13

Present Day

Emily

I t rained the entire drive. And maybe that was the exact foreshadowing I needed.

Before I even fully stepped onto the porch mat, Becca had pulled me into a massive, enveloping hug.

"I tracked you the entire drive!" she squealed in my ear as she bounced up and down, never loosening her hold.

From the kitchen doorway, Liz's voice chimed in, with FitzWilliam weaving between her legs. "She's not lying. Her face has been buried in that screen for the last three hours straight."

I grinned at Liz, then buried my face in Becca's shoulder. "I missed you," I whispered to my still-bouncing best friend.

"I missed you more," she countered, finally pulling back slightly. "Can we make a promise to never go this long between visits again?"

I smiled and nodded, though a quiet understanding passed between us. We both knew I wasn't the best at keeping promises.

We spent the next two hours huddled on her couch, lost in a comfortable drift of conversation that touched on everything and nothing. The weather, my father, my nursing job, becoming an NP, how Fitzwilliam was adjusting to life without me, her new position at the weather station and the hopeful glint in her eyes about going on air soon, Liz's utter loathing for her own job and equally stubborn refusal to quit.

For a fleeting moment, everything felt right. If I closed my eyes, I could almost believe we were back in college, sprawled in that half-wrecked apartment, plotting elaborate revenge fantasies against anyone who'd ever wronged us.

She twirled strands of my hair as I hummed along to some indistinct song playing in the background.

Then, the perfect bubble burst and reality crashed in.

"I have to tell you something," she whispered.

"Hmmm," I murmured as I suck deeper into the soothing rhythm she'd created.

"Emily, it's—" She stopped, not just her words but the gentle movements too. She shifted, pulling my head off her lap and turning to face me.

My brow furrowed as a thousand anxious scenarios flickered through my mind. "You and Liz, are ya'll okay? Wedding is still on right?"

She gave a watery laugh and nodded, but then I saw the tear. And not just one. Many. Judging by the tracks on her cheeks, she'd been crying for at least five minutes, and I'd been completely oblivious.

"Becca, you're scaring me."

"It's only stage two. Very treatable. I've already—"

"Stage two?" I repeated in disbelief as if I didn't know exactly what those two words strung together meant. "What does that even mean?"

"It's my cervix, cervical," she clarified and the word hung heavy in the air. "But we caught it early. It would have been stage one, but they just had to find it in a lymph node." She rolled her eyes in a transparent attempt to lighten the crushing weight of the moment.

It didn't work.

"I don't understand."

"We already did an egg retrieval. So you're still going to get your wish of little nieces or nephews to corrupt," she managed a weak smile through the tears. "It's just that Liz will have to carry them all." Her voice broke on the last word.

"No. You don't have that," I shook my head, as if I could physically erase the last few seconds and rewind time.

"I go in for a full hysterectomy next month. I started chemo two weeks ago."

She reached back, her fingers brushing through her dark auburn curls. When she pulled her hand back, a clump of hair clung to her fingertips.

"I'm sorry I didn't tell you. It all happened so fast," she rushed on and the words tumbled out as I struggled to process them. "One minute I was going in for a pap smear, and the next I was being bombarded with treatment options. Thankfully, we'd already set up the egg retrieval, because Liz is dead set on being pregnant, and we both know I can barely handle a headache. Maybe it's a good thing I won't be giving birth," she laughed but it was a fractured sound laced with tears, desperately trying to diminish the enormity of it all. "I just couldn't tell you over the phone," tears streamed down her face. "I tried so many times, and I just couldn't do it."

"Becca?" My voice was barely a whisper.

"I know I told you to come here for a night, and we could just relax, but I lied. I need your help."

I nearly shrieked as Becca emerged from the dressing room, a monument to bad taste. I choked back a gag. The dress, a frothy confection of ivory and lace, swallowed her whole. It wasn't a dress; it was an explosion in a pastry factory.

"Oh!" Becca's mother and aunt, identical bookends of manicured enthusiasm, beamed. "You look beautiful! Like a princess!"

"Like a pastry," I muttered under my breath, catching Aunt Jenny's disapproving glare. Becca's eyes met mine and a silent scream of shared horror passed between us.

"This is Mom's pick," Becca said to no one in particular with a strained voice and a forced smile plastered on her face as she stared at her reflection.

"And I know you best! You look radiant!" Her mother exclaimed. A chorus of coos and murmurs rose from the over-fifty crowd, a wave of approval that threatened to drown us both. Becca and I remained locked in our silent battle, desperate not to shatter the fragile bubble of their joy.

This was dress number twelve and location number two. What had started as a quiet afternoon had spiraled into an emotional rollercoaster. Tears, whispered anxieties, and finally, the stark reality of Becca's cancer diagnosis. The word hung in the air, heavy and suffocating. It had been a whirlwind since the diagnosis – the tests, the consultations, the grim prognosis that promised at least a year of chemo. But Becca wanted a wedding, a celebration of life before the debilitating symptoms stole her joy. And she wanted it now.

After I spent an hour consumed with countless questions and pouring over her medical charts, the stark black and white of lab results confirming the devastating truth, her mother and aunt had descended into the home, full of well-meaning but misguided energy. Their mission was to find the perfect off-the-rack dress but that was easier said than done. Becca, while still slender, didn't possess the kind of curves that sample sizes catered to and we had no time for alterations. Finding a dress that fit, let alone flattered, was becoming a... task.

"What about something a little more understated?" I suggested, walking toward Becca with my own pick clutched in my hand. It was a simple ivory dress with a clean silhouette of flowing lines and delicate lace. Not a cloud of tulle and definitely not a single sequin in sight.

Becca snatched it from my grasp and mouthed a silent thank you.

"Not really like the ones you've been trying on."

She let out a shaky laugh. "Trust me, anything is better than the monstrosities my mother is choosing."

She turned and vanished into the dressing room, the door clicking shut behind her before the startled assistant could even register her disappearance.

I curled up in the bed and wrapped my arms around her from behind.

"I don't understand," I whispered. "How could this happen to you?"

Becca squeezed my hand against her stomach with a laugh. "Oh come on, have you seen Liz? I'm marrying a fucking goddess. I mean have you seen her ass? Absolutely glorious."

I burst out laughing.

"The universe had to throw a curveball in there somewhere," she added in feigned exasperation.

I closed my eyes and took a deep breath. "I'm so scared." I sniffled. "And I shouldn't even be saying this to you. I should be comforting you and here you are comforting me. This is so fucked up."

"You can say whatever you want. I think I've learned that there are no rules to life. Except maybe taxes. Fuck taxes."

"I fucking hate taxes." I agreed. "I mean what's the point of taxing income and purchases and ..." I paused for dramatic effect. "You know I actually don't really know exactly how taxes work but I still agree, fuck them."

Becca turned to face me. "I'm glad you're here," she said. "Not really the bachelorette party or night before my wedding I envisioned but honestly I wouldn't change it. I'm glad it's just us hanging out for the last few hours of my singleness."

"Becca, you haven't been single in years. You haven't been single since yall locked eyes."

"You know that is so true." She snuggled in closer. "I want you to have that one day."

"Me too."

"I think you already found it."

"Ugh."

"You wanna talk about him or should I take a page out of your book and pretend he doesn't exist?"

I threw a hand over my eyes. "I wanna talk about him."

Becca jumped up with the excitement of a child on christmas morning. "Thank fuck. You know you're like pulling teeth when it comes to him. Okay, tell me everything."

Ford

Caroline stood framed in the doorway, arms crossed, a mirror of the pose she'd held the night I'd handed her the divorce papers.

"What are you doing here?" she asked in cool and guarded tone.

I ran a hand through my hair, knowing the gesture betraying a nervousness I fought to conceal. I'd rehearsed this moment a hundred times in my head, but the carefully constructed sentences seemed to have dissolved into a jumble of half-formed thoughts. "I'm not really sure," I admitted and the words sounded hollow even to my own ears.

"Ford, listen—" Caroline began, but I cut her off in a desperate attempt to steer the conversation.

"I wanted to apologize."

Her eyebrows arched in surprise as the severe line of her mouth softened for a fraction of a second. "Apologize?" she scoffed in disbelief.

"I just needed to tell you that I'm sorry." I met her gaze. "And I wanted to do it face to face, not when a bunch of lawyers were supervising us at the courthouse, dissecting every word."

She sighed. "And what exactly are you apologizing for?"

I swallowed hard, the lump in my throat making it difficult to speak. "Not being the husband you needed." The words hung in the air between us.

She rolled her eyes and a flicker of the old Caroline I'd once known flashed before me. "It's a small town, you know. People talk."

I furrowed my brow, confused by the sudden change in topic. "Are they gossiping about us?"

"Not us. More the fact that Anderson's sister is back in town and how you seem to find yourself everywhere she is."

"It's not—" I started to protest, but she held up a hand.

"If you're looking for permission to move on, you know that's not mine to give."

I shook my head. "I'm not—"

"But in all honesty," she continued, her voice dropping to a near whisper, "none of that matters. You don't need permission to move on from me because you were never mine in the first place."

She leaned forward, her scent, a familiar mix of vanilla and something faintly floral, washed over me. She placed a timid kiss on my cheek. Then, before I could respond, she turned and shut the door.

Chapter 14

6 Years Prior

Emily

The rain was a cold, driving sheet as I sprinted across the lawn. The parking lot, usually half-empty when I visited, was a whirl of moving trucks and stressed out parents meaning the closest spot I could find was a good hundred yards away.

It was the end of an era. Ford and Anderson were officially college graduates and embarking on their separate journeys into the world of medicine. Anderson was returning to Columbia but Ford was Charleston-bound.

I finally reached their door as I clutched a box of doughnuts to my chest praying it wasn't completely soaked through. I'd risen before the sun and driven like a woman possessed to get there early, ready to help with whatever last-minute tasks might be needed.

My key turned in the lock for the last time and a heavy sigh escaped my lips. Something about them leaving this place—the place where we'd forged so many memories, the place where Ford and I had actually become friends—felt profoundly wrong. It was a reality I stubbornly refused to accept.

I tiptoed into the cold, silent house. My parents wouldn't arrive for at least another hour or more and Anderson was likely still asleep with Lynn by his side amd Ford was probably nursing a hangover in his room.

I swallowed, pacing the hallway between his door and the living room. Each time I gathered the courage to knock, something held me back. This was our last weekend of freedom before he officially became a medical student and I knew if I didn't say something now, I probably never would. I needed to just bust in there and tell him how I felt.

> Emily: They say the way to a man's heart is through his stomach, right?

> Becca: You brought his favorite doughnuts, didn't you?

> Emily: What if he laughs in my face? What if I've completely misread everything?

> Becca: You haven't. That man loves you. Knock on his door and just be yourself.

> Emily: And what exactly would 'myself' do?

> Becca: Haha. She would proudly confess that she masturbates to his face every night.

> Emily: I do not!

> Emily: Only on Wednesdays.

> Emily: And Thursday-Tuesday

> Emily: And sometimes it's his ass or his hands, not just his face.

> Becca: Stop texting me and tell him. We practiced this a million times. You got it, babe!

A nervous smile stretched across my face, tightening the closer I got to his door. I lifted my hand to knock just as I heard movement from inside. He was awake which was honestly the best-case scenario. Waking him up to confess my feelings was not the ideal start to that conversation.

I rapped my knuckles against the wood, simultaneously twisting the handle and laughed when I realized he'd left the TV on, again. It was his one truly annoying habit. I needed absolute silence to sleep; Ford thrived on background noise. Twenty-three years old and he still hadn't learned to relax in the quiet of life.

The door swung inward, spilling light from his bedroom into the hallway and I caught a glimpse of the TV. The screen was a dull black. Then my eyes landed on a woman I'd never seen before perched on top of Ford.

"Oh, God!" I slapped a hand over my mouth and stumbled backward. "I'm sorry. I'm so sorry. Pretend I wasn't here. Oh my God." The words tumbled out in a rush as my mind scrambled for an escape route. Which way to turn? Was the front door to the right or left? How fast could I run the 90 miles back to my apartment?

161

I'd barely made it through the kitchen when a familiar hand closed around my wrist. I whirled around, finding Ford wide-eyed, as bewildered as I was.

"I'm sorry," I repeated, just as the unknown woman stepped into view.

"Who are—"

"I'm Emily," I blurted out, flashing the widest, most obviously fake smile I could manage. "I'm Emily, Anderson's sister." I sidestepped Ford and did the most mortifying thing imaginable. I reached out and shook the hand of the half-naked woman, still wrapped in a bedsheet, who I'd just walked in on. If the ground could have swallowed me whole at that moment, I would have welcomed it.

"Hi," the woman said, hesitantly returning the handshake. "I'm Caroline."

My cheeks felt as though they might crack from the strain of my forced smile. My muscles refused to cooperate which left me frozen, staring at the five-foot-eight vision of absolute beauty before me. Even post-sex, this woman looked ready to walk a runway.

I glanced back at Ford, who stood frozen in disbelief. He might as well have been a statue or maybe he was dead. He certainly wasn't breathing. Should I check for a pulse? He was looking a little pale.

My gaze darted between them as a million thoughts collided in my mind. The only reasonable course of action my brain could conjure was to grab the soggy box of donuts I was holding and thrust a glazed pastry into each of their hands.

"I brought you breakfast!" I exclaimed with a voice far too cheerful for the hour. Finally, Ford gave a small nod.

"Thank you," he mumbled as he tentatively placed the soggy donut on the counter beside him. His mouth opened and closed as the three of us stood trapped in the most awkward triangle I'd ever been a part of. Ford looked from Caroline to me, then shook his head as if trying to will the appropriate response into existence.

Thankfully, Caroline broke the tension. "I'm going to get dressed." She placed her own soggy donut next to Ford's and turned to retreat into his bedroom. The moment the door closed, leaving me standing in a literal puddle of rainwater, the tension intensified.

"Emily," Ford breathed. "You're here early."

"You know me. I'm either half an hour early or three hours late." I swallowed hard.

"Emily—" He reached out to touch my shoulder just as Caroline reappeared in the hallway.

"I'll see you later," she said, giving us both a small smile before leaning in to press a quick kiss on Ford's cheek. She then gave me a hesitant glance. "It was nice to meet you."

"Oh!" The ridiculous smile snapped back into place. "Of course! So great to meet you, too! Don't forget your breakfast!" I tried to press the soggy pastry back into her hands, then silently berated myself as she froze.

"I think I'll pass, but thanks." Caroline met Ford's gaze, then walked out and the sound of the closing front door echoed through the suddenly silent house.

"Well, that was awkward as fuck."

We both jumped at the sound of Anderson's voice from across the room.

"Just a little," Ford replied, then walked the fifteen feet to his bedroom door. "I'll be out in a minute," he called out just before the door slammed shut.

"You okay?" Anderson asked as he placed a warm hand on my now-freezing shoulder.

"What? Okay? Yeah. Yeah. Of course. I'm fine. Completely fine. Why wouldn't I be fine?"

Anderson gave me a sad smile and shook his head before disappearing back into his own room, leaving me alone, and replaying every second of the past five minutes in my head.

My plan was ruined. Under no circumstances was I going to confess anything to Ford. Especially not with Miss America having just strolled out of his bedroom. I mentally replayed every moment between us over the past three years, trying to understand how I could have misread everything so completely.

> Emily: Abort mission! I repeat ABORT MISSION!!! Miss America was warming his bed.

> Becca: NO WAY!

Emily: Yep. Total idiot move on my part.

Becca: No, he's the idiot!

Emily: I'm so embarrassed I could cry.

Becca: What did you DO?!

Emily: I basically shoved a soggy donut in her hand as she was leaving. Plus, I'm pretty sure I could nail a 50s Stepford housewife. Fake smile and all.

Becca: Okay...so no Ford, but maybe Broadway? Who needs a Ford when you could get a TONY?!

Ford's bedroom door swung open and he walked out half-dressed with a t-shirt clutched in his hand.

"You are a mess," he teased, but his words were softened by the smile that met my tentative one.

"So you've said," I countered and prayed the turmoil churning inside me wasn't visible.

He ran a hand through his hair and leaned against the counter beside me, so close our hips brushed and I fought the urge to pull away.

"I think I have a new nickname for you." A smirk played on his lips, and I groaned, rolling my eyes.

I playfully nudged my hip against his. "It can't be any worse than what you call me now."

He returned the push, then his gaze turned serious. "You know that nickname was born out of love."

164

I frowned. "How, exactly?"

He turned back to the mountain of boxes that filled the living room, beginning his confession. "You always forgot to eat."

"What?" I turned to face him, but he kept his eyes fixed ahead.

"You get in your little trances and you forget to drink water and eat." He glanced at me. "Except for cookies. You always remember to eat cookies."

I scoffed as I turned back to the room. "So, I like cookies." I shrugged. "You gave me that nickname because I like cookies?"

"No—" He reached behind him, opening a soggy box of donuts. "I gave you that nickname so that every time I thought of you, I would remind myself to make sure you'd had something to eat that day." He picked up the leats damaged donut and offered it to me.

A sudden rush of emotion threatened to overwhelm me. It was a stupid reason. A stupid nickname. And who cared if I got busy with homework or reading and forgot about eating? It wasn't like I did it on purpose.

"Stop." Ford's hand cupped my chin as he tilted my gaze to his. "Stop."

"Stop what?" I glared at him. "I'm not doing any—"

"You're overanalyzing everything I just said and trying to make it make sense in your head." He tapped my temple.

"That's a stupid reason for a nickname." I crossed my arms, turning to the morning sunlight streaming through the window.

"But I have a new one," he countered as he tore off a piece of pastry and stuffed it in his mouth.

I turned back to find him staring at me. "Are you going to tell me?"

"Chaos," he answered, and I frowned.

"Chaos?" I repeated, and he nodded. "You are the absolute most chaotic person I have ever met."

My eyebrows rose. "You're not selling me on why this is a good alternative."

"You're wild. You're loud. You're impulsive. You're blunt. You're stubborn."

I rolled my eyes. "Ford. Not. Helping."

"You can turn an organized room into an absolute mess in less time than it takes me to brush my teeth."

I laughed at the truth in his words.

"You say exactly what you mean. You don't give a shit what anyone thinks of you. But most of all, and even with all of that, you're free."

His words hung in the air. "I'm free?" I questioned.

He nodded.

"And I'm chaos," I added.

"You're Chaos," he confirmed, pinching off another piece of the sticky treat and pressing it to my lips.

I pulled back slightly, a playful smile forcing its way onto my face, the movement deliberate to avoid his touch. "And who is Caroline?" The question slipped out before I could stop it.

The easy atmosphere shattered.

"She's a friend."

"That's nice."

"Emily, I—"

"You know. I don't think you've ever had a girlfriend. At least not that I know of. You should ask her out. She obviously likes you."

He frowned. "You want me to ask her out?"

"Yeah. Why not?"

He swallowed as he stared at the floor between us. "Her mom knows my mom."

"Oh."

"They went to college together." He swallowed again.

"That's nice."

"Yeah. When Mom came up here last week to help take the initial round of boxes down she ran into Caroline's mom and we ended up all going out to dinner together."

"That's nice."

"She's moving to Charleston after graduation too." He continued.

"That's nice."

Ford tilted his head in confusion. "Is that all you know how to say?"

"No. I just think it's...nice." I exhaled.

June

Emily: Hey FitzWilliam... I'm coming down to Charleston next week, wanna meet up? And this time I don't even need a fake ID!

Ford: Can't. Too much going on. Have fun.

July

Emily: The group is hosting an ultimate frisbee day on Saturday. You should come up and hang with us. Take a break from all the medical nonsense. Maybe try to not end the day as a lobster and I'll go easy on you and only make you watch Pride & Prejudice twice.

Ford: Hey. Sorry I'm busy. Definitely will next time though.

August

Ford: Thinking about heading up there for the weekend. Wanna hang?

Emily: You're alive?

Ford: I think . . .

Emily: Haven't heard from you in weeks. I was prepping my eulogy speech.

Ford: Well I didn't die so…..

Emily: Sure text me when you get here.

Ford: Hey sorry got to cancel. Tell everyone I said hey for me though. Maybe next time?

Chapter 15

PRESENT DAY

Emily

The tears I'd been holding back finally broke free as my best friend spoke her vows. Beside her, Liz was radiant, completely absorbed in the moment, in Becca, while I fought a losing battle against a full-blown meltdown. Twenty minutes. Twenty agonizing minutes of trying to keep it together while the beautiful, horrific ceremony unfolded.

It was like reliving the nightmare of two years prior, the one where Mom... It was happening all over again, different faces, different circumstances, but the same suffocating fear. A phantom echo reverberated in my chest, a cruel déjà vu. I was torn between crying for their happiness and collapsing under the weight of the fear that clawed at me.

We all knew the statistics. Becca's prognosis was good, far better than the odds Mom had faced. Yet, the comparisons were insidious, whispering dark doubts in the corners of my mind. My hands clenched into fists, anger tightening in my chest. It wasn't fair. None of it was.

Becca deserved so much more than this hastily arranged ceremony, squeezed in before the chemo took its inevitable toll. She deserved the massive celebration she'd always dreamed of, a room overflowing with laughter and friends, not this rushed, bittersweet affair born from the shadow of illness.

Hot tears traced paths down my cheeks.

She deserved a life free from the fear that clung to us all, the unspoken understanding of what lay ahead, the potential for pain and suffering that loomed like a dark cloud. She deserved happiness, pure and untainted. She deserved peace. Why couldn't life just be fair for once?

A warm hand closed over mine, breaking through my spiraling thoughts. Becca's mom stood beside me, her eyes soft with a mixture of sadness and strength. "She's going to be alright," she whispered, her voice a soothing balm against the turmoil within me.

But no amount of reassurance could truly convince me, not with the memories that haunted me. Still, I managed a weak nod, a silent promise I desperately wanted to believe.

"Come on," she nudged my shoulder gently with a subtle encouragement. "Your best friend is getting married. Dry those eyes and try to smile."

"Easier said than done," I admitted in a choked whisper."

"I know," Her arm wrapped around me in a comforting embrace. "But this is one of the happiest days of her life. For all we know," a faint smile touched her lips, "an asteroid could take us all out before we even get to cut the cake."

I met her eyes, and a small, watery laugh escaped me. It was a ridiculous yet perfect thing to say. A sudden injection of humor into the heavy atmosphere.

"Okay, you win," I murmured, squeezing her hand back. I took a deep breath, trying to let the moment wash over me, and for just a little while I allowed the joy of it, the promise of it, to push back on the ever-present fear.

The back porch of Liz's house glowed with soft string lights, casting a warm halo around the small gathering. No grand ballroom, no tiered cake, no awkward toasts. Just Becca, Liz, their parents, an aunt, myself, and two of Liz's cousins.

It was intimate and perfect.

As we milled around, a low hum of conversation punctuated by the occasional burst of laughter filled the air. Becca and I huddled together, thumbing through a playlist on Liz's phone, our heads bent close as we debated the merits of a particular mashup—something that would bridge the generational gap and get everyone tapping their toes.

I nudged Becca's shoulder with a playful grin tugging at my lips. "You know," I began, lowering my voice slightly, "Ford was absolutely adamant about being at your wedding. You snubbing him on the invite might just mean he kills you before the cancer gets the chance."

Becca whipped around, her eyes wide, and mouth agape as pure astonishment radiated from her face. "Did you, Emily Ann Truse," she breathed barely above a whisper, "just make a joke about my cancer?"

A pang of guilt shot through me, and I cringed, instantly regretting my impulsive words. "I did," I admitted. "Is it...too early?" I held my breath, bracing for her reaction.

Then, a sound erupted from Becca's throat—a burst of laughter that started as a giggle and quickly escalated into a full-blown roar. She threw her head back as tears filled her eyes and the other partygoers turned to us with a mixture of confusion and amusement etched on their faces.

"Absolutely fucking not!" she said between gasps, wiping a stray tear from her cheek. "This," she declared, "is exactly why you're my best friend!" The laughter continued, a cleansing wave that washed away the momentary awkwardness and solidified the bond between us—the kind of friendship that could even find humor in the face of the darkest of realities.

I'd wrapped my arms around her as I whispered, "He's still going to kill you."

"What are you two giggling about?" Liz's voice sliced through our private moment. She snatched the phone, her thumb immediately selecting a song she knew was Becca's favorite with no consideration for the mood, and no glance to gauge what anyone else might think.

A slow smile bloomed on Becca's face as she shifted her gaze between us, then reached out to touch her new bride. "We should give it to her?"

Liz and I exchanged a bewildered look. Even Liz, with her usual unflappable air, seemed lost.

"Give what?" we asked in unison as our voices overlapped in perfect confusion.

Becca's eyes locked onto Liz's. "You know. The thing we've had since..."

"Oh, shit. I completely forgot we still had that." Liz tilted her head in concentration. "You think it's still in the attic?"

"Probably." Becca shrugged with a small, almost mischievous smile playing on her lips.

I snapped my fingers between them. "Um. Someone wanna clue me in?"

They both seemed to have forgotten I existed. Their silence only deepened the mystery and fueled my growing frustration.

"But should we?" Liz's voice was laced with skepticism.

"I think it's fine," Becca murmured.

I scoffed as I waved a hand back and forth between them and tried to break through their private bubble. "Hello? I'm right here."

Liz finally turned to face me with her arms crossed over her chest and her eyes narrowed into a piercing stare. The contrast was almost comical. Here were these two women, dressed to the nines, looking like absolute princesses in their elegant gowns, and yet they were both staring at me as if I was next on some unseen kill list.

"What's going on?"

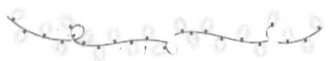

I stared at the engine letting its greasy metal become a cold comfort against my equally greasy hands.

"I asked if you'd found a place yet?" Anderson said and his voice cut through my thoughts. When I looked up I found him leaning against the side of Emily's RV and wiping his hands on a rag.

"Not yet."

He nodded, then scoffed. "Can we cut the bullshit?"

"What bullshit?" I asked, meeting his gaze in defiance.

"The bullshit of you not choosing to sleep on a blow-up mattress instead of finding somewhere suitable to live?" His eyes narrowed, and I knew he was pushing.

I met his stare and shrugged hoping to diffuse the tension in the air.

"I just haven't found the—"

"You applied to move hospitals. You're not going to complete your residency at Baptist." He cut me off, and I froze, the implication of his words hitting me like a physical blow.

"What?" The word was a choked gasp.

He shook his head, a grim set to his jaw. "You know you can't lie to me. You applied to finish out your residency at another hospital. Why?"

"How do you know that?" I countered, grasping at straws.

"What does it matter how I know? What I want to know is why I'm finding out from scheduling and not from my best friend?" His voice was tight.

I hung my head as a mixture of embarrassment and shame washed over me. "I can't do it anymore." The words were a painful confession.

"Can't do what?" He threw the rag down, the sound echoing in the sudden silence between us. "Can't get lunch with me every Friday? Can't come see James and Lynn on your weekends off? Can't hang out with me and Dad—"

"Fuck, Anderson." I ran my hands through my hair. "It's not always about you. You realize that, right?"

He stared at me with disbelief etched on his face.

"I love your family. Hell, they're my family too. But the last few years have been a complete shit show for all of us, and—"

"So you're running? Just like Emily." He balked. "Maybe y'all should get together again." The words were a cruel jab, meant to sting.

I balled up the rag in my hands turning my knuckles white. I knew if I let it drop, my fist would find his face.

"No one is running. We're just living our lives the best way we know how. And you know what, Anderson? Not all of us peaked in high school. Some of us want more than what this town has to offer. Some of us want—"

I froze as a searing pain exploded in my jaw. The taste of iron filled my mouth, and the world tilted.

Chapter 16

5 Years Prior

Emily

April

Emily: Hey are you coming up this weekend? The new Marvel movie is coming out and we're all going to see it. Let me know if you want a ticket.

Emily: Well you missed out. End Game is quite possibly the best action movies I've ever seen. Sadly Taylor Swift did not make an appearance. Text me when you can.

> Emily: Hey.

> Emily: You okay?

May

> Emily: Are you coming by my parents for dinner when you come to town?

> Ford: Not this weekend. I'm with Caroline.

June

> Emily: You okay . . . ?

"What's wrong?" Becca asked as she not so gracefully descended onto the couch beside me.

"Something's up with Ford." I clutched my phone, willing the three little dots of text-message anticipation to appear, yet they stubbornly remained absent.

"Why ou ay dat?" Becca mumbled around a mouthful of cinnamon toast crunch.

I shot her a withering glance. "Was that even English?"

She swallowed with a delicate gulp and flashed a charming, cereal-dust-tinged smile as she grabbed another handful straight from the box. "Yes. It was."

I rolled my eyes and stared back down at my phone. "He hasn't responded to me in two days. That's forty-eight hours of radio silence."

"You think he died?" Becca's eyes widened with mock horror.

I whipped my head back to her in disbelief. "What the—died? That's where your brain went? Straight to the morgue?"

Becca shrugged in complete nonchalant innocence as she shoveled in another handful of cereal. "Not really. But I doubt you want to accept what really happened, so that's the next feasible option. Like, maybe he's been abducted by aliens. Or maybe he's stumbled upon a secret portal to another dimension. Or maybe he's just being an idiot... like always."

I threw my head back and let out a frustrated groan. The truth in what she was insinuating hung in the air.

"You think?" I finally managed, my voice strained.

"I know. The question is, do you?" Becca's eyes twinkled with mischievous knowing.

I let out a shuddering breath and dramatically flopped over, placing my head in her lap. "I was hoping maybe he'd failed an exam or something and was pouting. You know, a classic case of temporary immaturity. Easily fixable with a pep talk and some pizza."

Becca started to run her fingers through my hair, but I dramatically halted her mid-reach. "Only the hand that's not covered in cinnamon, please. I need a comforting gesture, not a sticky surprise."

"Oops." She pulled back with a guilty but still utterly adorable smirk.

"You know what sucks the most?" I asked, gazing up at her with a pained expression as she started braiding my hair.

"What's that?"

"I'm not even jealous anymore. I'm just...mad. Like, explosively, volcano-level mad. I'm mad that he lets her turn him into a person I don't even recognize. It's like he's a different person now."

"How long are they going to do this?" Becca asked with genuine concern.

I scoffed and turned to face FitzWilliam, who was now curled up asleep between Becca's feet, oblivious to the emotional turmoil I was experiencing. "At this point, it seems like forever. How is this normal?

How many times can someone date and break up before they realize it just isn't going to work out?"

"I think the truth is she's jealous of you and doesn't let him text or call you," Becca said, voicing the unspoken fear we both shared.

"Then he's a fucking coward."

M y heart hammered against my ribs. This was my first solo shift. No preceptor, no professor, no clinical supervisor to catch me if I fell. I was officially a nurse. And not just any nurse, but one who'd landed the coveted Baylor shift at the region's top hospital, a gig that paid more than I'd ever dreamed. Friday night to Sunday morning, leaving the rest for the gauntlet of graduate school, as I chased my nurse practitioner license.

For the last twenty minutes, I'd been transfixed by my hands, willing the clammy film to vanish. At this rate, I'd make a complete fool of myself before I even wrestled on a pair of gloves.

A wave of relief washed over me as Becca's name lit up my phone screen.

"Hey." My own voice came out breathless.

Becca laughed. "Just checking. I assume you made it to the unit?"

"Yeah. I'm here." The words tumbled out in a rush. "I think the rest of my shift hasn't arrived yet, and apparently, we aren't getting report for another forty-five minutes, and—"

"Emily, what did you expect? You arrived over an hour early. I suspect you're going to be the only one there for a while." Becca chuckled. "But I'd rather you be early than late."

"Agreed." I sighed.

"I can't talk, I'm getting ready to interview some idiot about the housing market and I need to figure out how to become remotely interested in the conversation."

I burst out laughing.

"I just wanted to make sure you had arrived in one piece. But good luck. Love you."

"Love you, too," I replied, then ended the call and checked the time, confirming what I already knew. I was definitely over an hour early.

It was the one symptom that, even with medication, I couldn't seem to shake.

Time management was a bitch. A hideous, unmasterable, dreadful, abhorrent, hellacious fucking bitch.

No matter how hard I tried, time just seemed to slip through my fingers. It was why I always carried my Kindle—the one no longer tethered to my mother's library—everywhere. Because at least once a day, I'd arrive somewhere too early and need something to fill the void.

But early was better than late. So there I sat, alone in the empty locker room, waiting for the other nurses to arrive, losing myself in the most depraved smut I could find, hoping to quiet the rising tide of nerves.

"**Y**ou didn't kill anyone?" I jumped at the unexpected voice then whirled around to find Ford leaning against the bedroom door with a smirk plastered across his face.

"You scared the crap out of me," I whispered, my voice barely audible as I buried my face in my hands.

Ford chuckled and for the first time ever, the sound grated against my frayed nerves. "I could tell." He took a bite of his pizza and the cheesy aroma filled the room. "Kill anyone?" he mumbled through the chewing.

"No," I snapped as I pulled my hands away from my face and glaring at him. "Thank you very much, I didn't kill anyone." The words came out sharper than I intended, edged with a desperation I couldn't hide.

He tilted his head, still chewing, the casual gesture a painful reminder of how easily he moved through the world, completely unburdened. "I'm surprised. I was sure I'd be picking you up from the county jail."

A heavy sigh escaped my lips. "I hate you," I mumbled, the words feigned with frustration, but even I wasn't sure how correct they were.

The smirk vanished from Ford's face as he straightened and his eyes narrowed with concern. "What's wrong?"

"Nothing," I choked out. The word was thin and brittle, a flimsy shield against the tide of emotions threatening to overwhelm me. I closed my eyes, and in the suffocating silence, I heard his footsteps drawing closer.

"You're a horrible liar." His hand gently clasped my wrist, and he tugged lightly, a silent plea for me to turn to him.

But I remained stubbornly still with my gaze fixed on the floor. I didn't reply, couldn't reply. All I knew was that today had been hell, a relentless assault, and the thought of facing another day like it was a future I couldn't bear.

"Emily?" Ford's voice was soft and laced with worry as he gave me another tug.

"I'm fine," I answered the unspoken question, but my voice broke and the phrase ended in a sob.

"No, you're not," he countered, his grip tightening as he pulled me around to face him. "What happened?"

"Nothing," I repeated as I buried my face in my hands again only to find hot tears streaming down my cheeks.

But Ford Edward Thomas was just as stubborn as I was. He reached up and gently pulled my hands away from my tear-dampened face. "Listen, I didn't drive all the way up here to bring you pizza to celebrate your official first day of your big girl job for you to shut me out."

"I'm not," I sniffled as I wiped my nose with the back of my hand. The dam had broken and now the tears were flowing freely, "shutting you out."

"Oh crap," he murmured as a flicker of helplessness entered his eyes, "maybe I should have brought vodka instead."

Our eyes met and without a word, he tossed the half-eaten slice of pizza into the trashcan and pulled me into his arms.

"I would prefer to drown my sorrows in tequila if I get to choose," I mumbled against his shirt.

"What happened?" Ford whispered into my hair.

It was taking every ounce of my willpower to keep the tears at bay. I was strong. I had a degree and, as of today, a very good paying job. There was absolutely no reason I should be sitting here sobbing into Ford's chest.

Instead of answering, I played with the bandage at the hem of his shirt.

"Did you get new ink?" I whispered.

"Yes, and I promise to show you, but not now. Now you have to answer my question."

I took a long, shuddering breath. "I forgot to take my meds. Actually, I forgot to call in the script, and when I finally remembered last night, the pharmacy said they weren't going to get any in for another three days." Without a care, I wiped my face against his shirt as I forced down the emotion. "I can't go three days. I can't even go one." The admission was full of guilt as I leaned back to meet his stare. I cringed when I saw what I'd done. "And now I've covered your shirt in my snot."

He laughed. "I love snot. It's the newest fashion accessory."

I shoved his shoulder. "Don't make me laugh when I wanna cry."

"Okay, Bambi's mother dies in the first scene and—"

I punched him again as my smile rose. "Why would you say that?! Oh my god, that was so traumatizing!"

"Well, you said you wanted to cry soooo?"

"I hate you," I lied as I buried my head against his chest once more. "Ford, why am I such a fuck up?"

He brushed his lips against my hair. "What'd you mess up?"

"Everything." The muffled word vibrated off his chest, a shaky exhale against his warmth. He chuckled, a low rumble that did nothing to soothe the frantic flutter in my chest.

"But you didn't kill anyone." His voice held a careful lightness, a fragile attempt to pierce the heavy shroud of my despair. But nothing felt light.

"No." I pulled back, swiping at the tears that blurred my vision, leaving my eyes raw and red. "But I know the other nurses think I'm an idiot."

Ford shook his head, his expression turning serious as the weight of the moment settled between us. "You're not an idiot. You're one of the smartest women I know."

I scoffed. "Ugh! I just—" I buried my face back in his chest, finally surrendering to the only place that felt remotely safe. "I had to re-read everything twice to make sure I was taking it all in correctly, which made me take twice as long to do anything. The other nurses were grunting all day, and I could feel the frustration radiating off them in waves. And then I forgot to eat lunch because I spent my break making sure I was well versed on a diagnosis my patient had that I never really learned about in school, and then my blood sugar dropped 'cause I forgot to eat, and I practically passed out walking to the vending machine. And everyone—"

Ford pulled me closer, his arms tightening around me. "You realize that is all an easy fix. We'll call around and see if we can get your meds at another pharmacy. Then, when we get them you take them tomorrow and everything will be okay. I'll even text you a reminder in the morning, and then I'll text you during your break to remind you to eat."

The frustration twisted in my gut, coiling tight, and without warning, the anger burst free. I shoved him away, breaking the desperately needed contact and leaving a hollow ache.

"But I don't want you to!" I screamed. The sound echoed against the walls of my bedroom as my gaze fixed on some invisible point beyond him, unable to look him in his eyes.

"Ummm." He paused searching for purchase on the shifting ground between us.

I cut him off as the words tumbled out in a rush. "I don't want you to. I don't want to have to need you and Anderson and Becca to remind me of the basic life shit I need to do! I'm a fucking grown-ass woman and I'm a mess."

"Okay. I won't remind you," Ford said in an even tone and a fresh wave of frustration crashed over me.

"Ugh! That's not the point! The point is you shouldn't have to!"

"Yeah. I shouldn't. Like you said, you're a grown-ass adult."

I whirled around letting my furious glare burn into him.

"But I want to," he added quickly, before I could unleash another torrent of bitter words. "I want to text you, and I want to call you, and I want to rag on you for all the little details you miss, because you're my fucking family, and that's what family does for each other."

I cringed. The hurt in each word was a physical blow.

"I'm sorry." I ran my hands through my hair. "I'm so sorry." My head hung low, embarrassment a hot flush across my cheeks. The outbursts were rare now, but sometimes... sometimes the overstimulation just won. "I just don't want to be a burden. I want to be able to do things." I stumbled to the bed, collapsing face first into the spread. "I just want to do it without help." The last words were muffled against the fabric.

Ford's arms wrapped around my middle, strong and sure, and he flipped me over so I was facing him. I was on my back now, feet still planted on the floor, his hands braced on the mattress on either side of my waist.

"This is uncomfortable," I grumbled, trying to wriggle away.

"I don't care." He held firm, a stubborn glint in his eyes. "If life is hard right now, then we need to figure out a way to make it easier for you."

"I have a million planners. They don't work," I countered, rolling my eyes dramatically. They were a graveyard of good intentions.

A knowing smile tugged at his lips. "What about time blocking?"

"What's that?" I stared up at him, confused.

"Like, blocking out your day. Lists barely work for your brain anyway, so let's time block. Divide your day into timed segments with a specific goal for each." He pushed back to pace the room, the almost doctor in him taking over. "Your brain craves dopamine, and you tend to get that by procrastinating and doing things at the last moment."

I leaned up on my elbows, intrigued despite myself. "Not sure how time blocking will help that?"

"We trick your brain. Your morning segment can list out five things you have to accomplish within a certain time. It will trick your brain into thinking you're on a time deadline, and the dopamine will kick in, and you'll get a rush from doing things before the metaphorical timer goes off."

I furrowed my brow, considering his well-thought-out plan. "Holy shit."

"Right?" He nodded, a genuine grin spreading across his face.

"What class did you learn that in?"

He tilted his head, as if reluctant to reveal the source, but quickly gave in to the urgency in my features. "Honestly, social media."

I barked out a laugh and fell back onto the bed and the tension eased from my shoulders.

"Ugh. Why are you so damn nice? Could you not be such a good guy for once?"

Ford all but threw himself back onto the bed beside me as laughter bubbled up from him. The silence that followed felt heavy, thick, until I turned to face him. "Why are you here?"

He lifted a hand, ticking off reasons on his fingers. "Free weekend. Wanted to see Mom, your parents, check on you, see Anderson."

"You've been radio silent for weeks."

He winced. "Sorry."

I lowered my voice. "Where's Caroline?" The question hung in the air, a whisper I almost didn't want answered.

"I don't know."

"You don't know where your girlfriend is?" I propped myself up on my elbows.

"She isn't my girlfriend anymore. We broke up."

I jolted upright, sitting fully on the bed. "Again?"

He gave a wry smile. "Geez. Thanks for the support."

I shook my head. "Sorry. It's just... this is becoming a pattern. How many times have you two dated and then broken up now?"

"I haven't kept count."

I sighed. "Are you okay? Do I need to kill her?"

Ford actually laughed at that. "Nothing really happened. We just aren't good for each other. She's too—" He paused, searching for the right word.

"Pretentious?"

He shot me a look. "She's not pretentious, she's just—"

"Hella fancy and expects the best of the best at all times."

He grunted. "Fine, I'll give you that one."

I turned to face him squarely. "You know, the two of you together confuses the hell out of me."

"Me too," he admitted.

"Then why? Why keep going back?"

He sat up, staring at the wall. "It's complicated."

"Uncomplicate it for me."

"She's nice." He paused, as if the word itself was inadequate.

"Nice? She's nice?" I balked. "Are you talking about your girlfriend or the wallpaper you picked out for the stairwell?"

"Ex-girlfriend." He quickly clarified.

"She's your mom's pick." I said and he shook his head.

"Don't say that."

"Why? It's the truth. You could have any girl in the world, and you choose the one who makes you constantly feel like you'll never measure up, because she's the one your mom wants you to end up with."

He rolled his eyes. "Caroline doesn't make me feel that way."

"Ford, you wanted to go into psychiatry, and she pushed you toward trauma, because she thinks it's more prestigious or something."

"It has a lower burnout rate," he amended, wrinkling his nose.

"Doesn't matter. It's not what you wanted."

"Emily." He said my name like a warning, but I'd never been the cautious type.

"You deserve someone who is going to support all your dreams, not just the ones she approves of. Also, for the love of God, please stop letting your mom make all your life decisions."

He rolled his eyes again. "She doesn't."

"You wanted to go out of state and conceded to Clemson because of her."

"I got a full ride."

"Yeah, at five different colleges."

"So?" He shrugged.

"So," I nudged his side, "you also got into Duke for med school, and yet you ended up in Charleston."

"MUSC is a great medical school."

"MUSC is seven hours closer to your mom."

"Where are you going with this?" He rolled over, arranging himself against my pillows.

"I just want you to be happy."

"I'm happy."

I moved to sit beside him. "Are you really?"

"At least I didn't almost pass out on my first day at—"

I punched him in the side.

He groaned dramatically. "Too soon?"

"Too soon," I confirmed, then settled in beside him. "But seriously, how did your mom take the news? I'm guessing that's the real reason you came up here."

Ford groaned, burying his head in my sheets. On impulse, I ran my fingers through his hair, but pulled back the second he tensed. We hadn't touched much since he and Caroline had become official, but if that was over, then I sure as hell was going back to the way it was before.

"Exactly how you would expect."

"She cried?" I asked as I moved back to run my hands through his hair.

"Yep. You would have thought I'd committed murder and was sentenced to life in prison."

I knocked on the back of his head, and he turned to face me. "You realize that is a completely irrational response."

Ford closed his eyes. "You know what sucks?" He said without answering.

"What?"

"Sometimes when I think of the word 'mom,' I don't picture my mom, I picture yours."

"Ford—"

"Does that make me a bad person?"

"No," I answered. "Complicated? Maybe. But bad? No."

We both smiled.

"She's a pretty good mom," I whispered as his fingers laced with mine.

"I don't want to drive back to my mom's tonight and listen to her rant about Caroline. You care if I stay here?" he asked, staring at the ceiling.

"Not at all."

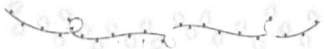

I woke to the scent of brewing coffee mingled with a roar of laughter that spilled from the living room and into the quiet of the morning. I blinked against the dim light filtering through the curtains and stretched before walking out to find Becca and Ford huddled together, heads bent in a conspiratorial way.

"What trouble are you two about to get into?" I asked, rubbing the sleep from my eyes and reaching to grab a cup.

Ford looked up and a grin spread across his face. The kind of grin that usually preceded some spectacularly bad idea. "Becca has a new girlfriend," he announced, "and you didn't tell me?" He actually looked hurt, as if he'd been personally slighted.

I huffed. "I didn't realize you were supposed to be kept apprised of Becca's love life?" A light laugh punctuated each word.

Ford looked baffled. "This isn't just a girlfriend. This is Elizabeth—"

"Liz," Becca corrected quickly.

"Whatever. Liz Bramlet. Her dad is Justin Bramlet. He was in the NFL." His voice grew louder with each word, rising to a near shout. "And not just the NFL, he played in the Super Bowl. The. Super. Bowl." Ford's eyes practically bulged from his head. "He's damn near royalty, and Becca could be his daughter-in-law one day!"

"Woah, now," Becca said, holding her hands up in a gesture of surrender. "We've gone on two dates. Two dates!" she emphasized.

"And she may not last past next week," I chimed in, and a look of pure confusion washed over Ford's face.

"What's next week?"

"I'm meeting her to give the best friend approval," I answered as if the idea of having to explain such a fundamental concept was utterly absurd.

Ford practically leaped from his chair, sending it crashing backward onto the floor. "You're meeting Elizabeth—"

"Liz!" Becca cut in forcefully.

"Liz Bramlet. You're meeting Liz Bramlet!" Ford finished, casting a mildly apologetic glance at Becca.

I chuckled in surprise, exchanging a look with Becca as we both tried and failed to contain the laughter that bubbled up at Ford's expense.

"Yeah. We're going to the Festival of Lights together."

"Fuck." Ford ran a hand through his hair. "What night? I have two labs this week, and a med—"

"Why?" I interrupted, scooping an obscene amount of sugar into my mug.

Ford furrowed his brow, as if the very idea of explaining his reasoning was the most ridiculous thing he'd ever encountered. "I'm going with you."

"Ford." I warned, glancing at my watch. "This is their date. I'm just meeting up after for drinks."

"Okay. So we go see the lights and then get drinks. What night are we going?" He pressed, pulling out his phone, presumably to consult his undoubtedly packed academic calendar.

"Wednesday," Becca answered. "We're going Wednesday since mid-week prices are cheaper."

Ford's hand raked through his hair again as his eyes darted across his phone screen. "Okay."

I burst out laughing. "Ford?"

He looked up, meeting our incredulous stares. "I can make Wednesday work. My Thursday classes don't start till ten." He slipped his phone back into his pocket with a shit-eating grin plastered on his face. "Holy shit. I'm about to meet E– Liz Bramlet!" he corrected himself without even glancing at Becca. "I'm guessing I shouldn't bring her dad's jersey for her to—"

"NO!" we both answered in unison.

By Wednesday, my phone buzzed incessantly—a relentless barrage of texts from Ford. Which I have to admit was slightly frustrating being as though we sent more text in the last four days than we had in the last four weeks.

But the Festival of Lights loomed, and he was in full panic mode, desperate for the perfect thing to say to impress Liz. Each message detailed a new, increasingly ridiculous approach, from quoting her dads football statistics to feigned knowledge of him in any capacity.

A rumble echoed from across the room, making me laugh. "We just ate dinner," I reminded him, incredulous and pointed to the empty pizza boxes.

He scoffed, clutching his stomach dramatically. "I'm a growing boy."

I turned to assess him, my eyes traveling up his impressive frame. He was easily over six feet, with biceps that strained against the sleeves of his t-shirt, muscles that seemed to possess their own gravitational pull. "I don't think that's physically possible," I said, shaking my head in mock seriousness.

"Definitely possible," he countered, a grin tugging at the corners of his mouth. It was then that I noticed something peeking out from beneath his sleeve—the edge of a bandaid. "You never showed me your new ink."

He hesitated for a moment, then silently pulled up his shirt sleeve, slowly revealing the artwork underneath. Little by little, black lines and intricate details emerged: flowing lines, delicate feathers, and finally, a pair of fearsome, piercing eyes.

"A phoenix?" I breathed, mesmerized by the detail. The tattoo stretched from his elbow to his shoulder, a powerful and evocative image.

He nodded as a faint blush crept up his neck.

"Are you a phoenix?" I asked, crossing my arms and leaning back in my chair with a playful smile on my face.

He shook his head as the blush deepened. "I don't know. It just...felt right at the time." He self-consciously rolled his sleeve back down, as if suddenly aware of the vulnerability of the gesture. I made it across the room before the sleeve fully covered the design.

"Wait. I wanna see it." I reached out and tugged the sleeve back up.

"It's just a tattoo. I have twenty four, nothing new."

I traced the lines with my finger, mesmerized by the design. "Do you really have twenty four?"

He laughed. "I don't know. Maybe?" He shrugged his shoulders.

"I like this one." I admitted. "It's really beautiful."

"Thank you." He blushed again.

"I feel like there is a story behind this?"

He shook his head but the move was less than convincing.

"Well, when you decide what that is, do you promise to tell me sometime?" I pressed gently, sensing there indeed was a story, just one story he wasn't quite ready to share.

"If there's ever something to tell."

"So, what's the plan?" Ford asked, his words tumbling out in a rush. "We just show up at the festival? Is there a specific spot we are meeting? Does Liz know—"

"Ford. Please," I pleaded, cutting him off. "I know Becca seemed real chill, but I think she truly likes Liz. Like, actually likes her. We can't screw this up."

"Screw this up? I'm not screwing up the chance to become family with someone who was in the Super Bowl."

I furrowed my brow. "What do you mean, family?"

"You and Anderson are basically my family, and you and Becca might as well be family, and if she ends up marrying Liz, then I'll get to be at the wedding, and that means I'm basically joining Justin Bramlet's family."

I laughed. "You stretched that so far I'm pretty sure it went to the moon and back."

"Ahhh, but it did come back." He winked.

The sun had dipped below the horizon by the time we'd paid admission and squeezed through the park gates. The twilight air seemed to have stolen some of Ford's earlier enthusiasm for expanding his family.

"So, what's the big deal with this festival? Just a bunch of light displays?" he asked.

I reached out, snagging two flashlights from the attendant. "I told you in the text. Honestly? I have no idea," I said, handing him one.

He chuckled. "I think it's a rich people thing."

"A rich people thing?" I echoed, raising an eyebrow.

"Yeah. Isn't the idea that you could buy some of these displays for your own house? Your backyard?"

"I guess?" I mumbled, as we started down the dimly lit, sparsely populated path towards the displays. He was probably right. The whole event stretched across two city blocks of the park, smack-dab in the wealthiest district.

"And neither of us are in that tax bracket." He chuckled, and I bumped my hip against his.

"One day you will be."

"Maybe," he countered.

We spent the next hour wandering from display to display, taking it all in, and surprisingly, actually enjoying ourselves.

"I really want to see the fireflies display," I said.

"Which one is that?" Ford asked, shining his flashlight down at the map.

"The last one. I looked them up online. They're so pretty."

"They fly?" He frowned.

"No." I shoved his shoulder playfully. "I think they're in different forms. Mostly these little sticks you stick in your garden, or attach to trees or bushes. When I have my own place, I'm covering my backyard in them. So many that even when it snows, you'll think there are a thousand little critters buzzing around."

"You know it barely snows here?"

"I'm not going to live here. I'm going to live in the mountains. Somewhere near Boone, maybe Beech Mountain," I said, a smile spreading across my face.

"Is that what you want?"

I nodded. "Though I doubt my nurse's salary will get me there. Maybe Liz has a brother I can seduce."

"Not if I don't seduce him first." Ford wiggled his eyebrows and I burst out laughing as we moved on to the next display: lights strung through the trees, flashing in time to music. We watched, mesmerized, as the colored lights danced on the breeze, like fireflies themselves.

The next display was a series of six-foot-tall towers, activated by movement. Before I knew it, Ford and I were racing between them, trying to outrun the bursts.

We moved through one display after another, a whirlwind of imagination, and for the first time since starting my new job that week, I could breathe.

By the time we could see the main entrance in the distance and the bar where we were meeting Becca and Liz, we were breathless from laughter and exertion.

"This was much more entertaining than I expected," Ford murmured, his voice barely audible.

"Did you think it wouldn't be any fun?" I tilted my head, studying his profile in the dim light.

"I don't know. I don't really like the dark," he stated, the words tumbling out as if by accident. He seemed to freeze a moment later, as if realizing the weight of what he'd just said.

"You don't like the dark?" I questioned, a slow dawning in my mind. When Ford didn't answer, I tugged on his arm. "That's why you always had the TV on when you stayed over!" The realization hit me like a physical blow. "Wait, you don't like the dark, or you're afraid of the dark?" I lowered my voice, attempting a spooky inflection as I raised the flashlight to illuminate my face from below.

He swallowed, his gaze fixed on something in the distance, his body stiff and unyielding.

"Ford?" I whispered in his ear, the playful tone gone as the serious-ness of the moment settled over me. "Are you afraid of—"

"It's not really the dark but more the quiet that fills it." His answer was clipped. "And it's not quiet here so I'm good."

A silence stretched between us.

He'd never spoken like that before... and certainly not to me. I glanced around, noting the painfully slow progress of the line leading to the final display. It would be minutes before we reached it. I tugged on his arm, pulling him sideways towards an empty bench.

"Explain."

Though the light was dim, I could just make out the exaggerated eye roll that preceded him turning to face me.

"Nothing to explain."

"Be honest, is that why you leave the TV on at night?"

Ford simply shrugged.

"Hey!" I nudged his shoulder. "Friends? Right? We're friends? We tell each other almost everything and—"

"There's nothing to tell," he cut me off as his gaze fixated on his hands.

"Ford," I urged. "Stop lying. If you don't want to tell me that's fine, but just don't lie to me. You know I won't judge you either way. It's just the dark, plenty of people are afraid of the dark. To be honest, I'm afraid of the dark. I probably wouldn't even be out here right now if you weren't with me."

A pause hung in the air, broken only by the hushed whispers of a family passing nearby. Then, he shook his head, as if fighting an internal battle.

Just as I thought he was about to dismiss the whole thing and get up to leave, he opened his mouth.

"I kept the TV on so I didn't have to hear the screams." The admission was quick, low, and took me completely by surprise.

"Screams?" I questioned, my voice barely a whisper.

"There were two types of nights in my home. The nights I slept in silence and the nights I slept with noise." He shifted with every word, as if desperate to escape his own skin.

"I don't understand?" I reached out, interlacing my fingers with his, trying to offer some semblance of comfort.

"My dad." Ford's voice cracked, and I stalled, trying to conjure an image of the man, but his face remained a blurred, indistinct picture in my mind.

I shook my head, trying to piece together the fragmented story he was weaving. I rarely ever saw Mr. Thomas. The only thing I truly remembered were the stern warnings my mom and dad gave Anderson and me about staying away from him.

"I know he's lived next door for most of my life but I don't really know him."

Ford took a deep, shuddering breath. "Lucky you."

"Hey." I squeezed his hand, letting him know I was there for him in whatever way he needed. "What happened?"

He stared straight ahead, avoiding my worried gaze.

"Some nights, if my dad had a particularly bad day at work and spent too long at the bars before he came home, my mom would send me to bed early and make sure to turn the TV on. It wasn't until I was older that I realized that noise had a purpose."

His eyes finally met mine, and even in the dim light, I could see the moisture gathering there.

"When I was really little, she screamed a lot. I think she stopped as the years went on because she realized it didn't matter. No one was coming. But then y'all bought the empty house beside us and it wasn't so easy to hide anymore."

My stomach churned with a sickening feeling. My jaw tightened as I fought the urge to speak, wanting to let him get it all out.

"For a while I thought it had stopped, but in all actuality I think she just got better at covering up the bruises. And then when I was nine, there was a particularly bad night. She hadn't screamed in months, but even with the volume turned all the way up, I could still hear her."

Dread filled the air as his words sank in.

"Your dad had gone out for something that night, or maybe he was coming home late, either way he heard her when he pulled back in the drive. I don't remember much except for opening my bedroom door and finding him and my dad having it out in my living room. The next day was the day your parents bought Anderson the bunk beds and they let me know I could stay over any time I wanted."

I felt a wave of nausea wash over me.

"Ford?" My voice broke as I pieced it all together. "I didn't know."

"I look like him."

"Okay," I agreed, unsure where exactly he was going.

"I look exactly like him, and we have the same mannerisms."

I reached out, cupping his chin and forcing his gaze to meet mine as the realization of what he was saying hit me. "You're not him."

"I know. I'm not him. I hate him." Ford turned back to face the darkness. "I hate him," he repeated, this time with more force. "I made a promise to myself that I won't turn out like him. I'm going to make something of myself, and then I won't feel the need to drink myself into oblivion so I'll forget about bills or money. I'm going to become a doctor and have a good life. I'm going to be able to take my family on vacation and not lash out when—" He paused, as if giving voice to the words was physically agonizing. "I refuse to stay cooped up in this town for the rest of my life." His words were filled with an unyielding resolve.

"I believe you," I said as a tear traced a path down my cheek. "Does Anderson know what happened?"

"Yeah." The word was heavy with defeat.

"Did he ever," I swallowed, my voice catching in my throat, "does he hurt you?" The thought was a sharp, painful jab.

Ford shook his head.

"Why didn't you tell me? I should have known. I could have—"

"You could have what?" Ford cut me off, and from the frustration in his tone, I could tell he was close to shutting down completely.

While we had spent the last few years building this odd, undefined relationship, we'd never allowed emotions or feelings like these to enter the equation—or at least, he hadn't. This was uncharted territory, and I had no idea how to navigate it.

"You were five when y'all moved in. Your parents couldn't even do anything because every time they called the cops, my mom would just lie and cover for him. There is nothing you could have done."

"But, I'm confused. He's still there right? Why hasn't your mom kicked him out? Why isn't he in jail?"

Ford scoffed. "Like I said. She is a great liar."

As soon as he said the words, the air between us shifted.

Ford swallowed, then stood and turned to face me. "I'm going to head out. I'm sorry. I know you wanted to see these lights and maybe Becca and Liz will go with you."

"Ford." I moved to follow him.

He shook his head. "My schedule is a little more packed than I realized." His forced smile faltered with the blatant lie. "I'll see you soon."

I stood frozen, stunned by the weight of his confession and his sudden departure, watching him walk away. A powerful urge washed over me to run after him, to wrap my arms around him and tell him I was there, but that wasn't who we were.

I paced by the bench, replaying every memory I could from our childhood. Had I missed something? Was I that oblivious and selfish? Why hadn't my family told me? A fierce anger burned within me for the little boy Ford had once been, and I was half tempted to call my mom right there and then and let her have it for never telling me.

Chapter 17

PRESENT DAY

Emily

T he hum of tires on asphalt was a dull counterpoint to the storm raging inside me.

Something about being with Becca and watching her and Liz experience so much happiness and devestation in the midst of hours broke me. They were going through absolute hell and still somehow were able to show up for each other and make the most out of the given moment.

That was something I had never been able to do. And that was something I needed to change.

Each mile marker on the ride home was a fresh wound, a reminder of the chasm that had opened between who I was and who I'd pretended to be. As the South Carolina state line sign blurred past, I wrestled my dad's truck onto the shoulder of the deserted interstate. The engine died, and a suffocating silence descended, broken only by the frantic thrum of my own heart.

In the rearview mirror, a stranger stared back. The girl I was supposed to be was gone, replaced by this...woman. This shell. A sharp ache pierced my chest as I took in her face.

She was breathtaking, achingly perfect in a way that made my stomach twist. *Her* hair, styled with meticulous care, cascaded over *her* shoulder in flawless curls. Each perfectly applied false eyelash, catching the headlights of the few passing cars, seemed to mock me with their pristine perfection. Had I seen *her* on the street, I would have been captivated, drawn in by a beauty that masked a hidden torment.

But that was the cruelest part of it, the flaw that had become *her* prison.

She drew people in with a lie, spun from silken threads of deceit. It was a masterpiece of fabrication, yet a lie nonetheless. And then once the lie had done its job it would, inevitably, fade. Some of the sparkle would drift away, repelled by the tarnished interior, the jagged edges of truth poking through the carefully constructed façade.

But she—I—clung to that manufactured shine with desperate ferocity. For years, it had been the only thing I knew, the only thing I believed could anchor me, could define me. I'd wanted to believe that this carefully constructed image was what built my life, what made me whole, what made me... me. But it had never truly been me.

A wave of nausea washed over me as the realization slammed home. This wasn't about procrastination, or a neurodivergent brain, or even the gaping wound left by my mother's death. It was about the lie. The elaborate, suffocating lie I had woven, not just for the world, but for myself.

I'd tried everything. Therapy, medication, the elaborate ritual of makeup and designer clothes. I'd bought the planners, scheduled every second of my days, obsessed over perfectly manicured nails, poured money into products promising flawless skin. I'd chased a phantom of perfection, desperate to fill the emptiness inside. Desperate to out-run the reality of life.

But a chilling truth echoed in my mind: a thousand band-aids could never mend a bullet hole.

I'd spent the last twenty-eight years carefully running away from every perceivable hell thinking running would help when in reality, all running ever did was tear me apart.

With trembling hands, I rummaged through my bag until I found the makeup wipes. The small, disposable cloths felt like instruments of liberation. In the dim light of the driver seat, I began to dismantle the lie, one careful swipe at a time. With each stroke, a layer of pretense peeled away, revealing the raw, vulnerable truth beneath. The act felt like a painful shedding, a necessary stripping away of the artifice that had held me captive for so long.

And once the paint was gone, I finally saw *me*.

Becca: Glad you made it home safe.

Emily: Stop checking my location and go fuck your wife.

Becca: Already done that a few times tonight. But since you asked nicely….

I sighed as I made it into the driveway, the exhaustion clug to me like a second skin. I hauled myself out of the car and trudged across the lawn, up the porch steps, and towards the front door.

"You're home late?"

Ford's voice cut through the quiet night, carrying across the yards. I stopped in surprise.

"You're up late." I turned and walked back down the porch steps and back into the darkness as he approached.

"It's almost midnight. You have a hot date?" he asked with a playful smirk tugging at his lips.

I scoffed. "I just got back from a wedding."

His brows furrowed in confusion. "Who got married?"

"Becca."

He stopped dead in his tracks. "To Liz?"

"Yeah, to Liz."

A look of mock horror washed over his face. "Holy shit. You didn't keep your part of the deal!" He said with a smile but all I could manage was a choked sob as tears I thought I'd shed already came rushing back.

He panicked. "Wait. I'm not really mad," he said quickly, concern lacing his voice.

I sniffled, trying to compose myself. "I just found out about it yesterday," I managed to get out.

"I'm confused," he said as his forehead creased with worry. "Why are you crying? Them getting married is a good thing, right?"

I nodded, leaning against the porch post, wishing the tears would stop. "It's a great thing."

"Then do you want to explain what all this is?" he asked as his eyes filled with a mixture of confusion and concern.

He stepped closer, his hand hovering hesitantly near my arm and I knew he was waiting for me to elaborate, to explain the tangled mess of emotions that had me falling apart on my doorstep. The surprise of the wedding, the sudden realization of whatever unspoken agreement we had, and the resurgence of old feelings—it was all swirling inside me, a chaotic storm I couldn't seem to contain. I took a shaky breath, ready to begin unraveling the truth.

"She has cancer." It was the first time I actually said the entire phrase out loud. Joking about it had been one thing, but this precise arrangement of syllables was something else entirely.

"Who?" Ford's swallow was audible in the sudden quiet.

"Becca." The whisper was barely there. "She has cancer."

He reached for my hand, and in my peripheral vision, I saw a rapid parade of emotions flicker across his face, mirroring the same journey I'd gone on yesterday.

"It's curable. Her prognosis is great." I wiped away a stray tear. "Honestly, I shouldn't even–"

He pulled me into a fierce embrace.

"I'm so sorry," he murmured into my hair. "I'm so so sorry."

I pulled back, meeting his concerned gaze. "Did you know cancer has a smell?"

Ford's brow furrowed.

"Well, not really," I amended. "Wait, actually, I think some animals can smell it, but that's not what I'm talking about."

"I'm not sure where this is going."

My small laugh broke into a sob.

"I mean, I should have known when I walked in her house. Liz is the opposite of tidy, but the house was perfect, every surface was clean. And let's be honest, we know she didn't do that for me." A small chuckle bubbled up. "And it seemed like she was hovering. Every few minutes she checked in on Becca and kept asking her how she felt. And in the kitchen, next to the sink, was what looked like an entire bucket of pills. And I didn't even notice. The freezer was full of popsicles, and there were ginger mints in little bowls in almost every room."

"Okay," Ford said skeptically. "All of that seems –" he paused. "For the nausea."

I nodded. "Becca has the freaking stomach of a horse. She could eat seven-day-old pizza and it wouldn't faze her. She doesn't get nauseous, ever."

"But now she's on chemo."

"Yeah."

"I get that, but when does the cancer smell come into play?" He tried for a lighthearted tone.

"It smelled like my house before Mom died. I was so worried about her catching something that she couldn't fight. I practically bleached every surface every chance I got. But sometimes chemical smells can make the patient sick, so I made sure to buy this specific brand of cleaner that was mostly odorless but has this soft lemon afterscent. Sometimes Becca would come home with me and help clean with it. Her house smelled the same. Becca had Liz buy the same cleaner that I used when my mom was–" I buried my face against his chest

"She's going to be okay," he said, and for some reason, I actually believed him.

"I know," I sniffled. "But I'm still scared."

Ford

The words echoed in my head, ricocheting off the faded paint of the room.

Her mom.

Now Becca.

A hollow ache settled in my chest. I'd give anything to erase the pain she carried, but I knew, with a crushing certainty, that some wounds couldn't be touched.

A soft knock broke through my thoughts. "Ford?" My mother's voice was hesitant as the door creaked open. "It's almost sunrise. You haven't slept?"

"Can't," I mumbled, leaning against the wall.

"Can I make up for lost time and give you some motherly advice?"

I laughed though the sound foreign to my ears. "Of course."

"You should take her up there."

I turned to face her. "Where?"

A dry laugh. "I may be old, but I'm not an idiot."

My breath hitched. "You know about the cabin?"

A slow nod.

"How?"

"Last month. When your laptop died and you used mine. You forgot to log out of your email, and..."

"You went through my email?" My voice rose in frustration.

"No," she said quickly as she shook her head. "I went to close out the pictures you'd opened. They weren't of this house, obviously. Then, when I clicked out of your email, I saw the draft to the contractor about redoing the heaters. Then I remembered all those light displays you had shipped here a few months ago. It wasn't hard to put the pieces together."

"You knew and you never said anything?"

"I figured you'd tell me when you were ready."

I buried my face in my hands. "I promise I'm not trying to get away from you or anything, I just..."

"Ford," she interrupted gently and placed a hand on my shoulder. "You're a grown man. You don't need to explain your decisions to me. And most importantly, you can't waste your life away here, trying to fix what he broke."

My voice cracked. "I'm sorry."

"Nothing to apologize for. You never did anything wrong. And what I said still stands. You should take her up there."

A scoff escaped my lips. "No."

"Why?"

"Because."

She gave off a small, weary laugh. "That's not really an answer."

"It's the only answer anyone needs."

She drew a steadying breath. "When do you plan to make it official?"

I turned to face her. "The house? It's ready now. But my start date at Watauga Medical isn't for a few more weeks."

"Have you told Anderson?"

"He already found out."

She nodded. "Am I right in assuming that's the reason for your black eye?"

"Partially," I admitted, swallowing hard.

Talking to my mother had never come easy. Perhaps because she'd never been there to talk to when it truly mattered. But she was trying now. Had been trying more in the last six months than in my entire life.

"You really should take her. You should let her see it."

I steadied my breathing. Taking Emily to the one place I'd ever found refuge...it was a dream I'd allowed myself to entertain, but lately, I'd learned not to let my mind wander into the territory of false hope.

Chapter 18

4 Years Prior

Emily

"You know, this is becoming a recurring theme, don't you think?" Becca said as she sat across the coffee table folding laundry.

"I know," I admitted but I wasn't sure I'd fully accepted it.

"Tell me what's on your mind," she prodded.

I chuckled, "You missed your calling as a therapist."

She rolled her eyes. "Weather is my calling. How many people can point to a greenscreen perfectly?"

I laughed again. "You want to be a weather woman because you can point to a screen accurately?"

"I am a weather woman because I love it. But yes, pointing correctly has its perks," she said, tossing me one of my shirts.

Becca had only worked at the current news station for two weeks and had already been on air twice. She was loving it.

"Promise to warn me if there's ever a tornado heading my way," I joked.

"Absolutely. Now stop avoiding the question and tell me what you're thinking!"

I sighed. "I'm thinking I lost a best friend."

"Yeah, I think you did too, and that really sucks."

I smiled sadly at the blanket in my hand, which I'd probably folded then refolded three times since we started talking.

"I can't believe he didn't show up," I said, trying to mask the hurt I felt.

I tossed the blanket aside and winced as it landed on the dress I'd thrown off in anger the night before. The same dress I was supposed to wear to the hospital gala that Ford was my plus one to, but he never showed.

"I don't understand why he's like this. Every time she's around, he acts like we never met. He completely forgets I exist."

"I think it's more her than him," Becca countered. "But that's not an excuse."

"I need to quit this cold turkey," I declared, tossing my unfolded laundry back into the basket.

"Now this sounds interesting. Tell me more!" Becca's eyes gleamed.

"I'm done. I'm deleting him from social media and blocking his number. If he can ghost me, I can ghost him."

Becca threw her hands up in mock celebration.

"It's about time!"

The jingle of the front door handle at 3 a.m. was accompanied by a male grunt. My phone was nowhere to be found, leaving me with two options: hide or confront the intruder head-on with my small baseball bat.

I screamed as the door flew open.

"What the fuck?" Ford's eyes widened at my defensive stance.

"What the fuck is right," I retorted, catching my breath. "What are you doing?"

"What am I doing?" He scoffed. "What are you doing?"

"Obviously about to kill an intruder!"

Ford glanced around the hallway, then back at me. "I don't see any strangers." He laughed, but my expression remained serious.

"I do," I said, dropping the bat.

His brows furrowed. "What's that supposed to mean?"

"What are you doing here?"

"I came to see you."

I rolled my eyes. "We haven't talked in weeks."

"Yeah, I've been busy with class but I wanted to surprise you."

Rage bubbled within me. "Surprise me? You wanted to surprise me?"

"I'm confused?" He raised his hand in mock surrender, but I wasn't having it.

"You're not confused." I turned to walk away. "You're just an idiot." I slammed my bedroom door, wishing Becca were there. "And you need to leave," I yelled, knowing he could hear.

By morning, I half-convinced myself Ford's visit had been a hallucination. Still, I tiptoed to the living room, fearing he'd be asleep on the couch.

"Why do you look like you're waiting for a bomb to go off?" Becca asked.

I exhaled. "Because I am."

"Hmmm." She finished her breakfast. "Wanna explain or should we play twenty questions?"

"Ford came over last night."

"What?"

"Yeah."

She jumped up, searching the room. "Is he still here? Is there a body? Should I call—"

"I kicked him out."

Becca paused, then hugged me. "Let me guess. They broke up, and he came here thinking everything would be the same?"

"Yep." I chuckled. "Actually, I'm not sure. I didn't let him elaborate."

Becca nodded. "And I fully support that."

I smiled, but the unease remained.

"So, what's today's plan? Queso and tequila or vodka and cheese fries?"

That time, I laughed. "Both."

Big Bear: What's going on?

Emily: Context would be helpful?

Big Bear: You and Ford? He said he's been trying to text you but you haven't answered.

Emily: UGH!

Big Bear: Seriously . . . what happened?

Emily: He ghosted me AGAIN the second Caroline was back in the picture. I'm tired of being his friend only when it benefits him. I blocked him.

Big Bear: Oh. Well y'all can figure that shit out. I'm busy. But at least do me a favor and hear him out. We are about to all have

> christmas together and I don't want to deal with y'all fighting like toddlers.

> Emily: Ugh...

The kitchen felt smaller as I paced, the silence only broken by the ticking clock. A week had passed since Ford's last unexpected visit, and this confrontation was the last thing I wanted. Anderson was right, though. We were days away from heading home for Christmas, and if we didn't address this now, it would only worsen.

I froze, nearly colliding with the counter, as a timid knock replaced the expected sound of the door opening. Peering through the peep-hole, I found Ford staring at the ground.

"Fuck," I muttered, jolting back when his head tilted up at the sound.

"You wanna open up, or should I knock again?" His voice was strained.

I rolled my eyes as I unlocked the door. "I expected you to use your key."

He scoffed. "Last time I used my key, I was met with a baseball bat."

He had a point. "Fine. Hi."

A forced smirk touched his lips. "Hey there, Chaos."

I stared ahead, unsure how to navigate this sudden awkwardness that had replaced our usual ease.

"You wanna let me in? Or are we talking in the hall?"

I stepped back, closing my eyes as he shut the door behind him.

"Where's Becca?"

"With Liz's family for Christmas."

Ford's eyes widened. "Oh shit. It's getting serious then."

"I think it's been serious since the first date."

He ran a hand through his hair. "Right."

"Look," I moved further into the living room, "I have an early shift, so you can't stay long."

He nodded. "I just wanted to talk. You haven't answered any of my texts."

"I blocked you."

He jolted back. "You blocked me?"

I nodded.

"Why?"

Swallowing, I wrapped my arms around myself. "Because it was the smartest thing to do in the situation."

"That's not an answer."

"You already know the answer."

He leaned against the wall. "Caroline?"

I shook my head. "You know, at first I would have said yes, but no, it wasn't Caroline. It was you. I blocked the number because my best friend wasn't being my best friend anymore."

"I'm busy. You know that."

"Oh my god! That's such a cop-out. You being busy had nothing to do with you ghosting me and missing the Gala. You allowing Caroline to control you is what led to you ghosting me."

"Wait, what?"

"The Gala. You ghosted me and missed the Gala."

"No, I didn't!"

I balked. "Oh, I'm sorry. You're right. The hospital Gala must not have been two weeks ago, and it was just me and the entirety of the hospital staff that mixed up the dates."

Ford frantically pulled out his phone and started scrolling.

"No. I have it in my calendar for next week. I saved it for next week."

He turned the phone around to show me.

"You saved it wrong. And maybe you would have known that had you actually answered any of my calls or texts the days leading up to it."

"Oh shit." He ran his hands through his hair one more time. "I didn't mean to. I was —"

"Busy with Caroline," I finished for him.

He paused and swallowed as he met my unwavering stare.

"How long are y'all going to keep doing this?" I crossed my arms.

"Can we not talk about her?" He buried his face in his hands, but I was done with the constant avoidance of the topic. If we were doing this, then we were going all in.

"No. I'm your family, and I'm going to talk about it. Last time y'all broke up, you said it was the last, and yet less than a week later, and you were back together. And I'm going to make a big assumption here, but I'm guessing you're currently in another breakup because there is no way in hell she would let you come up here to see me."

"It's complicated."

"You've said that countless times, but I think it's pretty simple."

He scoffed. "Sure . . ."

"Yes. It's simple. You wanna know what I see? I see my best friend who is flourishing in life, who is living his dream and making a difference in the world. I see a man who is happy and who laughs and who genuinely enjoys just being. And then I see a boy who for some reason, unbeknownst to me, decides to go back to the one woman who has treated him like crap time and time again. And you know what, fine, go ahead and go back to her every single time, but know this doesn't just affect you."

"And who else is it affecting?" He snarled.

"Anderson, our families, me." I practically screamed the final word.

"How?"

"Anderson says —"

"No. I honestly could not give a shit as to what Anderson thinks on the matter. How does it affect you? How does her and I being together and breaking up affect you?" He shook his head, and the frustration rose. We'd never really fought in the true sense of the word, but I had a feeling tonight was about to change that. "How is my having an on-and-off-again thing with her affecting you?"

I paused as I buried every word I wanted to confess.

"Because you aren't you when she's around. You aren't happy and funny and —" I froze as a sudden rush of emotion hit, and I turned to run to my bedroom. I couldn't do this right now.

"Emily, wait!" He rushed after me and moved to grab my arm the second I reached the bedroom door.

"I can't be myself around you when she's in the picture because she turns you into this shell of a person." I yanked my arm free then I moved across the room and fell back into my chair.

He immediately followed. "Then what would you have me do?" His hand landed on the armrest of the chair practically trapping me within it

I stalled, willing the answer I was desperate to scream out to come. He was so close, and there was a tiny voice screaming to confess everything I felt, but that wasn't what tonight was for. Tonight was to clear the air so Christmas would be bearable. If I confessed everything now, I was sure it would do nothing but turn this already shitty situation into a cataclysmic event.

He leaned in further. "Emily. What should I do?"

I shook my head as I willed the tears away

"Stop." I whispered.

"Stop what?" He cupped my chin, but I pushed his hand away.

"Just stop it." I begged, not knowing exactly what I was begging for. For him to leave Caroline for good? For him to walk away from her? For him to —

"Stop what? I need you to talk to me. I fucked up, okay. I fucked up and I missed the Gala, and that's on me, and I'm so sorry. You have no idea how sorry I am.

My chin trembled as I sealed my lips together and willed my self-restraint to remain.

"Please forgive me. I honestly can't function if you aren't a part of my life. I couldn't function if I thought you hated me."

I scoffed. He sure as hell functioned quite well every time Caroline was around.

"Please."

I shook my head.

"Emily." He whispered my name as his forehead met mine.

"Don't."

"Don't what?" He pleaded. "I need you to —"

I threw my hands in the air as I pushed him back.

"Stop using her as a fucking bandaid. Stop going back to her because you think it will take away some of your mom's pain. You can't fix your dad, and you can't fix your mom, and no amount of beauty queen perfection in six-inch heels is going to make your dad beat up your mom any less."

I clasped my hand over my mouth as soon as I realized what I'd said.

"Shit. I'm sorry. I shouldn't have —"

"Am I that easy to figure out?" Tears filled his eyes.

212

"Ford. I shouldn't —"

"You have me all figured out, don't you?"

He swallowed.

"I'm sorry." I reached out to him, but he took a step back.

"Trust me, I wish that was the entire story."

"What?"

He laughed, but there was no humor in his voice.

"I don't understand."

"I have been waiting for —," he paused as he turned to face the wall.

"Ford?" I was desperate to reach out but not sure if he would accept it after that little outburst.

"Fine." He turned back, and this time his face was filled with determination. "If you won't say it, then I will, only because I'm so damn tired of whatever the hell it is we are doing."

I swallowed, unsure of where this was going.

"You're right. I keep going back to her partly because of the shit show that is my family, but that isn't the only reason. Caroline isn't good for me. She's actually the exact opposite of good for me. Mostly because she isn't you."

I gasped as my breath caught in my throat.

"But you aren't ready to hear that right." He turned to pace my room as he buried his hands in his hair. "You aren't ready to hear that the only reason I even got with her was because she was the exact opposite of you. I just needed someone who didn't make me think of you. And you're right. I have ghosted you. But it's not all because of her. It's because being with her and not you but still trying to act like I'm fine just being your friend is making me miserable."

Tears streamed down my face, but I couldn't move. I couldn't breathe. This was happening, and it wasn't a dream or fantasy. It was real.

"All I want is you. All day. Every day. You're all I think about. I wake up and I wonder what you're doing. I go to the clinic and I worry if you've eaten or if you're having a bad day. I go to bed and I dream about you. I see you everytime I close my fucking eyes."

"What?" I scoffed in complete disbelief.

"I can't get away. I can't make it go away. And it fucking sucks. Because you are the girl I can't have and yet all I have ever been to you is this fucking messed up sort of brother who aggravates the shit out you and you—"

All my well thought out reason and judgement jumped off a damn cliff as I lunged forward and crashed my lips into his and the barrier between us finally shattered.

At first, he froze, and I pulled back, worried I had somehow imagined the entirety of the last sixty seconds. But then he smiled. An absolutely earth shattering smile.

I wasn't sure who moved first. All I knew was his hands had reached out to cup my hips just as mine had reached for him, and then he was lifting me up. My legs wrapped around his waist, his lips attached to mine, and *oh*, this was it. He licked and sucked and devoured me.

Oh god.

It was better than I could have ever imagined. It was better than every dream I'd conjured up.

I tightened my legs as he walked us backward and set me down on the desk.

"Ford?" I pulled back, breathless and still slightly confused as to what had happened.

"I've wanted to kiss you for so long," he whispered against my lips.

"Why did you wait?"

He shook his head. "I honestly don't know."

I swallowed as I cupped his cheeks and stared into his eyes. "I need to be completely honest with you."

He nodded.

"I'm fucking pissed at you. Like really fucking pissed at you."

"I know, I—"

"But I have spent the last ten years," I cut him off, "imagining what it would feel like to have your hands and your lips on my skin." He gulped and I smiled. "And I'm not about to let you stop what you finally started."

My words were all the invitation he needed. His lips met mine, and in those stolen moments—time seemed to blur, stretching into an eternity—his every touch, every kiss, was a desperate attempt to reclaim the years that had slipped through our fingers.

A moan escaped me as his hand slid beneath my shirt, followed by a whine of protest when he pulled away. His eyes traced the contours of my face, drinking in every detail.

His voice was a breath of warmth against my skin, a husky whisper that sent shivers down my spine. "So beautiful," he murmured as his lips brushed against mine and a tender smile played on his lips.

I met his gaze with a pounding heart. "You're not too bad yourself," I breathed. He chuckled and the sound was so deep and resonant is sent a thrill through me.

The air crackled with tension as his hands moved over my body igniting a fire within me. My shirt was discarded, my bra following suit. His lips trailed a path of fire down my throat, and I gasped and arching into him as he reached a pebbled nipple.

His body, taut with barely restrained passion, pushed against mine with a newfound freedom that both thrilled and captivated me. Every muscle quivered, every touch was like nothing I'd felt before. My fingers threaded through his hair, guiding his lips on a journey across my skin as a symphony of whispered adoration filled the air.

A playful grin graced his lips when I reached for the edge of the desk, desperate for leverage to pull him impossibly closer. My body moved instinctively in a silent plea for the friction that would set my soul ablaze.

His laughter, husky and low seemed to land right between my thighs. "You're insatiable, aren't you?"

My breath hitched as a whimper escaped my lips. "You've been teasing me for so long."

He kissed my lips. "I bet your pussy is soaking just for me."

Holy. Fucking. Shit.

My eyes went wide in shock as I pulled back to stare at him.

"Ford Edward Thomas. Did you just ask me about my pussy?"

"Not yours. Mine."

I threw my head back to laigh but the sounds morphed into a moan as he licked his way back up my throat.

"Are you wet for me?"

I gasped as my lungs struggled to find air. This was beyond anything I could have imagined. Who knew Ford was a dirty talker?

"Wet and needy just for me?" He said as he frantically kissed my jaw line. "Is this what you fantasize about when you read your naughty stories?"

I couldn't even mumble a response. I was so wound up I barely remembered how to breathe let alone form actual words.

"I bet you're such a good girl too." He unbuttoned my pants and teased the edge of my underwear. I bucked in response. "Little miss perfect who always got straight A's and never caused any trouble. I bet you excel in everything." I shook in anticipation as he hummed against my collar bone. "You like getting all those little praises don't you."

Holy. Shit.

Who knew I had a thing for academic dirty talk, hell I didn't even know academic dirty talk was a thing to begin with but here we were.

"You're such a good girl Emily."

"Ford." I whispered his name just as his hand slipped between my legs but paused just before reaching where I needed it most.

"I need to ask you something."

"Hmmm." I lifted my hips in search of more but Ford pulled back to look me in the eye.

"You know I respect you, right?"

"Yes." I moaned in his ear as my lips skirted across the shell desperate to taste his skin again.

"Good. Because it's not going to look like it for the next while."

I swallowed as realization hit.

"I can feel the heat burning off of you," he whispered into my ear and then lightly bit the lobe. My body shook with need as I yanked harder on his hair, searching for control.

"Touch me." I begged with no idea how I actually formed the words.

"How do you touch yourself?" Ford's thumb skirted over my clit and my ragged breathing increased. "Like this?"

"Please!" I screamed just as he lifted us away from the desk and sat me down on the nearby bed making sure his hand never wavered from the teasing strokes that were driving me wild.

"Come on, baby girl," he cooed as he grabbed my free hand and brought my fingers to his lips. He slowly slipped my middle finger in his mouth, sucking and licking until he popped it out. "You never answered my question. Do you use this to fuck yourself when you think of me?"

My pussy clenched on instinct as his tongue lapped at the pad of my finger.

How on earth was he able to formulate sentences?

"What about this one?" He sucked my ring finger into his mouth. "Has it been covered in your cum as my name slipped from your lips?"

Well, yes . . . yes it most certainly had but hell if I could verbalize that at the moment.

I tried to speak, tried to formulate some form of a response, but my brain and mouth were on two completely different wavelengths. Actually, I was pretty sure they weren't even in the same universe.

His fingers, warm and possessive, traced the curve of my jaw, tilting my gaze upwards and forcing me to meet the smoldering intensity in his eyes. His voice, a husky whisper against my lips, felt like a claim. "Did you know," he murmured, his breath mingling with mine, "that I'm a jealous man?"

The words were laced with possessiveness. Every nerve ending thrummed with anticipation. "I don't like things," he continued as his voice lowered, "taking what's mine." His thumb brushed against my lower lip, sending a jolt of desire through me. In that moment, I was completely his.

His gaze darkened. "You," he breathed with such authority I damn near melted at the sound, "are not allowed to touch yourself again, unless," he paused as his voice dropped to a whisper, "I give you permission."

The words hung in the air, thick with tension and unspoken promises. My breath hitched in my throat, and I knew, with a thrilling certainty, that I wouldn't deny him anything. I wasn't sure where this insanely possessive and slightly, scratch that, massively in control men had come from but I knew without a doubt I loved it.

"Okay," I panted as my breaths came in ragged gasps. His fingers tightened on my chin, tilting my face upwards and forcing me to meet his intense gaze.

"Emily," His voice was a deep rumble I felt in my core, "I said you aren't allowed to touch yourself again. Not unless I tell you to." Every word was a command, and I couldn't help but obey.

"I prom—" My protest died in my throat as his hand wrapped around it, his touch both threatening and thrilling. He pushed me backward onto the bed as his body hovered over mine.

"That's not how you respond when I give you a fucking command."

The words pierced through me. I swallowed, my throat suddenly dry but understanding his unspoken demand.

Oh fuck. This was the Ford I'd been missing out on? This was about to be so fucking good.

"Yes, sir," I breathed as submission and desire mingled within me. His grip on my throat tightened slightly, sending a pleasurable shiver through my body and a satisfied smile curved his lips. .

"That's my good girl," his voice a caress against my skin. "I want to take care of you."

I could only nod in acceptance.

"I *need* to take care of you."

I licked my lips as his breath ghosted against my cheek.

"I need you to relax and let me."

I nodded again still unsure how to respond

His touch lingered as his hand traced a tantalizing path down the center of my chest, leaving a trail of heat across my stomach. A shiver coursed through me, a mix of anticipation and surrender. He paused, his gaze sweeping over me with a hunger that mirrored my own and my body responded, melting into his unspoken desire and yearning for the touch.

When he looked back up, I found his eyes clouded in feral desire. "You're mine."

The soft whine that escaped my lips quickly transformed into a breathy moan as his hands expertly ripped his shirt away, revealing the sculpted, tattooed masterpiece of his chest. I barely had a moment to register the sight before his lips were back on mine and with one swift, precise motion, he pulled my pants and underwear down, leaving me bare and exposed before him.

In less than a heartbeat, I was completely vulnerable. Ford's strong hands lifted my legs, gently placing my feet on the top of the bed, ensuring I was fully spread out before him. He stepped back letting his gaze rake over my body, making me tremble with anticipation and a hint of trepidation. My hands fisted the sheets in a desperate attempt to not cover myself.

"I love the view," he murmured and licked his lips as he continued to stare, letting his eyes conveying the depth of his hunger and I knew he could see exactly how much I wanted him, how much I needed him. "You're a masterpiece," he whispered. "You know that, right?"

I swallowed as I nodded.

"Fuck." He trailed a hand from my calf to my stomach just barely grazing the slickness I knew he saw.

"Please." The word was barely past my lips before he was moving. His mouth met the sensitive skin behind my knee and a low moan escaped but I couldn't tell if it was him or I that made the sound as his hand moved lower.

"You're shaking," his lips ghosted my inner thigh. "Do you want to come?"

"Yes," I breathed as my hips arched instinctively towards him.

He stilled and I whimpered at the loss of contact. "Yes what?" he growled as his grip on my leg tightened.

"Yes Sir."

He slapped my clit and I screamed before jerking upwards and meeting his stare.

"That's my good girl." His said just as his lips reached their destination and I collapsed back against the bed.

I was going to die. I was going to die right then and there. Ford Edward Thomas was devouring me as if he had trained for this his entire life.

Forget football, med school and sports. If there was ever a cunnilingus event at the Olympics, I was sure he would take home bronze, silver, and gold.

I'd never been more thankful for soundproof walls as I moaned his name over and over.

Just when I thought I couldn't take any more, his fingers joined in, and fuck . . . holy fuck. Holy mother fucking shit hell fuck . . . There were not enough words to explain this feeling. My body arched and I cried out as waves of pleasure soared through me.

By the time I felt as if I could fully breathe, he'd pulled what had to have been at least three orgasms out of me, though at that point I wasn't fully confident in my counting abilities.

My eyes fluttered open.

"Hi."

Ford smiled.

"Hi yourself." He crawled over me, blocking out all the light from the small lamp to my side. "You taste so good." He whispered against my cheek. "I could live between your legs."

I let out a satiated laugh as his eyes roamed my body.

His voice was husky and filled with awe, "You're so goddamn beautiful, and you don't even realize it."

I shook my head as my fingers threaded through his hair and a playful smile graced my lips. "Oh, I realize it. I was just wondering why in the hell it was taking you so long to notice."

His eyes softened, "I've always known you were beautiful."

"Then why didn't you do something about it?" My voice was light, but there was a hint of challenge in it.

He trailed soft kisses along my jawline and I soaked in the warmth tickle of his breath against my skin. "I was a coward," he murmured as his lips moved down my neck, "and to be honest," he chuckled in a low rumble, "you scared the shit out of me."

"I scared you?" I laughed as my fingers traced the lines of the tattoo on his arm.

"Correction," his voice was serious now, "you scare me."

I raised an eyebrow, "Is that right?"

"Hmm," he hummed , "And now I think you are due for some punishment for all that."

I pretended to be annoyed, but a thrill of excitement ran through me. "You avoided me like the plague," I pointed out, "We never even really spoke until the last few years."

Ford kissed my neck as his hand grazed my naked side. "Why do you think that is?"

"Cause you were too cool for me?" I moaned as his hand slipped between my legs touching the exact spot his tongue had just spent the last few— was it hours, days, months— lavishing.

He shook his head as his eyes clouded over.

"Fuck, you're so wet." He kissed the skin between my breasts. "It was cause everytime I would start to say something I froze." His lips met my belly button as his fingers teased the soaked spot between my legs and I had to focus on tracing the path down his arm. "And anytime I was near you I had to run and hide my massive boner." He whispered the last words with a laugh as his lips returned to my neck.

A laugh that was immediately cut short when I sat up and reached down to cup the exact evidence he was telling the truth.

"Jesus Ford." I palmed him through his boxers and he crawled up closer to me.

"I'm going to fuck you." Ford whispered in my ear and this time his voice was deep and commanding. "I'm going to fuck you until you come and then I'm going to flip you over and fuck you again." He slid his boxers down and I gulped at the size of him.

"Well, shit." I bit my lips as I leaned up on my elbows.

"Like what you see?"

I swallowed as I nodded and he spread my legs. "I may need to call in sick tomorrow. I don't think I'll have the capacity for walking."

He laughed but then went still. "I wasn't planning on this. I didn't bring . . . I don't have anything to —"

"I'm on birth control." I lifted my hips desperate for some form of friction. "And I'm clean."

"Me too." Ford met my gaze as the tip inched inside.

I turned to the side and moaned into the pillow as he settled.

"You feel so fucking good Em." He kissed my cheek. "So good baby."

I lost every thought as he rhythmically sent me soaring.

I woke with a start and turned to silence my alarm only to realize I had Ford's phone in my hand.

"What the —" I froze as the last few hours came rushing back; Ford, me, the desk, the – oh fuck.

The phone screen lit up.

Caroline: I'm sorry about yesterday, please come back and

It was all I could see without knowing the code to read the rest. Not that I couldn't figure it out. But secretly rummaging through someone else's phone just wasn't who I was.

> Caroline: I love you. I know you love me too.

The self restraint needed to suppress the rising nausea could have won me a gold medal.

Chapter 19

PRESENT DAY

Emily

"What are you doing?" I said as I halted abruptly on the front porch.

Ford slowly emerged from beneath the RV's, every movement a testament to the effort expended. The grime that streaked his face and arms spoke of hours spent fixing my home while I'd wasted away the morning indoors and tethered to my phone.

"I changed the tire," he replied.

"Obviously," I retorted, folding my arms across my chest as I walked his way then stopped and leaned against the hood. "You don't have to. I don't wan—". A gasp escaped me as I noticed the dark bruise marring his face. "Why do you have a black eye?"

A flicker of embarrassment crossed his features.

"Ford?" I reached out instinctively and brushed aside a lock of his disheveled hair. He winced at my touch.

"You should see the other guy," he teased, attempting a laugh that fell flat.

"Who is the other guy?" I pressed with a voice laced with concern.

He shook his head as his lips pressed into a thin line.

"Ford? Who punched you?"

"It's nothing. Really," he insisted, but his evasion only confirmed my suspicions.

"Anderson?"

"Emily, it has—"

"Was it because we went to lunch? I mean, we aren't—"

"No. It wasn't," he interrupted firmly. "It's because I lied to him about something and said shitty things to him."

"That's still not okay."

"It's better than it looks," he offered a weak smile, turning his gaze back to the RV. "I can't say the same about Ramona, though."

I mirrored his stance, arms crossed and begrudgingly allowed the shift in conversation but a mountain of worry churned within me. "I figured. She's older than me anyway. Maybe it's just her time to go," I attempted a laugh that sounded hollow even to my own ears.

He leaned back against the hood, mirroring my posture. "You gave her a good final few years," he murmured with a hint of sadness in his voice.

A bittersweet smile touched my lips.

"But truly, I think you need to have it towed. Anderson and your dad can do a lot, but I don't think they have a clue as to what happened."

I sighed as I ran my hand along the hand-painted floral design on the hood and a wave of nostalgia washed over me. "Do you know anyone in town who I can trust with my baby?"

Ford gathered his tools. "I'll ask around on Monday when I get back."

"Where are you going?" I inquired as I turned to find him stalled and staring at the ground in uncertainty. "Ford?" I ventured closer and gently bumped my hip against his. "I asked where you were going?"

His tentative gaze met mine. "Just a little trip up north to check on something."

"Check on what?"

He took a steadying breath which only fulled my growing curiosity. "Do you still like skiing, hiking?"

"What?"

"Do you still like to go skiing?" he clarified and I couldn't help but laugh.

"I live in a freaking RV, of course I still like—"

"I'm going up to the trails for the weekend," he interrupted. "Nothing special, just to clear my mind."

"Oh," I replied with a hint of disappointment in my tone. "Why didn't you just say that? Same trails we all used to venture down?"

Ford nodded. "Yeah. Same ones."

"Well, I hope you have fun," I offered and had to swallow down the disappointment at not seeing him for the next few days. "And when you get back, maybe—"

"Do you want to go with me?" he blurted out so quickly I wasn't sure if he actually said the words or if I'd imagined them.

"Go with you? To the trails?"

"Yeah," he replied and an awkward laugh escaped his lips before he shook his head. "You know what? That was dumb. I know you're supposed to be having dinner with Anderson and Lynn tonight, and I'm sure you want to soak in every bit of James before you head out."

I nodded, unsure of what to say. But the mere thought of seeing Anderson, especially after his last visit and the revelation that he was the reason behind Ford's black eye, made him the last person I wanted to see.

"I'll go with you," I blurted out and Ford's head snapped up in surprise.

"But what about—"

"Did you forget I'm not going to Florida anymore?"

Ford's eyebrows rose. "Ah. No, I didn't. I'm just not really thinking, I guess."

"And besides," I added, "I'm not really in the mood to see Anderson right now."

"Emily, don't avoid him just because he—"

"It's not just the fact that he hit you," I interrupted. "It's also some stupid brother-sister stuff we have going on. We're just not used to seeing each other this much. Normally when I pass through it's for a day or two, not for a week. Maybe we need a break from each other."

Ford nodded in understanding. "Okay."

"When are you leaving?" I asked as the anticipation built.

He tossed the dirty towel back and forth in his hands with a contemplative look on his face. "I'm not expected back into the hospital until Monday. We could drive up tonight in order to get started early in the morning."

I shifted my weight from one foot to the other, weighing the pros and cons of this unexpected adventure. Was this really okay, or was I simply falling into the exact trap Anderson had warned me about?

"Three days?" I questioned, seeking clarification.

"Or two or one," he replied. "I don't really have any plans." Despite his steady words, his body language betrayed his nervousness. He shifted back and forth as his eyes darted from me to the ground and then to the sky.

"Okay, let's do it," I responded with a smile and let the excitement bubble within me. "Only if you promise we can continue our wallowing."

"Really?" he asked as a surprised laugh escaped his lips. "I mean of course but–," he paused as he stared directly at me. "You sure you want to spend four hours stuck in a car with me?"

I gazed into the distance, already envisioning the escape that awaited us. "It beats the hell out of staying here."

"Okay. Let's do it," he agreed with newfound enthusiasm. "I need to get a shower, but maybe we could plan on leaving within the next hour? I'd planned to beat the five o'clock traffic."

I nodded as my heart fluttered in anticipation. "I'll be waiting."

An hour had passed, marked by the slow crawl of the sun across the cloudless sky and I walked outside to find Ford exactly where I'd left him, his tall figure a silhouette against the backdrop of Mona. The only difference was the phone now pressed to his ear, his expression a mixture of impatience and amusement.

Curiosity gnawed at me as I approached. "Can we meet in the walk over to the parking lot and trade there?" he spoke into the receiver with a voice laced in exasperation then gave an oscar worthy roll of his eyes. "We'll be there in twenty. That work with you?"

He listened for a few more moments, then a smile slowly spread across his face as his gaze caught mine and he hung up the phone.

"Who was that?"

"Your brother."

My brow furrowed. "Anderson?"

Ford arched an eyebrow. "Do you have another brother I'm unaware of?"

I rolled my eyes. "Stop. You know what I mean. Why are we meeting him? Aren't we supposed to be avoiding him?"

Ford laughed. "Because my truck is also in the shop and my car won't make it up those hills, so we're switching vehicles."

"Oh." A strange sense of relief washed over me. "You have a car and a truck?"

"It's the same truck I've always had."

I nodded. "Then why add the car?"

He shrugged and I noted a hint of self-consciousness in the gesture. "Doctors are supposed to have nice cars, right?" He rubbed the back of his neck. "Give me five minutes to grab one more thing. I'll be right back."

With that, he turned and disappeared inside, leaving me to grapple with the lingering warmth of his presence and the unsettling flutter of my heart.

The minutes stretched, each one feeling like an eternity as I leaned against the hood and contemplated exactly what I was getting myself into. When the dreaded twenty-minute mark arrived, I nervously made my way towards Ramona. It had been five days since I'd last stepped inside, and an unexpected wave of loneliness washed over me as I stood in the heart of what had once been my sanctuary. My hand traced the countertop's edge, then my fingers ghosted over the outlines of smiling faces in the photographs pinned to the bulletin board.

A pang of uncertainty twisted in my gut as I gazed at the space that had once been my refuge. The day I bought it, I'd been determined to shed my former life – the designer shoes, the clothes, the endless bottles of shampoo and seventeen different types of bronzer. Though I hadn't fully grasped it then, buying Ramona had been a way to force myself to shed the skin of the girl I no longer wanted to be. How ironic that I'd spent the next two years hiding behind makeup and flashy jewelry, only to finally wash away the last layer when I returned to the one place that represented freedom from anything fancy.

I'd sought escape from the chaos, trading it for the promise of quiet peace but now looking around, I realized, I never accomplished what I set out to do.

The slam of the door behind me made me jump.

"Sorry," Ford's voice was soft as he leaned against the counter. "Ready?"

He nodded as his gaze swept the interior.

"I haven't been inside yet. I like it."

A nervous laugh escaped. "It's tiny." My eyes fell to the neglected corners, a testament to my perpetual state of disarray. "And it's a mess."

His lips curved into a mirror of my own smile. "It's a little chaotic."

Our eyes met, and a flicker of vulnerability passed between us. "Just like me?"

His smile deepened. "Just like you."

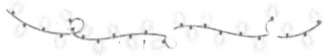

Ford

I'd hoped for a simple exchange with Anderson in the shadowed hallway connecting the lobby and the garage, away from Emily's watchful eyes by the car. Perhaps there, in the dim light, we could avoid the impending confrontation I felt brewing in his gaze.

But as we rounded the corner onto the third floor of the parking garage, Anderson's silhouette leaned against his truck, with his keys dangling from his fingers, and a mask of frustration etched onto his features.

"Picture of serenity, isn't he?" Emily's sardonic tone mirrored my own unease. I could only offer a tense exhale in response.

An awkward silence descended as keys were exchanged and a car seat for James was transferred from Anderson's truck to my backseat. Then, Anderson's eyes locked onto Emily's in a silent plea for a private moment.

"I'll be in the truck," I declared as I turned away.

By the time Emily slid into the passenger seat beside me, her earlier composure had vanished and was replaced by a steely resolve.

"Need me to rearrange his face before we go?" I offered as I attempted to break the tension with some dark humor.

A sharp bark of laughter escaped Emily's lips but her head shook in defiance.

We had just crossed the state border into North Carolina, a whole two hours into the drive, when Emily's voice finally broke the silence.

The noise was so unexpected and jarring that my hands instinctively tightened on the steering wheel as I fought to maintain control of the car.

"Anderson said he's sorry for punching you, but you still deserved it."

My lips curved into a sarcastic smile.

"And that he is worried about what we're doing. And he's worried about you."

I cleared my throat. "Is that so?"

Emily's gaze remained fixed on the mountains that loomed ahead. "Yeah."

"Did he mention why?"

A bitter laugh escaped her lips. "Your divorce. Me coming into town the exact week everything was finalized. Us possibly repeating the shit storm that happened two years ago."

My muscles tensed at the implication. "Understandable."

"He's worried you're too broken to fully consent to whatever it is we're doing."

A laugh burst from my lips and echoed through the car. I was in complete disbelief. "He thinks you're taking advantage of me when I'm down?"

A flicker of a smile played across her lips. "Something like that."

I shook my head as the absurdity of the situation washed over me. There was absolutely no universe in which Emily could take advantage of me. The thought was ludicrous. But then, a devilish grin tugged at the corner of my mouth, and I entertained the idea that perhaps, just maybe, there might be one situation in which I would very much like for Emily to—

"How are you doing it?" Her question broke through my thoughts.

"Doing what?" I kept my eyes focused on the road ahead, unsure of where this conversation was headed but certain it would be easier if I didn't have to look at her.

"Acting so perfectly fine after your life just exploded. I mean, you got fucking divorced, and you seem cool as a cucumber."

I couldn't help but laugh. "Seriously?"

She rolled her eyes. "You know what I mean."

I swallowed a I contemplated my response. I considered deflecting, shifting the conversation to safer territory, but I was tired of hiding behind carefully constructed facades. There was only one way forward: the truth. I had to tell her the truth.

Summoning my courage, I spoke before it could slip away. "I didn't love her."

Although I didn't meet her gaze, I could sense the exact moment Emily's head turned toward me.

"What?"

"Exactly what I said. I didn't love her. The divorce, while I admit was sad, it didn't break me, because she never made me whole to begin with."

Emily swallowed audibly, and just as I turned to face her, ready to bare my soul, I found her gazing out the window.

"You could have fooled me."

"Emily, I think we are both very good at fooling people."

Her brow furrowed. "And what's that supposed to mean?"

My grip tightened on the steering wheel as I struggled to find the right words. "I hid behind the lure of money and status in order to appease my mom — a woman that barely knows me and you hid behind your makeup and your clothes and your wonderful ability to run away from things that scare you in order to not have to deal with the fact that your mom isn't here anymore."

"That's not fair." I saw her clench the seatbelt from the corner of my eye. "You don't get to say shit like that to me."

Frustration surged through me, and I pulled the car onto the emergency lane, slamming on the brakes. "Stop. I'm not doing this with you. We're almost there, and I refuse to fight with you over something we both know is true, even if one of us hasn't yet figured it out."

"Ford." My name was a warning on her lips.

"I didn't drive two hours up here for us to devolve into mindless bickering." My voice trembled with emotion. "You asked me a question, and I answered it honestly."

The small wooden cabin materialized at the end of the snow-laden drive. Its silhouette seemed to jump straight out of a fairytale against the canvas of the setting sun. A scene straight out of a movie, and yet, a gnawing fear twisted within me - had I already ruined it?

The silence that had filled the car since our near-argument pressed in and desperate to salvage the situation, my mind raced through countless scenarios, but each was more implausible than the last.

Doubt crept in as I finally turned to face Emily but the sight that met my eyes banished all thoughts as Emily's eyes widened and mirrored the awe and wonder reflected in the cabin's warm glow.

"I thought we were staying at a motel or something along the ridge?" Her voice, the first sound to break the silence in two hours, held a note of hesitant curiosity.

I chuckled, "Emily Ann Truse, I've known you since we were kids. There's no way you'd stay somewhere that screamed 'potential crime scene'."

A quizzical look crossed her face, "What do you mean, a crime scene?"

"You used to watch all those crime shows and listen to true crime podcasts," I reminded her, "Remember telling me about the statistics? Creepy mountainside motels were practically a staple."

Her laughter filled the air, "Oh my God, I did! I still do! And you're right!" The tension dissipated with each chuckle, "I can't believe you remembered that."

"I remember a lot," I replied as our eyes met and a flicker of vulnerability passed between us.

"Come on. Let's see what you got us. I'll decide if we're more or less likely to be murdered in our sleep tonight."

My heart pounded as I watched her every move. Grabbing her bag, she stepped out of the car and into the serene winter landscape.

"I'm paying for half the nightly fee!" she called over her shoulder as she walked from the driveway to the front steps, "No way this didn't cost a fortune! I can't believe you even found something so cute last minute, especially with it being prime skiing season."

As she reached the porch and turned to look at the lock, I tossed my keys towards her. She squealed in surprise as she playfully ducked to dodge them.

"That was an assault!" she yelled as the keys landed at her feet.

"Ha!" I retorted, "Death by terrible hand-eye coordination. I wonder if that would make it into one of your podcasts?"

She crossed her arms with a mock glare on her face, "You're dumb."

"You're uncoordinated."

A smile bloomed on her face, "I know."

But the smile faded as she picked up the keys and weighed them in her hand, "These are your keys."

"I know," I replied and gestured towards the door.

"Where's the key to the cabin?"

"The sparkly pink one on the second ring."

Confusion knitted her brow, "When did you get the key? We didn't even stop to check in anywhere."

Ignoring her questions, I plucked the keys from her grip, unlocked the door and swung it open.

"After you," I stepped aside, allowing her to enter.

"But I don't under-"

"Emily," I interrupted gently, "Walk into the damn house already."

She hesitated, then took a tentative step forward and I reached out to turn on the light. A gasp escaped her lips as the cabin's interior was revealed.

"What is this?"

Chapter 20

3 Years Prior

Emily

I laid naked on the bed as Ford's finger moved along my back.

"Umm." I tilted my head sideways to meet his stare. "A sun?"
He laughed. "No."

"A ball?" I scrunched up my nose, knowing the answer was probably wrong.

"Nope." He pulled his hand back as he leaned opposite to me against the headboard with an absolutely devilish smile.

This had become our newest normal. Surprise visits, sex, aggravation, sex, fighting over things we could never control, sex, dirty memes, sex.

"Do it again," I pleaded.

He shook his head. "Not a chance. One finger drawing and one guess is the rule. I already gave you two."

I rolled onto my back with a groan, then laughed when he poked out his bottom lip as I pulled the sheet to drape across my bare chest.

We were positioned opposite each other on the small bed; my head rested against the headboard while his hand now traced delicate circles on the sole of my foot. A soft moan escaped my lips as I closed my eyes. "Nevermind," I murmured, "I like this much better."

Ford chuckled, before abruptly shifting to mirror my position. I playfully kicked his side and a whine escaped my lips as I longed for him to resume his ministrations.

Instead, he settled on his stomach beside me as his lips pressed a tender kiss to my bare shoulder. "My foot rubs are very expensive," he whispered.

I felt his words as much as I heard them. "Good thing I'm rich," I countered breathlessly as his lips trailed a fiery path towards my collarbone.

Ford laughed, a deep throaty noise that was so enticing I had to physically restrain myself from reacting. "Is that so?"

"Yep. And I know the exact payment you require," I said with a grin as he found that sensitive spot where my neck and shoulder met.

"And what would that be?"

I yanked the sheet down in answer, baring my naked chest to him.

He groaned in earnest at the sight of me, and then laughed when he caught the smug look on my face. "Yep. You're rich. Very, very rich." He scooted lower to bury his face between my breasts as his hands cupped me. His next words came out muffled. "I like this form of payment. From now on, all your payments for my services will be in the form of titties."

I burst out into a laugh that quickly turned to a moan when his face shifted and his teeth scraped along the sensitive nipple.

"I hate you," I whispered as he moved from one side to the other.

"That's a weird way to say I'm your favorite person in the entire world."

I scoffed. "Definitely not what I said." My hands found his hair as he teased me, and I pulled, encouraging him further.

He looked up and caught my gaze just as he shuffled to move atop me. "I know. That's why I said it was weird." He smirked, and then I forgot the quip I was going to throw back in his face as he planted a line of kisses down my abdomen.

I moaned as he moved to my inner thigh and I yanked on his hair, trying to guide him back to where I needed him.

Ford didn't budge.

He wanted to tease me and though I feigned frustration at the notion, I secretly loved every minute he spent torturing me, knowing it would end in the most delicious ecstasy.

"Please," I whined as he hooked a hand under my right knee, pushing it upward and spreading me more fully for him.

"Please what?" He kissed the crease of skin that separated my right thigh from the heated spot between my legs before repeating the absolutely torturous move on my other side.

"Please. I'll do anything. Please," I frantically urged as I rolled and shifted my hips, hoping to force his lips and tongue to my center.

He lifted his head as I spoke. "While I love a good beg...," he trailed off as another round of wet kisses were placed a mere breath away from my swollen and throbbing clit. "Tell me what you want. I want to hear you say it."

"Fuck me." My eyes rolled back as the sensations flourished.

Ford laughed.

"That is the end game, no doubt." He moved his tongue a little closer, just close enough to taste me without fully giving in. "Damn. You taste so good." He licked again and I arched just as he pulled back. "But I want to know what you want me to do. Right now, what do you want?"

I whined and yanked on his hair once more.

He'd always been the more talkative one in our little duo. He was more experienced, and thus knew exactly what to do or say to drive me wild. But recently he had wanted me to take a bigger role in these moments.

We weren't technically together-together, but weren't just friends either. Somehow we'd carved out this little space for just the two of us with no titles or name or rules. We just were.

And I'd finally figured out why Ford liked having so much control in the bedroom... and the car...and the back of the movie theater... and the park. Well, at least I had a good guess. The answer was as simple as the question. It was about control. He had no control over his life. Not his mom or his dad or the way he grew up. There was never control. But I could give him that. I could give him the control he so desperately needed and in return, I received some damn good orgasms and maybe I was able to pretend, even if it was just for a few hours, that we were'nt just fuck buddies who had made a pact with no pressure for a future.

In those moments when I gave over all my control to him, I was his and he was mine and no one could take that from us.

While almost every visit led to at least a few orgasms, it wasn't the only thing that made us...us. At the heart of the entire calamitous situation, we were best friends. And maybe that was why it worked so well. We were each other's person in a way that no one else could be.

"I want you to kiss me," I whispered, and he leaned back to place a kiss on my knee. I groaned in frustration.

There were times in which he led the entire encounter, barely allowing me a breath between orgasms, and damn near killing me with the intensity of everything I felt. But there were other times where he wanted me to say it. He wanted me to have a hand in my own pleasure.

"Is that what you want?"

My chest rose and fell as the nervous anticipation surged.

How was I already this worked up?

We'd just finished our second round of morning sex less than thirty minutes ago, and now we were starting again. This man was relentless. He was ferocious. He was everything I – I paused the thought before it fully formed.

"Ford."

"Yes?"

Though we never laid down any specific ground rules, there was an unspoken agreement between us. We weren't in a relationship. I think we both knew neither of us could commit to that with him starting residency and me jumping straight into my own clinicals. And though I knew the parameters to this situationship, it didn't stop me from imagining what exactly a small step further might look like.

"I want you to kiss me . . . between my legs."

He leaned forward and placed a kiss inches below my belly button and directly above my center. "That's technically between your legs, right?" He cocked his head in that devilishly innocent way only Ford could do.

I groaned in frustration.

"Fuck." My head was damn near thrashing on the pillow as the words came out in a garbled rush. "I want you to lick my clit, and I want you to finger me and make me come, and then I want you to fuck me."

He let out a small chuckle at my obvious embarrassment, and then without another word, he sealed his lips directly onto my center.

A mumbled, incoherent string of curses spewed from my lips as he took his time making sure he followed my every command. He could have been down there five minutes or five hours. I wouldn't have known the difference. Time seemed to pause whenever Ford loved me.

The thought came so quickly I barely had time to process it before his finger was rubbing that sensitive spot and I was careening into a parallel universe.

I forced my heart rate to slow as he buried his face in the back of my neck and breathed me in.

I wasn't ashamed to admit that post-sex cuddles were always one of my favorite moments. But this time... this time I couldn't relax, because a singular thought seemed to play on a loop in my head.

I wasn't falling in love with Mr. Three First Names himself. Despite my most prolific efforts, I was completely, totally, and madly in love with him and the worst part was I was pretty sure he was in love with me as well.

Chapter 21

Emily

My breath hitched as I waited for him to speak.

"What is this?" I repeated as my voice became a fragile balance of excitement and trepidation.

"Emily, listen—"

He hesitated, appearing to search for the right words and my gaze flickered towards the breathtaking view beyond the cabin's expansive windows. The sun was beginning its descent, casting a warm glow across the snow-laden landscape.

Without a second thought, I let my bag fall to the floor with a soft thud and in a rush of adrenaline, I crossed the hardwood floor, letting my hands press against the cool glass as I peered out at the mesmerizing scene. I felt his presence behind me the his fingers gently traced the curve of my lower back.

A shiver coursed through me at his touch, but my gaze remained fixed on the spectacle outside. The snow-covered yard shimmered

241

with an ethereal glow, as though a thousand tiny stars had descended upon it. "Are those—"

"Firefly lights," he murmured as if he was finally voicing a long held secret. "I stole your chance at seeing them that night and—"

"This is *your* cabin." The words escaped my lips, not as a question, but as a realization. I took in the familiar details of the room – the lamp that had once graced his dorm room, the rug my mother had helped him choose, the blanket I'd once wrapped my naked body in, the Indian Ghost Pipe painting I'd discarded in a moment of anger.

"Yes, this is my cabin."

I nodded, unable to refute what I was seeing. "That's my painting."

"You threw it away," he countered.

A sniffle escaped, betraying the carefully constructed mask I wore. But this was Ford. My Ford. The same Ford I'd been so comfortable with all those years ago. The same Ford I'd loved since childhood. The same Ford who had shattered my heart.

My head bowed as tears filled my eyes and I tried to make sense of the situation. This was supposed to be a simple getaway, two friends seeking solace in each other's company. He wasn't supposed to have a cabin, let alone one that was my favorite mountain with my painting on the wall and my firefly lights covering the back yard. But most of all he wasn't supposed to make me fall for him again.

I'd promised myself to not fall for him again

But, oh, how I always failed to keep my promises.

If I was being completely honest with myself, the moment I told Ford we could be friends again, I knew it would never work. Before the words had even finished tumbling past my lips, I knew I was going to fall for him again. Or maybe fall wasn't the right word, because that had already happened. I had fallen, and he hadn't picked me up. I'd picked myself up as he left me lying like a broken vase on the ground—shattered and scattered off in a million different pieces.

I'd spent the last few years patching up every single one of the cracks he formed. And now I was doing the one thing I promised myself I would never do again. I was going to let him love me in his own way, knowing that there was an expiration date stamped between us. I swallowed as I accepted what the future would soon hold. And maybe this time, when it was all over and I was left to piece myself back together, it wouldn't hurt as much. Maybe it would be a dull sting and not the sharp pain that once filled every moment of my existence.

My heart rate slowed as I placed all the pieces of Ford that I'd once loved into their little metaphorical box in my heart and sealed the lock. And then I felt his touch. Warm and soft. Gentle and delicate in a way that could only mean one thing as he cupped my chin and brought my gaze back to his.

With a sharp intake of breath, I forced myself to move. "Can you—can you give me a—a minute?" I stammered, retreating towards the front door. "I just need a minute," I repeated, stepping onto the porch and closing the door behind me.

I sank to my knees as the urge to run overwhelmed me. I couldn't do this again. I couldn't stay here with him in this house and pretend that everything was normal.

Anderson had been right, and I hated him for it. I never did learn my lesson.

Even I knew that coming here with Ford under the pretense of escaping Anderson and the chaos of my life was a lie. I wanted to be here with Ford simply because he was Ford. He could have said he was going anywhere, and I think I would have followed. But following him had only led to heartbreak in the past.

In a moment of sheer panic, I did the only thing I could think of. I bolted.

Leaping off the snow covered porch, I sprinted down the drive, my heart pounding in my chest. My destination was unknown, my future uncertain. All I knew was that I had to escape.

The driveway gave way to a winding path, and I followed it blindly as the cold night air burned my lungs. My bag, my phone, my entire life lay abandoned back at the cabin, but none of it mattered. I had to get away from him.

Snowflakes fell, numbing my fingers and gathering on my eyelashes, but I didn't stop. As I rounded the final bend, the lights of the small mountain town twinkled in the distance, offering a beacon of hope. with a trembling body, I stumbled into the first bar I saw.

The warmth of the bar enveloped me, but the stares of its patrons sent a chill down my spine. College students and locals alike turned to gawk at the disheveled woman who'd just burst through the door.

A gentle tap on my shoulder startled me. "Are you okay?"

"Can I borrow your phone?" I blurted out not caring about the desperation that clung to my words.

The woman nodded as led me to a table in the back and away from prying eyes. "Sure," she said, handing me her phone.

My hands shook as I dialed the number. It was one of the few I knew by heart.

"Hello?" Becca's voice answered.

"It's me," I choked out.

"Oh god, are you okay?"

"Yes," I lied as my voice cracked and I dropped the phone. "Sorry, my hands are shaking."

"But you're okay?" she pressed.

"Yes. No. Not really. I'm so sorry, Becca. I know you just got married and you have a million things to do, but—"

"Emily, stop rambling and tell me what happened," Becca interrupted.

I cursed as the phone slipped from my grasp again, but thankfully, its owner caught it, set it to speaker, and placed it on the table in front of me.

"I think he built me a house," I blurted out realizing how insane those words were.

"What?"

"I'm with Ford in the mountains."

"You're with Ford... in the mountains?"

"Beech Mountain, to be exact," I clarified. "He said he was coming up here to get away for a few days and asked me to tag along. I only said yes because Anderson pissed me off and punched him in the face, but—"

"Anderson punched Ford?!" Becca shrieked, but I continued on.

"—but then we got here, and it isn't a motel, it's a cabin. Becca, it's an actual cabin, like on the side of the mountain, and my painting is on the wall," I hiccuped as the tears flowed.

"Okay, that's a lot to take in," Becca said in her now calm voice. "I need you to take a few breaths for me. But first, tell me, are you physically okay?"

"Yes," I sniffled and reached for a napkin to wipe my tears.

"Good. That's good. Take another breath. Second, whose phone are you calling me on?"

"I don't know," I admitted as I looked up at the woman who'd lent me her phone. She offered a sad smile. "I'm at a bar."

244

"Are you drunk?" Becca asked as the concern inched back in her tone.

I shook my head as if she could see the motion. "No, I just got here."

"And where's Ford?"

"At the cabin," I replied, burying my face in my hands.

"Emily, how did you get to the bar?"

I hesitated. "Becca, I can't do this."

"How did you get to the bar?" she repeated, firmer this time.

"I ran," I confessed in a whisper.

"You ran? Where?"

"His cabin is on a road up the mountain, and I just ran down it to the town."

Becca gasped. "Holy shit. Does he know where you are?"

"I doubt it," I squeaked as I wiped away more tears

"Okay. It's going to be okay," Becca reassured me.

"He has a cabin," I repeated, still in complete disbelief.

"That's what you said."

I sniffled. "And he has my painting."

"Okay."

"And there's a rug in the kitchen that my mom bought," my voice broke, and a glass of water appeared before me.

"Oh, Emily," Becca sighed. "Listen, you need to let Ford know where you are. He's probably worried sick."

"I can't do it again," I sobbed.

"Do what?"

"I can't lose him again. I can't love him again just to know—"

"Emily," Becca interrupted, her voice stern yet gentle. "I need you to listen very carefully. That man has a cabin in the mountains, some of your favorite mountains if I remember correctly. And in that cabin, he has a painting on the wall that you made and a rug your mom bought."

I nodded. "And there's a blanket on the couch that I gave him in college."

Becca laughed softly. "Emily, you're a fucking idiot. While I'll admit that man is also an idiot and has done some shitty things in the past, he's an idiot that's head over heels in love with you."

"No, he's—"

"Honey," the woman whose name I didn't know but whose phone I was using chimed in, "I literally have the barest amount of knowledge concerning your situation, but I can tell you without a doubt that man loves you."

"He can't," I protested.

"Why not?" they both asked in unison.

"Because I'm a mess. I have nothing figured out. I stabbed someone with the wrong medicine last week—"

"She's a nurse," Becca interjected. "I promise she is only stabbing people with medicine in the legal sense."

"Noted," the woman replied.

"Well, that legal stab got me fired," I huffed, blowing my nose into a tissue. "I don't have a job, and I'm almost thirty, and I live in a broken-down camper van, and my mom is dead."

"Well, that is a lot," the woman acknowledged, reaching for my hand. "But not unmanageable, especially if you have someone by your side."

"Exactly," Becca added. "And you have so many people by your side. Also, I had no idea about all of that."

"I didn't tell you because you were—"

"I know." Becca chimed in.

"I'm a mess," I repeated, laying my head on the table and feeling utterly defeated.

"You are," Becca agreed. "But you're our mess, and we love your mess, and we wouldn't have it any other way. So, here's what we're going to do. First, I need you to find out whose phone you have taken over."

"My name's Sheila," the woman replied.

"Hi Sheila, I'm the best friend, Becca."

"Nice to meet you," Sheila said, leaning closer to the phone.

"Same to you. Now that we have that squared away, I need you to take a few more breaths and make a decision."

"What decision?" I sniffled.

"I need to know what you want because I have a detailed text ready to send Ford's way so he can come pick you up and you two can spend the night confessing what we already know. But I can delete that text and jump in my car and come get you if you never want to see him again."

"But you just got married," I protested.

Becca sighed. "We wore fancy dresses, ate cake, and signed a piece of paper. We're just as married today as we were two months ago."

I sniffled as she spoke.

"So I need you to make a decision. Am I coming to get you, or do you want to see Ford again?"

"I want to see him again," I confessed, my voice barely above a whisper.

"Good. I just hit send," Becca declared.

"Wait," I gasped, my anxiety returning. "What if we're wrong and he—"

A ding blared through the phone. "He's headed your way," Becca announced with a hint of triumph in her voice.

Ford

The heavy wooden door creaked as it swung open, revealing a dimly lit, smoky room. Every head in the small bar turned towards me as their conversations were momentarily forgotten.

"She's with Sheila," Doris's voice cut through the tension as her weathered hand pointed towards a back room. "I don't know what you did to that girl, but she's a mess." Her tone wasn't accusatory but laced with concern and maybe a hint of exasperation.

I nodded as my eyes found the familiar flash of golden curls through the crack in the door.

"You going to take care of her?" Doris's voice echoed again, filled with an unspoken challenge.

My gaze never wavered from Emily. "Hopefully, for the rest of my life."

As I stepped into the back room, Emily's head snapped up and her eyes went wide, filled with a mixture of relief and trepidation.

"I'm sorry I ran."

"I'm sorry I tricked you about the house," I countered as I stopped just inches from her.

A nervous laugh escaped her lips. "You know, it seems like all we do is apologize to each other."

A small smile tugged at my lips as I turned to Sheila, who had been sitting quietly beside Emily. "Thank you for taking care of her until I could get here."

Sheila stood and clasped my hand as she looked between us with a serious expression. "Don't fuck this up. I like this one."

I laughed out loud. In the year I'd known Sheila and Doris, the sisters who owned this little mountaintop haven, I'd never heard either utter anything close to a curse word. "I promise."

Sheila patted my arm reassuringly and walked away. "Feel free to use the back door to avoid the prying eyes," she advised with a hint of amusement in her voice. "I should probably thank you for the income we're about to receive. I think the entire town is currently trying to be a fly on the wall for this catastrophe."

I chuckled. "Thank you, Sheila."

"And don't forget, I know where you live," she added with a wink as she shut the door behind her.

I turned back to Emily, who was watching me with a curious expression. "You know Sheila?"

"I do," I replied. "She and Doris taught me how to repair most of the house."

"What?"

I smiled. "They also own the hardware store next door. By my third visit to get supplies they took pity on me and gave me advice."

Emily nodded as she looked down at her hands, which were trembling slightly. "I'm sorry I ran," she repeated with a voice filled with remorse.

I shook my head gently. "I'm the one that needs to apologize."

"Ford–"

"Please," I cut her off. Just let me say this.

She nodded in acceptance.

"Emily Ann Truse."

She chuckled at my use of her full name.

I took a deep breath as the weight of my past mistakes pressed down like a physical burden. "I've been an absolute fool," I began. "I've been selfish, thoughtless... I put my own wants and needs above yours, time and time again. And I fully recognize I don't deserve a single moment of your forgiveness." I paused and my throat tightened as I searched for the right words only to realize there weren't any right words...just my own. "You were right, I went to her because the little boy in me was desperate to make my mom happy. I chose her for the simple reason that when my dad left it broke my mom and despite her being a ghost during most of my life, she was still and will always be my mom."

Emily reached up and wiped away a tear I hadn't even known had fallen.

"You may have run away from that town and everything in it but you weren't the only one running away. I ran away from you. I ran away because what I felt for you scared me. But I'm not that little boy anymore," I reached out and clasped her hand in mine, "I love you. I have since we were kids, and I don't have any excuses for why I pushed those feelings away for so long. I was wrong, plain and simple." My eyes met hers in a silent plea for understanding. "I love you more than I ever thought possible and I want nothing more than to spend the rest of my life showing you how sorry I am."

Chapter 22

2 Years Prior

Emily

T he doctor's words hung heavy in the air, each one a weighty stone dropped into the still pool of the room. Too many words, too many thoughts. It was all a chaotic whirlwind inside my head. I sat, a statue amidst the storm. I was a nurse who knew the medical jargon, understood the implications, yet I found myself utterly lost in the moment.

Stage IV. Metastasized. Untreatable. Hospice. Weeks. Morphine.

Anderson fired off questions like bullets, each one piercing the silence but missing the target as my parents remained locked in a silent, desperate embrace and I counted the ceiling tiles in a futile attempt to escape the stark reality that was crashing down.

This wasn't happening. It was supposed to be a bump, a lump, a cyst – that's what I'd reassured mom with last summer when the concern was first voiced. A quick "get it checked out, but don't worry" had been my only advice before rushing back to my busy life.

Now, that dismissive "cyst" had transformed into a monstrous tumor, an orange-sized mass lodged in my mom's chest as its tendrils reached into lymph nodes, blood, bones... The details blurred, too horrific to fully grasp. I was adrift in a nightmare I never imagined could come true.

This happened to other people. Not to me, not to us, not to my mom.

"What about chemo?" I blurted out, interrupting Anderson's relentless questioning.

He met my gaze with weary frustration. "We already discussed that."

"Radiation?"

He sighed with exhaustion. "That too. It wouldn't work on this. It's too far progressed." The curtness wasn't directed at me; he was grappling with his own helplessness. The fourth-year medical student who always had a solution, a fix, was now facing the unfixable.

My eyes shifted to mom, and for the first time, the stark reality of the situation truly hit home. The gauntness, the loose clothing, the tremor in the hand my father held so tightly – mom had been sick for far longer than I'd realized.

Consumed by my own life, I hadn't noticed. My mom had been dying right in front of me and I hadn't even seen it.

Nausea twisted in my gut as I replayed every recent interaction with my parents. I should have known. If I hadn't been so self-absorbed, maybe...

The elevator ride down stretched into an abyss where time lost its meaning. No one spoke and the silence became a suffocating blanket. The search for my car in the sprawling parking lot only prolonged the agony.

Just before I reached for the handle, I turned to face them. Three pairs of eyes, red-rimmed and brimming with unshed tears, met mine. We were all a dam of emotions bound to burst.

Ten minutes ago, we were a rush of words, grasping desperately for a solution that remained out of reach. Now, there were no words. Only silence.

A heavy weight settled in my chest as the future I had so carefully constructed crumbled before my eyes. The life I had envisioned, now tainted with an unwelcome reality. My palms grew clammy, my breath hitched, and my bottom lip quivered uncontrollably.

"I don't know what to do. I don't know what to say." The words tumbled out, raw and broken, as my tears finally escaped their fragile confines.

My mother's smile was a lifeline amidst the chaos. A knowing smile, filled with empathy and love and the world around us faded into a blur. The hum of a nearby car engine, the distant honk of a horn, all became inconsequential. The world could have been ablaze, and I wouldn't have noticed.

"I don't know—"

Mom's hands enveloped mine. Her touch was my grounding force against the tremors that wracked my body.

"Say yes to lasagna." It was a gentle plea. "I'll have your dad stop by Cavilla's on our way home. Come by the house tonight, and we can have a big dinner. A good dinner."

I nodded in silent acceptance.

"Make sure to get the—"

"Fresh garlic bread from the bakery next door, and ask for an extra container of garlic spread for you and lots of those little packets of parmesan cheese they have," Mom finished my thought. "I know how you like your pasta."

A weak smile flickered across my face. Numbly, I got into my car, the motions automatic and detached.

I hadn't even made it out of the parking lot when the tears overwhelmed me and the world blurred as my vision became obscured by a torrent of emotion. My hands shook as I fumbled with my phone, dropping it twice before I finally found his name.

Ford.

He picked up on the second ring.

"Emily?"

"She's dying." My voice cracked on the word.

"What?" Confusion laced his tone.

"She's dying. Ford, she's dying." My body shook violently, teeth chattering, and hands trembling.

"Oh, fuck. Where are you?"

"She's dying." My words were barely coherent amidst the sobs.

"Emily." But his voice was a calm anchor in the storm. "Please tell me where you are."

"What am I going to do?" Each word was punctuated by a ragged breath. "What am I supposed to do?"

The phone dinged repeatedly. In my haze of panic, it took a moment to realize it was Ford, frantically typing.

Guilt washed over me. This wasn't fair to him. Mom was practically his second mother. She'd cared for him, nurtured him, loved him.

"What's going on?" I felt Caroline's voice as if it was a punch to my gut.

I sniffled as the reality of the situation crashed down. Last time he had come up he'd been more distant than usual and I couldn't figure out why. But now I had my answer. Ford wasn't mine. He never had been and he never would be.

"I'm sorry. I'm so sorry." I shouldn't have called.

"Emily. Where are you?"

I shook my head, as if he could see me, as if I could will myself to regain control. But my emotions were a runaway train, and I was merely a passenger along for the devastating ride.

The next words came out in a rush, a desperate attempt to articulate the fear and uncertainty that consumed me.

"Oh my god. I can't believe you are back with her. This is so fucking stupid. I'm so fucking stupid."

"Emily, I—"

"I shouldn't have called."

"No. Don't hang up. I'm headed up there now just tell me what happened." His plea was desperate.

I shook my head as the reality of the last few hours hit. Who cared if Ford wanted to fuck Caroline. Maybe it was for the best. All I had the mental capacity to focus on right now was what was right before me.

My mom was dying. My mom was fucking dying. And while he was most certainly an asshole of the most epic proportions, he had a right to know what was happening. Maybe I should have waited for

Anderson to fill him in but reason and logic seemed like a foreign language.

"I just started my new job, and we were supposed to go on a girls weekend next month to celebrate." A hiccup escaped. "Six weeks. That's what the doctor said. Six. Weeks." Disbelief tinged every syllable. "That's before Christmas. She always fills our stockings for Christmas. I know I'm an adult, and I don't believe in Santa anymore, but she always makes sure to fill—"

"Emily—"

"—the stockings. And this is so dumb, but I just called her last week because I couldn't remember my social security number for the new hire paperwork, and she had to tell me what it was." Panic surged. "What am I supposed to do when I can't call her? What if I forget my social again? I don't know what my blood type is or when I got my vaccines. What do I do? Who do I call?" My breath came in rapid gasps, my heart pounding against my ribs.

"Emily," he soothed, "I need you to breathe. You're going to pass out."

"Who do I call?" My voice broke with the scream.

"You call me. You call me. Just like you did right now. You call me, and I'll be there."

"I want to call her."

"You can. You can always call her. Maybe not with a phone, but she'll be there. She always has been." His words were meant to comfort, but the pain in his voice was unmistakable.

"I want to call her," I mumbled through the tears. "I want to call her every day."

"Emily. Are you at your apartment? Are you in the car?"

The sound of his car engine roaring to life jolted me back to the present. I grabbed a crumpled napkin and wiped my face but the gesture was futile against the onslaught of tears.

"I'm fine." I sniffled, wiping my nose on my sleeve. "I shouldn't have called. I'm so sorry."

Before he could respond, I hung up, silencing the ringer as I merged back onto the highway.

The drive back to my apartment was a blur. I walked into the quiet darkness, the silence confirming Becca's absence. The clock on the stove read 1 p.m., a stark reminder of the three hours that stretched before me until dinner.

By the time I reached my bed, exhaustion claimed me. I curled up, clutching my pillow, staring at the wall, and willing the day to end.

The sunlight crept across the ceiling, its warmth a stark contrast to the chill that had settled over me. The once-vibrant sounds of the park outside had faded into an eerie silence, mirroring the stillness that had enveloped me.

Had the front door opened? Perhaps. Maybe I'd mistaken it for Becca returning from work. Or perhaps this entire day was a cruel figment of my imagination, a horrific hallucination that would dissipate once I could finally command my body to move.

The creak of my bedroom door was like a knife slicing through the silence, but I remained motionless, not even a allowing a flinch to betray the inner turmoil. Deep down, in the recesses of my subconscious, I knew it was him.

His warmth enveloped me. His strong arms were a comforting contrast to the fragility that had consumed me. He buried his face in the nape of my neck and for the first time in hours, I moved as my grip tightened on the arm that he draped over my side.

The soft kiss he pressed against my shoulder was the final straw that shattered the fragile dam I had constructed around all my emotions. My body convulsed with the force of grief as sobs wracked my frame and I cursed the cruel universe and the insidious disease that had invaded our lives.

I forced a smile as the camera flashed.

"One more," the hospice nurse chirped, turning the phone sideways for a different angle. I froze as pleasantries and thanks were exchanged between the group, none of us still quite sure how we had ended up here. The whole scene felt like a terrifying nightmare disguised as a dream, a horrific ordeal that I knew would haunt me for years to come.

"Emily?" My dad's voice broke through the fog. "You want a piece of cake?" He gestured toward the store-bought pastry masquerading as something more.

"No thanks," I mumbled, turning to find my mom as the nurse and aide adjusted the pillows and blankets.

Despite the smile on her face, I could see the pain lurking beneath. She'd spent the last twenty minutes sitting up during Anderson and Lynn's exchange of vows in front of the living room fireplace, and it had clearly taken a toll on her.

"You okay?" I scooted onto the bed to face her, cupping her cheek.

"Oh, I'm fine," she replied as a tear escaped and she forced a smile. I quickly wiped it away before anyone else could notice.

"You don't have to be so strong all the time," I whispered, "You're allowed to cry."

She chuckled softly, "Not like this. Not on my son's wedding day." Her grip on my hand tightened.

"I thought most moms cried on their children's wedding day."

Leaning back, her hand found mine against her cheek. "True," she conceded.

We both glanced over to see Anderson playfully wiping icing off Lynn's nose. Mom groaned, and I turned back to her with concern. "What do you need?"

She smiled through the pain, "Nothing. I'm perfectly fine."

"You're a bad liar," I smirked in hopes of lightening my own anguish.

"You had to get it from somewhere."

I balked in feigned annoyance and she smiled.

"How are you?"

"Mom, I'm fine," I forced a more convincing smile, hoping that just this once, she wouldn't see through the facade.

"And how's Ford?"

My jaw clenched at the mention of his name. He was standing not ten feet away, and yet we had barely spoken since he arrived that morning. In the three weeks since her diagnosis, meaningful conversation had been scarce. Consumed by the need to spend every waking moment with Mom, the days we did see each other were filled with an unspoken grief. He never brought up he fact that he was with Caroline the day our world broke and neither did I. It was as if the mention of her would be the final straw the shatter what little life was left and neither of us was brave enough to risk it.

"He's great."

"Has he figured out he loves you yet?" she whispered conspiratorially.

"Mom!" I hissed, hoping no one else heard.

"Have y'all made it official yet?"

I shrugged, "It's complicated."

Mom's smile wavered, and I decided then and there that I had to give her something, even if it wasn't the truth.

"Can I tell you a secret?"

Her eyes lit up with excitement.

"We're kinda together, but we don't want anyone to know. His mom—"

"Emily Ann Truse! Are you still worried about her?"

I laughed at the conviction in her voice. "No. Not really. But we don't want to mess it up."

"I think he's scared."

I sighed, "Maybe. Or maybe he's just an idiot?"

Mom's laughter boomed through the room, turning every head in our direction before she shushed them away and pulled me closer.

"Can I let you in on a little secret?" She raised her eyebrows, and I could see that even that small movement was exhausting.

"And what is that?"

"Most men are idiots."

I chuckled, "Not Dad."

She scoffed and shook her head. "Oh honey. You should have seen him when I first got him. It took many years to get him to where he is now."

I smiled at her teasing, "You're so bad."

The funeral dress still clung to my body. The once-vibrant bouquet of roses, a gift from a well-meaning family friend, now lay overturned on the backseat floorboard. Water, meant to sustain life, had become a destructive force when I'd slammed on the brakes, staining the once-cream floor mats a depressing beige. I despised those mats almost as much as I despised the car itself. Maybe as much as I despised this town and all the people in it who would, in less than a week, would inevitably go back to living their perfect lives as if my mom hadn't just died.

I hated everything here.

This town, with its suffocating familiarity, felt like a prison. The supermarket where Mom shopped, the streets I'd walked a thousand times, even the sympathetic glances from acquaintances—it all fueled a growing rage within me. Anderson, with his practiced composure and ability to express gratitude through his grief, only highlighted my own inability to maintain a façade of normalcy.

Anger pulsed through me in a volatile cocktail of sorrow and resentment. Everything and everyone became a target for my bitterness.

A sudden honk jolted me back to reality, and I responded with a well-placed middle finger before hastily pulling into the first available business parking lot. My head fell against the steering wheel, seeking a moment of respite.

"Just five minutes," I pleaded silently, "Five minutes to regain control and finish this drive back to the house." But as I envisioned the inevitable return to my empty house, a knock on the window shattered my fragile peace. I looked up to find a middle-aged man with a receding hairline, filled with an unnatural amount of black dye, peering at me.

"Need any help?" he inquired as I rolled down the window.

"I need to get away," I blurted out, the words escaping before I could filter them.

His laughter, loud and unexpectedly cheerful, startled me. "Well," he chuckled, surveying the surroundings, "I think you picked the right spot."

Confusion furrowed my brow as he pointed towards where I'd parked. "She's an oldie but runs like a champ. Even had a few modifications. I'm sure we could work something out..."

His words trailed off as my gaze fell upon a clunky RV, at least as old as I was, with a large "For Sale" sign in the window.

"...we could get you—"

"Is this a car lot?" I interrupted, finally taking in the full picture of the area.

"We specialize in RVs and Motorhomes," he corrected, a hint of pride in his voice.

Chapter 23

PRESENT DAY

Emily

"How long have you had this place?" My voice broke as we stepped on the porch.

"I bought it last year."

I nodded in acceptance as I walked back into the home and to the back wall of windows. "And when did you put in the lights?"

He cleared his throat.

"The week after I bought it." His admission knocked the wind straight from my lungs. "It was the first renovation I made."

"You were still married." My whispered voice was barely holding together.

With every word, a little more of the chasm he'd once created began to mend, and then break apart and mend once more. I had no idea what to feel . . . how to feel.

"I was separated," he corrected.

I cleared my throat, closed my eyes and willed the chaos in my mind to slow for just a moment so I could make sense of what was right in front of me.

"I was on the other side of the country and we had no plans to ever see each other again."

"I know," he whispered as his fingers brushed mine from behind. This time I didn't push him away.

"And you still put in the lights?"

"They made me think of you."

A timid smile filled my face. I cleared my throat, forcing that silly thing I was feeling to bury itself somewhere I hoped I would never find. "I want to see them." He lifted a hand and motioned to the door. "After you."

The snow-laden ground felt like a secret valley nestled within an enchanted forest, a scene both foreign and strangely familiar. As I ventured further into the expanse, my fingers brushed against the tiny, twinkling bulbs that peeked through the rising foliage. Hundreds, maybe thousands, of them spread out like a starlit sky, each stem swaying in the wind as if imbued with life.

"It reminds me of when we were kids," I murmured, my voice barely above a whisper.

"The beach?" Ford's voice boomed from behind me, closer than I'd expected.

I nodded, unsure if he could see the gesture in the dim light. "We spent hours on that beach."

Memories of that summer flooded my mind - a time of innocence and carefree laughter. It was the first time Ford had joined our family vacation, and we'd spent the days splashing in the waves and building sandcastles. One evening, under the watchful eyes of my parents on the porch, we chased after fireflies that danced in the twilight. The memory of that night, the sand between my toes, the sound of our laughter, remained a vivid dream, a reminder of a time when nothing else mattered.

A smile touched my lips as the cold air whipped around me. The contrast between the present and that memory was stark, but my imagination bridged the gap.

Turning, I found Ford's gaze fixed on me and a playful smirk dancing on his lips. Before the memory could fade, I took off running and letting laughter echo through the yard as the lights blurred around me.

Ford's strong arms enveloped me, pulling me close to his familiar face. "You're beautiful," he breathed, his voice now barely audible above the wind.

"I thought I was chaos," I retorted, breathlessly, as I tightened my arms around his neck.

"My chaos," he whispered against my lips. "My beautiful chaos."

"Ford," I warned, though my fingers threading through his hair and my legs now wrapped around his waist betrayed my tone.

"I honestly thought you would never see this place."

"Why did you really ask me to come?"

Ford shook his head. "It wasn't a decision. It just happened."

"Is this why you haven't found an apartment?"

Ford nodded, his eyes holding mine.

"You plan to move up here, don't you?"

Another nod, as he gently lowered me to the ground and I leaned my head against his chest, the warmth of his body a welcome contrast to the cold night.

"Is there a fireplace inside?" I whispered, shivering as I pressed closer.

"Yes," Ford murmured into my hair. A shiver ran through him, and I knew it had nothing to do with the cold.

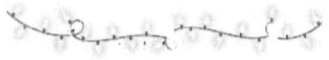

The moment I stepped back into the house, a wave of nostalgia washed over me.

"I remember a lot of this stuff," I murmured, my fingers trailing along the blanket draped over the back of the leather couch. My now bare feet tiptoed across the cool wooden floor, the silence punctuated only by the soft thud of my steps. "Does anyone else know you have this?"

"Only Caroline, my mom and my lawyer," Ford replied. "I had to disclose it as an asset, and she agreed not to fight for it if I gave her our place in the city."

"Her loss," I hummed with a hint of a smile playing on my lips as I glanced over my shoulder to find Ford standing exactly where I'd left him. The wind had picked up outside, and the twinkling lights swayed in the distance, casting an ethereal glow on the darkened cabin.

I continued my exploration, letting my fingers trace the mantel and then the rough stone of the wall. "This place is beautiful," I whispered, more to myself than to him.

The clinking of glasses from the kitchen pulled me from my thoughts and I made my way back to the couch, wrapping the familiar blanket around myself as Ford emerged with two glasses of wine. He handed me one, then knelt to light the fireplace. A sigh of contentment escaped me as the warmth reached my toes.

I set my glass down as Ford took a seat opposite me. "Tell me about this place."

For the next hour, Ford wove a captivating tale of the old woman named Adaline, and how he'd spent an entire night listening to her stories about the home she and her late husband had built. He spoke of the town, of Doris and Sheila, and how he'd poured his heart and soul into transforming the cabin into the haven it was now. By the time he finished, I couldn't suppress a knowing smile.

"What's so funny?" Ford asked, his brow furrowed.

"Nothing, really," I chuckled. "It's a truly beautiful story, and I'm so happy you were able to make that happen." I paused, a playful glint in my eyes. "But..."

"But?" Ford echoed, drawing out the word.

I took a deep breath, mock seriousness settling on my features. "If one of us were going to show up on a true crime podcast, it would have for sure been you."

Ford burst out laughing and the noise filled the cozy space. "She was a sweet old lady!" he exclaimed, swatting my foot playfully.

"Sweet old lady?" I retorted, leaning forward with a mischievous grin. "There's an entire Netflix documentary dedicated to 'sweet old ladies' who commit murder. You're just lucky that hot chocolate wasn't laced with something. You could be buried under this floor instead of sitting on the couch right now."

He shook his head, still chuckling. "Well, next time I help an old woman up her ice-covered steps, I'll be sure to send you my location so you can recover the body."

I nodded in acceptance, then drained my glass and pulled the blanket tighter around me.

"So what happens now?"

Ford swallowed as if he wasn't quiet ready for the shift I had just catapulted us into.

"What do you want to happen?"

I smirked. "Probably something that will end up breaking my heart in the long run."

He shook his head with a determined look in his eyes. "No more heart breaking allowed."

I laughed. "We kinda have a track record of fucking it up."

"Our past doesn't have to dictate our future."

I nodded in response as I stood. The blanket trailed behind me as I walked the few steps to Ford's side of the couch. I knelt, my knees sinking into the soft leather between his legs, and brushed a lock of dark hair from his brow.

"Emily," he murmured and I couldn't tell wheather my name was a warning or a plea.

"I have no idea what's going to happen in the future."

He looked at me with an unreadable expression. "Okay?"

I took a deep breath. "I don't even know what's going to happen tomorrow, let alone next week."

Ford's eyes searched mine.

"But I do know one thing," I continued, my voice laced with new-found confidence.

"And what is that?" he asked, his voice husky.

I swallowed the lump in my throat, my gaze unwavering.

"I want you. I've always wanted you."

His eyebrows rose in response as he cupped my outer thigh and then downed the remaining liquid that swirled within his own glass.

"Always?" He challenged, kneading my leg.

I nodded.

"I need you to know I didn't bring you up here just to—" he paused, "Actually, maybe I did. At this point I don't know what I'm doing. But I know I'm not going ot lie to myself or to you anymore."

"I know." I answered honestly.

"I would never force anything of you. But I can't lie and say us getting back together in some capacity didn't cross my mind."

"It never left my mind." I confessed and he gave me a tentative smile.

"And what if I want there to be something after tonight?"

I shrugged. "I can't promise you anything."

His shoulders fell slightly but he quickly recovered with a smile. "Okay."

His grip tightened as he pulled me in further.

"I don't want to force you into doing anything–"

He laughed as he cut me off. "Emily, there is no way you could force me into anything. I have always been and always will be a willing participant in whatever you choose to give me."

I smiled as the moment stilled and the warring emotions collided.

This is exactly where we were not supposed to be. We had spent the last two years in what could only be described as radio silence and yet a few days back in each other's worlds and all our self control had vanished.

"What exactly do you want to happen tonight?" His smirk grew as his eyes darkened.

"Whatever you want," I answered as I leaned further in, my knee teasing the growing bulge in his pants.

He laughed, the sound so low it vibrated through me. "My choice?"

"You're choice."

A wicked grin spread across his face as his gaze swept over me. Then, with a deliberate motion, he reached up to trace his thumb across my lips before grabbing the back of my neck and pulling me down into a searing kiss that stole my breath. Our lips collided, hot and demanding, a silent battle of tongues. Each movement felt familiar, a perfectly choreographed dance our bodies remembered, a melody we had played countless times and would never forget. A spark of heat flared at my fingertips as I traced the sharp angle of his jaw, and—

He pulled back.

"I want you on your knees for me." He stated without missing a beat and I swallowed. "I want to see those pretty eyes water and ruin that pretty makeup as you choke on me." My heart rate was rampant as desire pooled within. "I want you begging me to take you, and when I finally do . . . when I finally flip you over, bury myself within that sweet cunt, and remind you exactly why you never forgot me . . ." He leaned in further and my breath caught in my throat. "I want you to be a good girl and come only when I say."

I bit my lip as that little whisper of warning disappeared. He looked me up and down as his beautiful blue eyes turned molten, and a devious smile spread across his face.

"Emily." His voice was rough and commanding and I startled at the power that filled it. "I said I want you on your knees."

My breathing turned ragged as I immediately dropped to the floor, awaiting his next command. I licked my lips, wondering if he could see the slight tremble, and hoping he knew it was built only from excitement and want. My eyes remained trained on his hands as he undid and slid off the leather belt, laying in gently at his side.

"You're so pretty . . . sitting there . . . waiting for me." He unbuttoned his pants and lifted up to slowly push them down his legs. The bulge of his cock strained against his boxers. "You want this, don't you?" He cupped himself as I nodded in agreement. "Words, Emily. Use your words."

"I want it," I panted, my body growing immensely heated under his stare. And that was the truth, I did want it. I wanted all of it, all of him. I just couldn't figure out if that was for only tonight or for forever.

He slid his boxers off, and I damn near whimpered in relief at the sight. His free hand came up to cup my chin as he caressed a thumb across my lips. "It's a shame. Your makeup is so pretty. So perfect." He pushed down, swiping some of the lipstick off my bottom lip and dragging the reddened dye across my chin. "It's about to be all messed up." His voice was low and teasing. And then his hand moved as he traced the outline of my face and buried it in the crown of my hair. "Come here, baby," he cooed and I leaned forward with his movement.

He stopped right before his cock met my mouth. A bead of moisture leaking from the tip. It took more restraint than I knew I possessed not to reach out with my tongue and taste it...taste him.

Thankfully, Ford didn't want to put either of us through any more torture, and just as he pulled me in, he rubbed his wet tip around my red lips. "While I love the red," he paused as he took in the sight, "you look much better covered in me."

I damn near passed out at the insinuation as I realized right then that being covered in him, in every way possible, was exactly what I wanted.

Before he could utter another command, I parted my lips and slowly teased him as my tongue swirled around the head. Ford groaned, the sound filled with relief and desire, and it did nothing but rouse me further as I took him fully into my mouth. I peered upward, catching the sight of his face through my lashes just as he threw his head backward. The sight of his undoing only served to spur me on further.

I'd never considered giving a blow job to be something I yearned for, but kneeling here with Ford's cock in my mouth, I felt as if there was nowhere else I wanted to be.

"Fuck, baby," Ford growled out as the hand buried in my hair tightened its grip. I hummed in appreciation, and his hips bucked upward. "Your mouth feels so good. Sooo good," he dragged out the word.

I looked upward once more, taking him further back and hoping to cause a few more of those delicious sounds to leak from his lips.

"You look so pretty. My beautiful chaos with my cock between her lips," he praised me, the words tight and muffled, and I knew he was moments from release.

I took in every drop as his body shuddered in relief. When my eyes found his sultry gaze, he reached out, letting his finger swipe across my swollen lip to gather the lost drop. He pulled my chin down, exposing my tongue, and I obediently licked off what was left.

I sat, still and waiting, not yet sure what would happen next as I watched Ford pull up his boxers. He stood and I leaned back, keeping my obedient gaze trained on his face. It had been a few years since we had been together but I remembered well the control he commanded.

His silence was profound, yet his message was clear, resonating within me as he gestured me forward with an alluring command.

A short journey of five feet brought us to a partially open door, hinting at a darkened room within. Ford's hand reached out, his touch a gentle restraint on my wrist, halting my movement. I turned to meet his gaze, his expression a complex tapestry of emotions I couldn't decipher.

"Ford?" My voice was a breath, a whisper in the charged air.

His touch ascended, a tantalizing trail of heat along my arm, my shoulder, my collarbone. My breath hitched, a wildfire ignited within me by his caress. Reaching my cheek, he cupped my face, and I found myself leaning into his touch, an instinctive surrender.

"I had this dream," he began, his voice hesitant, as if coaxing the words to form. "I had this dream when I was little. I was so consumed by it, I didn't see what was right in front of me." He swallowed, the sound heavy in the silence. "I didn't see you."

A pang of sorrow pierced my heart.

The carefully constructed box I had confined my feelings within only moments ago thrummed with a desperate need for release. I almost yielded, almost reached down to unlock the chains and unleash a torrent of confessions. But one thing held me back.

I had allowed those emotions to escape once before. I had dismantled my own barriers, confessed everything to him all those years ago, and I wouldn't repeat that mistake.

"I'm here," I said, the words a comfort, a reassurance, though their full meaning remained elusive even to me.

Ford's lips curved into a tender smile, and he reached up to cover my eyes. I tensed as he turned me, his breath a warm caress against my ear. The creak of the wooden door as it swung open filled the air. He flicked the light switch, and even through the veil of his hand, I could see the soft glow seep between his fingers.

His hand pressed gently against my lower back, urging me forward. As the dim light began to expand, he lowered his hand, revealing a sight that stole my breath.

"Oh. My. God." The words escaped me in a hushed whisper as my eyes took in the breathtaking scene.

The dark wooden ceiling soared upward, converging at a central point. A low-hanging chandelier, crafted from wood with intricate carvings, seemed to have sprung directly from a tree, suspended in the center, directly over a massive four-poster bed.

The chandelier branched out in various directions, like the limbs of a tree adorned with vines of greenery woven around its massive structure. But what truly made the room a masterpiece wasn't the chandelier itself, but the thousands of lights that cascaded like a luminous river from its center, ending along the molding that encircled the room.

"Ford!" Awe filled my voice as I absorbed the beauty of the room. So distinct from the rest of the house, yet unimaginably perfect in a way I could never have envisioned.

"It was the first room I renovated," he admitted, his words bringing a smile to my lips.

But then my gaze fell upon the intricate carvings adorning the chandelier, and my world seemed to shatter.

"Indian ghost pipes?" I whispered, my feet carrying me closer to the bed. A lone tear escaped, tracing a path down my cheek.

Ford

I caught her hand in mine, the warmth of her touch igniting a spark that traveled up my arm. With a gentle tug, I spun her to face me, our bodies coming close, breaths mingling.

"I never expected you to see this," I began, my voice husky with a mix of surprise and desire, "But then, you—"

My words were stolen by Emily's touch. Her hands reached up, cupping my cheeks, grounding me in the moment. With a boldness that took my breath away, she pulled my face down to hers, sealing her claim with a kiss that spoke of longing and possession.

Time seemed to slow as I surrendered to the moment, letting her guide, letting her take all she wanted. My arms instinctively snaked around her, pulling her closer until there was no space left between us. A hum of pure pleasure vibrated through me as I buried my hand in her hair, eliciting a soft, appreciative sound from her lips. That sound, that small sigh, was the catalyst to something I hadn't felt in so long – a raw, primal desire.

I twisted us as I walked her backward, never breaking the connection between our lips, and pressed her against the door, our bodies molding together. Pulling back slightly, I gazed down at her, the woman who had always held my heart captive, the one who would forever be my undoing.

We were so close, an electric current ran between us, a fire that threatened to consume us both. I licked my lips, my tongue barely missing her own as I gathered her small wrists in my hand, raising them above her head. She tilted her head back, her body arching into mine, and I took the opportunity to lavish her neck with a thousand kisses, each one a promise, a declaration of my devotion.

A war raged within me. I wanted to take my time, to savor every inch of skin she was so generously offering me. But I also wanted, needed, to let her know she was mine, that she always had been. Releasing her hands, I watched as she panted, gasping for breath, her eyes filled with a heady mix of lust and anticipation. Without breaking eye contact, I walked backward and sat on the foot of the bed, a silent invitation.

She was breathless, her chest heaving, her lust-filled eyes searching the room, desperate to decipher my next move.

"Ford?" Her voice was laced with a frantic need as she stared at me more intently. I crossed one leg over the other, my gaze never wavering from hers. The air thrummed with unspoken promises, the silence a prelude to a passion that was about to be unleashed.

"Crawl to me." My command was sudden.

Emily's eyes went wide, but she immediately complied. Before the order was fully stated, she had dropped to her hands and knees as she moved on shaking limbs toward her prize.

"Slowly," I stated, my voice deep and husky, and from the way the visible shiver ran through her body, I knew this was affecting her just as much as seeing her on her knees was affecting me.

Fuck if she wasn't the sexiest woman I'd ever seen.

I leaned forward just as she came within reach, and stroked the side of her face.

"Undress."

She swallowed, but stood and peeled off her thin top. Then she hesitated and I gave her a look of warning. She knew the rules to this game. She had played it far too many times.

"Undress." My voice was deep and forceful. A warning I wasn't sure she was happy to receive.

She mewled at the noise but this time she didn't hesitate as she ripped off the sports bra and slipped out of her pants. My heart pounded with every inch of skin she gave me.

"So beautiful," I murmured as I took in everything that lay bare.

"It's yours," she whispered.

I smirked as I reached out to pull her forward, my hands grazing her sides as I appreciated every curve.

Emily met my stare with a devious smirk as she climbed on top of me. I let her rest a leg on either side as she ground her body into mine and chuckled when my hand slid along the curve of her hip, pausing just before it reached her center. She whined in protest.

"So damn needy for me," I whispered into her ear as I dragged my lips along her jaw. My hand slipped further south, and I barely held my composure as my fingers found the slick wetness gathered at her center. "So damn wet for me." My voice was rough as I teased her.

She threw her head back as the sensations rolled through her and I took the opportunity to prolong that torturous pleasure. I played with her, letting that want and desire build. I knew she was close when her wide hips began rolling against me, fighting for more friction. I pulled back, knowing I had to make this last, and she whimpered in protest.

Just as her lust filled gaze met mine, I grabbed her hips and flipped us over. She sucked in a breath as I leaned over her, spreading her legs further apart and exposing all of her.

"You're still dressed," she whimpered as she reached upward for my shirt, but the motion was halted as I took her hands in mine and peered down. I couldn't let her see what was hidden beneath just yet.

"This isn't about me right now." My free hand slid down her inner thigh, and she bucked upward when I skirted along the outer edge of her swollen clit.

"Please," she begged, but I was on a mission, and no amount of begging would change that.

"I'm going to lick that sweet cunt." My fingers traced her lips, becoming coated in her arousal. "I can't wait to have that taste on my lips . . . my tongue. I want to drown in you." I kissed down the length of her right thigh, stopping just before I met her center. "I want you to be a good girl," I whispered, the tendrils of warm air snaking around her thighs, and she bucked upward in need. "You have to be a good girl and not come until I tell you," I commanded, and from the way

272

her body shuddered, I knew there was very little chance of her actually complying.

I stared at her a moment longer, eyes closed, head thrown back in need as if waiting for heaven to arrive. And then just when she started to move, I leaned in and circled her clit with my tongue. A slew of mumbled curses fell from her lips.

I did it again, knowing there was nothing more in life I wanted than to hear her breathy voice ring out like that for years to come. I took my time, torturing her clit with sucks and licks, and drinking in everything she gave me. Her pleas became louder, her whines and whimpers seemed to permeate the walls.

"Not yet, Chaos," I breathed against her. "Hold on, baby." I licked again, knowing she wouldn't last as I sealed my lips around her clit and plunged two fingers into her hot wet cunt.

"I—" she started, but the words ended in a scream as the pleasure surged through her.

I let her finish as I coaxed out every sound from those beautiful lips. And just as her breathing was starting to slow and her eyes were fluttering open, I crawled upward to hover over her languid form.

"You didn't listen," I stated as my lips planted light kisses on the swell of her breast.

"I'm sorry," she whispered the apology low, as if anything louder was unattainable.

I leaned back and stood from the bed. "Bad girls get punished."

She audibly swallowed at my words.

My hands found her hips, and I flipped her onto her stomach and pulled her backward, just enough to allow her feet to graze the floor. I cupped her ass, and swore she lifted it slightly, begging for whatever was about to come.

"I want to see this pretty skin turn pink," I teased as my fingers trailed over her goosebump covered skin. She groaned and this time she definitely pushed her ass further into the air. I used my knee as I pushed her legs further apart, exposing that wet slit I wanted nothing more than to claim again.

Her body was shaking, and though I knew it was from want, I paused my hands as I forged a path of delicate kisses up her back. I ended right below her ear.

"I'm going to spank you for being bad, and then I'm going to fuck you," I whispered and she nodded, a moan of relief falling from her lips. "If you need me to stop—"

"Don't stop," she cut me off. "Please don't stop," she whined once more, and I couldn't hide the triumphant smirk that erupted.

"I'm going to spank you five times."

There was only a moment's hesitation before my hand landed firmly on her ass and she called out, a scream of desire ripping from her lips. The second slap was a tad harder, and I pulled back to assess the changing color of her skin.

"You're so beautiful," I praised her just before the third slap rang out. This time, she arched her back with the moan. "Only two more." I rubbed the sensitive skin between her legs and she whimpered into the covers.

She was thrusting, desperate for relief as she tried to find release. But I was not letting her off that easily. She tried to bring her legs together, and I kicked them further apart. The fourth slap caused her entire body to shake.

"You're doing so good, baby girl." I rubbed the heated skin as my own heart rate began to spike. "So good for me," I praised once more just before I leaned forward to whisper along her spine. "Now, you can come." I leaned back, letting the fifth slap land at the junction of her thighs and not letting go as I cupped and rubbed her throbbing pussy, my fingers becoming soaked with her release.

The world seemed to pause its rotation, holding its breath as she lay nestled in my arms. The night had been a rapturous blur of tangled limbs, stolen breaths, and shared warmth. Now, dawn painted the room in soft hues, and the steam rising from my coffee cup mirrored the uncertainty swirling within me. Could last night's magic ever be replicated? I gazed at the chandelier's shimmering crystals, their light a stark contrast to the darkness lurking beyond the cabin walls.

This place, this sanctuary, was meant to be my refuge, a secret kept from prying eyes. Yet, Emily Ann Truse had an uncanny ability to breach my defenses, to unravel the carefully constructed barriers that separated me from the world.

A tender smile curved my lips as she stirred, her hand reaching out instinctively for the warmth of my body, only to find the space beside her cold and empty. Panic flashed across her features, replaced by a serene calm as her eyes met mine, standing silhouetted in the doorway.

"Good morning," she murmured, her voice husky with sleep and a hint of overuse from the passionate hours of the night before. Her blonde hair, still tousled with curls from yesterday, was a delightful mess, and in that moment, I had never seen anything more captivating.

"Good morning," I replied, moving to her side of the bed and handing her a steaming cup of coffee.

She took it eagerly, inhaling the rich aroma and sighing with contentment as the warmth spread through her.

Our eyes met, a silent conversation passing between us as we savored our much-needed coffee. Though I appeared calm, my mind raced, searching for the perfect words to express the emotions swirling within me.

"You're tense," Emily observed with a gentle laugh that I mirrored. "Is everything okay?" A flicker of worry crossed her features. "Was last night–"

"Last night was perfect," I assured her, my hand reaching out to gently caress her knee through the covers. I gazed out the window at the breathtaking view beyond. "I never planned to show you this," I confessed, my voice low, laced with an emotion I couldn't yet name.

"But you did." Emily's hand cupped my chin, turning my face back to hers. "Do you regret bringing me here?"

"Never." My response was instant and unwavering.

"Then what's on your mind?" She chuckled softly.

"I have a present for you."

Her eyebrows rose in surprise. "You do?"

"I do."

"Are you going to give it to me or do I have to guess?" She teased, running her fingers through my hair.

I shook my head, throwing back the covers and leaving the room. My heart hammered against my ribs as I stared at the book tucked safely in my bag. Uncertainty gnawed at me, but I pushed it aside, determined not to let fear ruin this moment.

When I returned to the bedroom, Emily was sitting up, the blanket draped around her shoulders, a hesitant look in her eyes.

"I bought it a year ago."

She tilted her head in confusion. "Bought what?"

I ignored her question, my voice filled with a nervous excitement. "It was at an estate sale in Highlands. I don't think the young man realized what he had, and I wasn't about to enlighten him."

"Ford," she chided playfully. "You're speaking in riddles." She gestured towards my hand. "What's that?"

I walked to her side and carefully unwrapped the protective cover.

A gasp escaped her lips as the cover came into view.

"What is that?" She straightened, her eyes wide with anticipation.

"It's not a first edition," I explained, my voice trembling slightly. "It's technically the second. It's the leather-bound peacock edition."

"Oh. My. God." Her breath hitched as her hands shook with emotion. "You bought me the second edition of Pride and Prejudice."

Tears welled up in her eyes, and in that moment, I knew I had given her more than just a book; I had given her a piece of my heart.

Chapter 24

18 Months Prior

Emily

I sat on the front porch steps and willed the last few hours to disappear.

"Emily?" My dad stepped out and crouched to sit beside me.

"Yeah?" I twisted the weed I'd plucked between my fingers.

"I didn't know how to tell you." He confessed. "I should have but–"

I reached out and grabbed his hand. "It's okay dad. I'm okay." I lied.

"It's okay if you're not. And it's okay if you wanna get away for a while and pretend it isn't happening."

I barked out a laugh that sounded more like a sob.

"You know I feel like I should have seen it coming." I confessed and dad placed his arm around my shoulder. "When did it all go down?"

Dad shook his head. "I have no idea when he actually left. I can't recall his truck in the drive for the last few weeks, maybe more."

I nodded. I had an idea when Mr. Thomas officially left. If I had to guess it would have been somewhere around the time Ford conveniently stopped responding to my every message.

"And the next thing I know Ford had stopped by to tell me the news."

I had to hold in the bile that threatened to erupt.

The *news*.

He said it so casually as if that *news* didn't shatter my entire world.

"Do they have a date picked out?"

"I'm not sure but I am assuming it'll happen sooner rather than later,"

I nodded as he patted me on the back, stood and walked back inside.

Ford was getting married.

Ford was getting married.

Ford was–

A tear landed on my fingers as I continued to twist the now destroyed weed in my hands.

All it took was for his father to officially leave. That was the catalyst for it all. Though no one had confirmed the exact situation, I had already figured out the details.

Ford was a fixer. It's probably what would make him a wonderful doctor.

But he wasn't a doctor yet. Right now, he was just a son whose shitty father walked out and most likely destroyed his mom. And Ford had to fix her. Just like he had tried to fix me.

And there was only one way to fix Mrs. Thomas; make sure Ford's future was set up for perfection. And perfection would never be the lost girl who had no real plans.

The unexpected warmth of a hand on my shoulder made me jump.

"Hi," Ford's voice was so casual, so normal, that I had to force myself to breathe, to anchor myself in the reality of the moment and dispel the idea that this was just a dream... or maybe a nightmare.

"It's good to see you." He shoved his hands into his pockets as his gaze shifted away from mine. "Are you meeting up with Anderson and Lynn?"

I stood frozen, my jaw clenched so tightly it ached. Every fiber of my being screamed to throw a punch, to inflict pain in return for the agony he'd caused.

"Emily?"

"What are you doing?" The words were like shards of glass, sharp and edged with a fury I could barely contain.

"I'm coming to see Anderson, Lynn, you." His voice faltered, a hint of uncertainty creeping in. "We always hang out on—"

"You haven't gotten drinks with us in six weeks," I spat. "Actually, you might as well have been dead for all I knew."

He seemed to shrink under my words. "I'm sorry."

"Sorry?" I scoffed, the sound bitter and disbelieving. "You're sorry?"

"Yes, I'm—"

"How's the wedding planning?" I interrupted, my voice dripping with sarcasm. "Did you think I wasn't aware?"

He swallowed, his Adam's apple bobbed nervously. "No, I knew you—"

"Were you even going to tell me," I demanded, "or just pretend like I didn't exist in that world? Am I invited? Maybe I could be the flower girl, but then again grooms don't normally fuck the flower girl weeks before they get engaged to the bride."

Ford froze as his eyes darted around to gauge the reactions of the surrounding people who had undoubtedly heard my outburst. I couldn't care less.

"Emily, it's not—"

"But it is." I stepped out of the line, my patience utterly spent, and turned to walk back to my waiting car a block away.

"Emily, wait!" He reached out to grab my arm, and that touch, that unwelcome contact, was the final straw. I whirled around to face him, my anger finally erupting like a volcano.

"Wait!" I snarled, my voice laced with disbelief. "Wait?" I shook my head, a bitter laugh escaping my lips. "You're horrible, you know that?"

He had the audacity to nod in agreement, his expression was a strange mix of defiance and resignation.

"What are you doing?" My voice was a hushed scream, barely contained fury simmering beneath.

"What do you mean what am I doing? What are you doing?" His tone was sharp, a defensive edge creeping in.

I balked at Ford's audacity. "You are so predictable."

"Are we really going to do this right now?" His voice held a warning note, but I refused to back down.

I shrugged my shoulders, feigning nonchalance. "I don't see any better time than the present."

He raked his hands through his hair, his agitation evident as he paced in a tight circle, his movements jerky and erratic.

"I can't," he shook his head, his voice strained. "I'm leaving. I ca–"

"Oh, you are –," I started, my retort cut short by a passerby on the sidewalk.

"Y'all wanna take this someplace else?" The stranger's voice was laced with irritation.

We both turned instinctively as a synchronized "Shut the fuck up" erupted from our lips.

I grunted in frustration, my gaze colliding with Ford's once more. "You know what, I don't even care. I'm leaving."

I turned to walk away, my strides fueled by anger and hurt, only to be halted a few paces later by a hand clamping around my wrist.

"Wait. Don't. Please just talk to me. You're my best friend." Ford's voice was urgent, pleading, and it took every ounce of my self-control not to whirl around and punch him in the face.

I shook my head, my voice thick with emotion. "You've got to be kidding me. This is a joke, right? This is a stupid joke."

"Just talk to me." His voice was hushed, desperate. "I won't leave. I just need to talk to you."

I yanked my wrist out of his grip, my anger flaring. "I can't keep doing this."

"Just wait. It's not–"

"Why? So we can work out the details of how I become your mistress?" My voice dripped with sarcasm, each word a lash.

"Emily, no. That's not–"

"You haven't been back together for more than a month." My tone was accusing.

"I don't know what to do." His words were frantic, his composure cracking.

"What to do? What do you mean you don't know what to do? I'll give you a hint. It's not proposing to that on-again, off-again train wreck the second you see her after your dad walks out." My words were harsh, but they were the truth, and I refused to sugarcoat it. "You can't fix your mom's broken heart by getting married."

"Don't call her that." He grunted, but I could hear the lack of conviction in his voice.

"Then what is she? What is this? Is she going to fix all your problems with her daddy's Amex and her shiny black Porsche?" My voice was laced with bitterness, my resentment bubbling to the surface.

"It's not her money." His defense was weak, and we both knew it.

"No, you're right. It's not her money. It's her daddy's money and the idea that she is your ticket out of this godforsaken town with all its bad memories. It's the idea that with her you won't end up like—"

"You have no idea how hard it is to make everyone happy all the time. You have no idea what it was like growing up in that house and never being good enough for anyone. You have no idea what my mom went through. I just –"

"You were good enough for me," I whispered, tears streaming down my face. "You were good enough for me."

He shook his head. "No, I wasn't. You deserve someone so much better than me. You deserve someone who can put you first and not..." His voice trailed off, the unspoken words hung heavy in the air.

"Think of me as a reminder of your shitty childhood," I finished bitterly, the sharp edge of my words mirroring the ache in my heart.

"Emily," he sighed, the sound laden with sorrow. His non-answer was answer enough.

"It doesn't matter what you think I deserve," I retorted, my voice laced with frustration. "All that matters is the fact that I am tied to here and she isn't. But guess what? Joke's on you, because I'm leaving too."

His head snapped up, surprise etched across his features. "What?"

"I'm leaving," I repeated, my voice firm.

"And where are you going?" he asked, a hint of desperation creeping into his tone.

"Anywhere but here," I replied with an unwavering gaze.

Ford took a step back, as if the distance would somehow create space between us. Then he turned to face me, his expression a mix of sadness and remorse. "I'm sorry. I fucked it all up."

"And what is that supposed to mean?" I challenged, my voice thick with emotion.

"I'm too fucked up, Emily," he admitted, his voice raw. "I'm too much like him."

"What does that mean?" I pressed, my heart sinking.

"I don't want to hurt you or let you down," he explained, his gaze averted.

"Newsflash, Ford," I retorted as my voice cracked. "You are hurting me."

He shook his head, his lips pressed into a thin line, but no words came.

"You know what, Ford?" I said, my voice trembling but resolute. "I'm done."

"Emily, I—" he began, but I cut him off with a sharp gesture.

"No!" I exclaimed, my voice firm. "For once, I'm going to talk and you are going to fucking listen."

I swallowed hard, fighting back the tears that threatened to spill over.

"I have been in love with you for longer than I can even remember," I confessed, my voice heavy with the weight of unspoken emotions. "I loved you as a brother when we were kids, and then I loved you as a man when we grew up." My chest ached with the burden of my confession. "I have waited for you to realize what we had for so long, and yet you spent the majority of that time toying with me. Letting me love you with my entire damn heart while you only gave me half of yours. You kept me dangling on a string, just tight enough that you knew I would crawl back to you whenever you needed me, and I was so weak that I let it happen."

My voice broke, but when he opened his mouth to speak, I threw my hands up to stop him.

"I get it, you had a shit childhood," I continued, my voice raw. "I won't ever know what that was like, but I know it doesn't excuse what you've put me through."

I turned to walk away, my heart heavy with the finality of my decision. But after only a few steps, I paused. When I met his gaze,

I found only sadness filling his features. The sight of his pain twisted my heart, but I knew I couldn't stay.

"I'm done," I repeated, my voice barely above a whisper. This time, when I turned to walk away, he didn't follow.

Chapter 25

PRESENT DAY

Emily

The warmth from the crackling fire on the back porch did little to stave off the chill that was settling into the air. I watched him, muscles flexing as he prepared more wood, and a wistful ache took hold. If I just surrendered, let him take care of me, this scene could be my everyday reality.

"It's going to get cold," he called out, his voice carrying across the yard.

"It's already cold," I retorted, a playful lilt to my words as he made his way towards me.

"Well, it's supposed to drop well below freezing tonight, and I haven't fully repaired the heaters," he explained, a hint of concern in his tone.

My eyes widened in mock frustration. "And you're just now telling me this?"

He chuckled as he passed me, his breath visible in the crisp air. "You seemed perfectly fine and cozy last night while wrapped in my arms."

"That's because you're a heater," I teased, my voice laced with warmth. "Who needs a fireplace when they have you wrapped around them?"

He turned, cupping my cheek with a gentle touch. "I like the way you think."

As we walked back inside, the scent of breakfast still lingering in the air, I couldn't shake the feeling that the next few hours would be pivotal.

"What's the plan for the rest of the day?" I asked, my heart pounding a nervous rhythm.

"What do you want to do?" he countered, his voice laced with a tempting offer. "We could venture into town, stay here, maybe see how this heater works during the daylight hours?"

I laughed outwardly at the suggestive undertone, but inwardly, my nerves were screaming.

This could be easy. This could be so damn easy. No next placement to worry about, no rent or lease to break. I could easily have Mona towed up here while I settled into what I was sure would be my forever home.

But I always took the easy way out, and easy never seemed to work in the long run. A wave of uncertainty washed over me.

"I'm going to take a shower," I declared, placing my steaming mug of hot chocolate on the counter.

"You need company?" Ford smirked, but I shook my head.

"I think this one is just me," I replied, my voice firm though my insides were in shambles.

He nodded in understanding. "I'm going to run into town for a few supplies. I'll be back when you get out, and we can get lunch."

"Sounds good," I murmured, already turning towards the bathroom. As the door clicked shut behind me, the silence amplified the turmoil within.

The bathroom became awash in a haze of steam, the mirror fogged over from the scalding water cascading from the showerhead. Yet, I remained outside the torrent, my body untouched by the warmth that filled the small space.

As if that room and isolation suddenly gave me the moment to process it all. Unseen tears traced paths down my cheeks, mingling with the condensation that clung to my skin. Time seemed to blur as I sat there, enveloped in the misty embrace of the room.

The night before had been a dream come true, a culmination of every whispered hope and longing. The man I loved with every fiber of my being had finally confessed his own love, a love that mirrored my own in its depth and intensity. He was ready to give me everything, to love me completely.

But that was the problem.

My hands trembled as I stared at them, a stark reminder of the years spent trapped in a cycle of self-doubt and unfulfilled promises. Change was impossible if all I ever offered myself were empty assurances.

I wiped my eyes and reached for my phone.

"Emily?" Her voice wavered, thick with emotion.

"I think I figured it out."

"Okay?" Becca's voice was tentative. "And what does that mean?"

"He loves me." The words felt foreign on my tongue. "He loves me for me. And it's everything I ever wanted."

"Then what's wrong?"

A humorless laugh escaped my lips. "What if I don't love me?"

"What?" Becca's incredulity was palpable.

"What if I ruin it? What if I just end up sabotaging everything? What if I—"

"Stop." Becca broke through my tangent. "Just stop."

Silence hung heavy on the line, the only sound Becca's sharp intake of breath.

"Emily, what if you don't ruin it? What if you don't sabotage it? What if you just don't? What if you just allow yourself to be with him and love him. I know it's scary and I know you are afraid that this will end up in a broken heart but babe," she paused as she took a breath, "he doesn't love you despite your chaos. He loves you because of it."

Ford

I placed the bags on the counter, the weight of them a stark reminder of the domesticity I craved but knew, in that moment, was a distant dream. The cold items should have been put away immediately, but the allure of her, the warmth of her skin, the taste of her kiss... it had been a much-needed indulgence I thought about from the moment I walked out the door to the moment I crossed back inside the cabin.

I peeked into the bedroom, half-hoping to find her nestled amongst the sheets, my sheets, our sheets. But the bed was empty, the covers undisturbed. Instead, my eyes fell upon a folded piece of paper, resting on my pillow.

I'm on the bench by the slopes.

My heart rate slowed as I realized this wasn't a goodbye letter as I had originally assumed. I tucked the paper into my pocked as I put my coat back on and walked through the backyard to find her staring at the few skiers we could see.

"Hi," Emily breathed with her arms crossed nervously.

"Hi," I echoed barely above a whisper.

"I have some ground rules," she declared, her tone allowing no argument.

My brows lifted in silent question. "Okay."

"Sunday movie marathons. Classics only."

My heart swelled at the implication. "Okay."

"Laundry will never be fully done. Ever. Deal with it."

I chuckled, "Warm and straight from the dryer is my preference anyway."

"I didn't say it'd be warm," she countered with a hint of a smile playing on her lips.

"Slightly damp is perfect too," I replied, my voice now laced with amusement.

"No coffee after lunch time, I get irrational. Like, really irrational and I can't sleep."

"I happen to only drink coffee in the morning," I assured her.

"And monthly sleepovers for Becca and Liz. You're either out of the house or joining in on the cocktail-fueled gossip-fest."

I nodded, then added, "On one condition."

She gave me a playful eye roll. "Which is?"

"I want to meet Liz's dad."

She sighed in feigned frustration. "Fine. A 'coincidental' visit with her parents, then."

"Okay."

She balked. "That's it? That's your only condition?"

My laughter bubbled up at her naivety.

"Emily, you could've asked for the moon and I'd have built us a rocket. There are no conditions. Only you. It's always been you." I pulled her close as her smile mirrored my own.

"Sorry it took so long," she murmured.

"You're here now," I whispered as I kissed her brow.

Pulling back, her gaze met mine. "I said I didn't need saving, and I didn't. But I'm glad you wanted to. I'm glad you *want* to."

"We saved each other," I replied as I wiped away a stray tear.

A laugh escaped her lips as she picked up some fabric I didn't realize had been sitting beside her. "By the way, this is for you," she said as she pulled out a wrinkled Aaron Bramlet jersey, complete with a signature.

"What the—"

"Becca and Liz gave it to me at their wedding."

Laughter erupted as I pulled her close once more.

"My beautiful chaos," I murmured against her lips.

"My handsome calamity," she whispered back.

"Is that what we are?" I asked as my breath ghosted over her skin, memorizing her scent.

She nodded. "Yes. I'm your Chaos, and you're my Calamity."

I smiled, testing the words, "Chaos and Calamity."

Epilogue

2 Years Later

Emily

I placed the flowers in the vase and stood back to silently assess the site. They weren't my best creation, but I was slowly learning. It turned out growing flowers wasn't as easy as I'd thought it would be, an even harder task knowing I had been doing it out of a small wooden box and not in a field of my own. In all actuality, I hadn't even grown these particular flowers. I ended up buying them from a florist once I'd finally accepted gardening wasn't something I could do. And that was okay. I didn't need to be perfect at everything. Perfect wasn't the goal anymore.

I hesitated, knowing what I needed to say but not knowing how to start.

"Do you know why I picked this flower?" I said to the headstone, shaking my head with a sad smile. "It was such a stupid decision. They are hard as hell to grow. But we both know I'm more stubborn than most." I laughed. "But I can't lie to you. You would figure it out anyway." I huffed. "I bought them."

While this would officially be my fourth visit to mom's gravesite over the last year, I'd yet to do anything other than replace the dying flowers with new ones and turn to walk away.

But this time, I had something I needed to say.

"I used to draw them a lot, but you know that. Indian ghost pipes were one of J Emily Dickenson's favorite flowers. I don't know if you know that." A tear rolled down my cheek.

"I mean you're my mom and she was… is one of my favorite authors so you should definitely know that," I teased, trying to lighten the mood.

"I used to like them because I read that they were once used to help treat people with anxiety, grief, and frankly a lot of the symptoms of ADHD. Think of them as the original Adderall." I laughed. "Painting them felt like a little secret I had with just my own mind." I reached down and ran my fingers along the stems.

"Anyway, I recently found out that they also symbolize resilience because unlike other flowers they can thrive in the dark." My voice broke.

"You see, I don't do well in the dark. Actually, the dark really fucking sucks. Maybe that's why I always tended to gravitate towards shiny things. I thought that maybe if I covered myself in something shiny and filled my room with paintings of these flowers then I could pretend to thrive. But pretending never really worked out for me." I stepped back, my voice thick with emotion.

"So, I wanted to tell you what I've decided. I decided to stop pretending. I know I've been saying that for a long time but this time is different. I decided to stop pretending and to stop being scared. And I can't do that unless I fully acknowledge who I am."

I swallowed as the words stuck in my throat.

"I used to hate my chaos. I used to hate how unorganized I was. I used to hate how much I had to focus on the smallest of tasks just to complete them. And I'm not saying I'm not thankful for the medication or the therapy because those have truly done wonders."

I kneeled down and ran my hand across the grass.

"But I finally figured something out. I'm chaotic and wild and loud and messy because I'm a part of you. And I don't want to ever leave that part behind. So, I want to tell you that I finally did it. I finally fell in love with who I am in the same way that you always loved me. And I wanted to say thank you for making me weird and loud and crazy.

Thank you for giving me this chaos because being normal would be so fucking boring." I laughed as I swiped at the tears.

"I also should probably tell you that my Kindle Unlimited library is so much worse than it used to be." I smiled as I sniffled. "Seriously, Mom, I feel so bad for you. You have no idea what you're missing when it comes to tentacles and vibrating knobs." I laughed. "Okay, that may have crossed a line but all I'm saying is I hope wherever you are that they have an abundance of smutty books for you to waste your days away reading."

I kissed my fingers and placed them on the warm earth.

"Also, Becca is okay. It took longer than we initially thought but as of last week she is officially considered to be in remission." I smiled.

"James is getting so big! But I'm sure you already know that. Also, I haven't told Anderson yet but he definitely said *fuck* the other day when he dropped his bowl of cereal." I laughed knowing I was probably the cause of his newly learned language.

"Lastly, I want to tell you that I am totally and completely in love with Ford Edward Thomas. I have been for quite a while now."

I breathed what felt like my first full breath in hours.

I pulled the cardigan tighter. "I know we had a rough start and our path wasn't always smooth but I finally realized that he loved me before the mask or the makeup or the extensions. Though he had his own demons to fight and his own lessons to learn, I know he loved me before I ever loved myself just like I loved him before he tried to change into whatever he thought he was supposed to be."

"You coming?" Ford called out from the car. "It's about to rain."

"I'll be right there." I said and then turned back to the headstone.

"I just want you to know that I'm happy. And I mean that with all my heart. I'm happy. And not just because of Ford or anyone else. It's because I am happy with myself."

I blew a kiss towards the stone. "And just in case you ever were unsure, I just want you to know, you are a really great mom."

Ford opened the door of his truck and I slid into the seat. "Apparently Doris said that new murder mystery documentary you wanted to watch is pretty intense."

My eyebrows rose. "Did she?"

He walked around the truck and slid into his own seat. "I figure if we leave now we can make it back home by lunch and then have all afternoon to binge it."

"Good plan. I got called in anyway so I need to be at the hospital by seven in the morning which means I'll need to get to bed early."

He pulle dout of the cemetery. "Maybe if the day goes smoothly we can synchronize our lunches?"

I laughed. "I wish but we both know that never happens."

"Then what about dinner? And then breakfast and dinner again the next day?" He smirked as he reached over, picked up my hand and kissed the finger that held a shiny new ring.

"Oh fuck!"

His eyes went wide. "What?"

"I completely forgot to tell mom we got engaged."

He laughed as he made a u-turn in the road and turned back into the cementary. "Wasn't that the entire reason we came by in the first place?"

I rolled my eyes as I kissed his cheek and he parked at the same spot we had just vacated.

"Yep. But I wouldn't be me if I wasn't consistently and chaotically forgetting everything."

He rolled down the window as I walked back to the gravesite and called out, "That's okay, I love your chaos."

The End

Acknowledgements

In true transparency, I have written, erased and rewritten this acknowledgement page multiple times. There is so much I want to say and so many people I want to thank that I'm scared I'll forget someone or mess up...that being said to everyone who played a part in this journey, THANK YOU!

First, I want to thank my amazing PA, Miranda, and the wonderful Alpha/Beta/ARC readers that helped me turn this messy story in my head into the amazing journey you see on paper! Thank you for listening to my every text, marco polo, phone call and rant about my chaotic brain and all the ideas I had.

Thank you to my friends (those IRL and on the internet) who supported me and loved me through all the chaos of getting this book to you.

Thank you to my family for loving my chaos. Thank you for always supporting me, loving me and (let's be honest) putting up with me.

Thank you to the sweet RV salesman at Blue Compass RV in SC who offered to show Ashley and I the RVs knowing we weren't buying but were researching for a book and then stood by, completely red in the face, while we made sure Emily could logistically have copious amounts of sexy time in said RV. If you need therapy please reach out.

To my husband, thank you for being you. Thank you for loving me not despite of but because of all my chaos. Thank you for not being mad when I lose something and not hating the fact that you search through a clean laundry hamper for clothes each morning because I have no idea how to completely finish a load of laundry. Thank you for letting me sit in my library dungeon for hours on end while I researched and wrote this book. Thank you for seeing my chaotic little 14 year old self and still wanting to ask me out on a date (y'all don't get your panties in a twist, he was only 15 lol). Thank you for everything. I love you to "confinity".

And lastly, to the readers...I wouldn't be here without you. I wouldn't be here without your support and your love and your constant cheering me on. You have truly changed my life and I am so thankful for every moment of this crazy journey! And it's all because of you.

About the author

Hannah is a current Medical Speech and Language Pathologist, who has turned her love of language into a thriving career as a published author of spicy adult romance and romantasy novels.

Her debut series, "The Celestra", became an international best-seller within its first year and has captivated readers with its rich story-telling and compelling characters. "The Celestra" and "The Shadows Within" (books 1 & 2 in her romantasy trilogy) are now available on

Amazon. In addition to her fantasy works, Hannah has also ventured into contemporary romance with *Shattered*, and *Chaos & Calamity*, both new adult novels that focus on self acceptance and mental health awareness while also making you swoon over that hot tattooed bad boy.

A devoted South Carolina native and die-hard Gamecock fan, Hannah finds joy in spending time with her husband, two sons, two beloved Labrador Retrievers and also their ball python named Bob (who Hannah hasn't fully warmed up to yet). Through her writing, she continues to inspire readers with passionate stories that transport them into worlds of love, adventure and self-discovery.

You can find Hannah on most social media platforms with that handle @hannahtillauthor or @hannahtillbooks and she also has a website www.HannahTill.com where you can find lots of goodies and information about upcoming releases and signing events.